THE SUNQUEST

THE LEGEND OF Q'NTANA
BOOK THREE

MARK DAVID GERSON

THE SUNQUEST

First Paperback Edition 2014. Fourth Edition 2024

Published by MDG Media International
Sedona, AZ 86336
www.mdgmediainternational.com

Library of Congress Control Number: 2024941081

ISBN: 978-1-950189-03-8 (paperback)
ISBN: 978-1-950189-06-9 (ebook)

Cover Image: Kathleen Messmer
www.kathleenmessmer.com

PRAISE FOR THE LEGEND OF Q'NTANA

Leaves you turning every single page, hungry for more!
DAVID MICHAEL – AUTHOR OF "THE UNITED SERIES"

Compelling…a magical journey!
KAREN VAUGHAN – AUTHOR OF "DEAD TO WRITES"

An intriguing and exhilarating magical tale.
DAN STONE – AUTHOR OF "ICE ON FIRE"

An evocative and emotionally moving tale.
"MIDWEST BOOK REVIEW"

*I read "The MoonQuest" three times and couldn't wait for
"The StarQuest" to come out. Well, it was worth the wait.
I loved this book, and you will too!*
AMY ROBBINS-WILSON – AUTHOR OF "TRANSFORMATIONAL MOTHERING"

*An enjoyable journey into a wondrous world
that will leave you yearning to return again and again.*
JUDY SMITH ADAMS – SPRINGFIELD, MO

Stunning, magical and inspiring.
PAOLA RIZZATO – GLASGOW, UK

*Magic, music and universal truths
masterfully woven into a gripping tale.*
BETTY DRAVIS – AUTHOR OF "1106 GRAND BOULEVARD"

*Of the hundreds of books I own and hundreds more I've read, this is
the only book I've ever finished and immediately picked pack up and
read a second time. Amazing masterpiece of literature.*
LYNN HUDSON – ALBUQUERQUE, NM

*A fantastical ride to another world...the kind of book
the world should clamor for and read more of.*
MICHAEL HICE – SANTA FE, NM

*Fans of quest-centered fantasy and visionary fiction
as well as New Agers should enjoy this emotionally solid tale.*
"LIBRARY JOURNAL"

More from Mark David Gerson

FICTION

Sara's Year

After Sara's Year

The Emmeline Papers

MEMOIR

Acts of Surrender: A Writer's Memoir

Dialogues with the Divine: Encounters with my Wisest Self

Pilgrimage: A Fool's Journey

SELF-HELP & PERSONAL GROWTH

*The Way of the Fool: How to Stop Worrying About Life
and Start Living It…in 12½ Super-Simple Steps*

*The Way of the Imperfect Fool: How to Bust the Addiction to Perfection
That's Stifling Your Success…in 12½ Super-Simple Steps*

*The Way of the Abundant Fool: How to Bust Free of "Not Enough"
and Break Free into Prosperity…in 12½ Super-Simple Steps*

The Book of Messages: Writings Inspired by Melchizedek

RESOURCES FOR WRITERS & ASPIRING WRITERS

The Voice of the Muse: Answering the Call to Write

The Voice of the Muse Companion: Guided Meditations for Writers

From Memory to Memoir: Writing the Stories of Your Life

Organic Screenwriting: Writing for Film, Naturally

Birthing Your Book…Even If You Don't Know What It's About

The Heartful Art of Revision: An Intuitive Guide to Editing

*Writer's Block Unblocked: Seven Surefire Ways
to Free Up Your Writing and Creative Flow*

A genuine odyssey is not about piling up experiences.
It is a deeply felt, risky, unpredictable tour of the soul.
Thomas Moore

On ne découvre pas de terre nouvelle sans consentir à perdre de vue,
d'abord et longtemps, tout rivage.
André Gide

To my Muse, who wouldn't take no for an answer.

*As you step from your world into the worlds of Q'ntana, you
will experience foreign lands, sample exotic foods and encounter
all manner of uncommon individuals and peculiar creatures.*

*Look for "The Worlds of The SunQuest" at the back of the book
to ease your journey through this unfamiliar territory
(and to assist you with some unusual pronunciations).*

*If you'd prefer to have this guide by your side as you travel these
pages, download a free copy of "The Worlds of The SunQuest"
at www.markdavidgerson.com/qntanaworlds.*

§ § § § §

*With its compelling story, engaging characters and rich,
multilayered themes, "The SunQuest" is an ideal selection
for any book club.*

Prologue

I will die tonight. I need no oracle to predict it, no dreamwalker to reveal it. The moon and the stars sing of it, and the sun calls me home. Yet like my grandfather before and after me, I must write my story before I can set off on this final journey. Unlike Toshar, though, I know to which realms I travel…to which I gladly return. Nor do I carry Toshar's reluctance to share my saga with you. I do it willingly, and the words of my SunQuest flow with ease from quill to parchment in my anticipation of what next awaits me.

My name, for those who do not yet know it, is Ben, and I am twice aged…just as I have twice lived and twice served as Elderbard of Q'ntana. To have lived twice is not exceptional. To have lived twice with the same body and name is rare. To have lived once at the beginning of time and once again at its endpoint is unprecedented. But, then, little of this SunQuest is commonplace.

The story that spills onto page after page is not mine alone. It is Q'ntana's story, and M'ranna's before that. Even more, perhaps, is it is the story of Bo'Rà K'n, whose lust for power never faded, whose villainy never dwindled, and whose nightmares never ceased to hover over this land, even during times of peace.

My mother has already shared one part of my story with you, through her StarQuest. Through that StarQuest, we were parted and reunited, only to be parted again. Through that StarQuest, Bo'Rà K'n was stilled but not vanquished. Through that StarQuest, time spiraled back in on itself, and I became my mother's ancestor as well as her son.

In the part of the story that has not yet been set to parchment, the people of Q'ntana named me as their first Elderbard and I married Y'glana Tori'à, the most beautiful and heartful woman in all the land. Y'glana, bore me one child, a daughter, Mìr'gn'ma, and thus was the line of Elderbards inaugurated and the Law of Balance established.

From father to daughter, mother to son,
The mantle passes, the Balance is done.

I served nearly four score of years alongside Q'ntana's first queen, Karenna Kihanna, and when I died I finally learned who my father had been and why it had been his destiny to leave my mother before I was born.

But that is part of The SunQuest, this final story that begins, as do all stories, once upon a time.

"Death to the
Storyteller!"

one

A mother rocks her boy-child in her arms, singing softly the same lullaby her mother once crooned to her. It is midday, and Q'ntana's two suns draw slowly together in that sacred moment of union that disperses all shadows from the land. The infant gurgles contentedly, his spittle spurting tiny bubbles at the corner of his mouth. The mother wipes the baby's lips with a corner of his blanket then leans back into the smooth riverside boulder that has been a favorite refuge of hers since childhood. She shuts her eyes and lets the focused warmth of the suns spill over her face, even as the cool breeze off the water refreshes her.

Something, she senses, is not right. Her eyes fly open, dart in all directions. She launches herself off the rock and again scans her surroundings. Upstream, blue-breasted mirika'as thrash noisily in the suns-dappled river, puffs of their cottony down floating silently up into the sky. Downriver, the Alanda ferry bobs over the gentle current, its crimson prow aimed for the weather-worn wooden dock. A dirt road winds lazily up the hill from the dock, slicing through the broad, sloping Great Lawn of Castle Rose, the sprawling storybook fortress that has been her only home.

Nothing has changed…yet something has. Something ineffable. Her son must have noticed it too, for his eyelids flutter anxiously and his breathing rasps into a whimper. What is it? She studies the landscape one more time. The breeze. That's it. She can see the breeze. There is no time to question how. Its dusky tendrils eddy around and past her now, draining color, form and substance from everything they touch. Nothing is spared their ghostly kiss. Everything washes out…fades out…dissolves. Boulder…river…castle… Everything.

Everything.

"Ben!" she cries as her son, too, washes out, fades out, dissolves…vanishes from her arms.

"Ben!" cries the dreamer as she thrashes in her bed.

Covers knot around her legs. She kicks them free, simultaneously kicking free the nightmare as one dream image melts into another…

Once again, it is moments before midday. This time, though, the mother stands just inside the Castle Rose courtyard, its pink stones glinting in the noonday light, the same light that spotlights a young man as he strides forward to join her. The courtyard is jammed with people of all ages and rank, all dressed in their brightest holiday finery. Many sing. Some dance. Others sway unsteadily, frothy mead slopping over the rims of their pewter mugs as they trip over the uneven cobble. In one corner, a trio of musicians mimes a lively tune, their pipes and lythe a poor match for the raucous laughter of a nearby throng. In another, children press hungrily against a trestle table laden with colorful sweets. High in all the courtyard's pennon-draped archways, heralds stand at stiff attention. They press trumpets to their lips, poised to blast the fanfare that will still the crowd and focus attention on a raised dais upon which now stand a strikingly beautiful woman and an elderly, yet ageless-seeming man.

The woman's full, red lips, dark eyes and creamy complexion are framed by raven hair that tumbles freely to her waist. She wears a plain, bleached-cotton shift and stands barefoot next to the man. Bald and clean-shaven, he wears a simple white robe flecked with gold and silver runes. His claw-like hands, four-fingered on the right, six-fingered on the left, are clasped loosely in front of him as his piercing yellow eyes scan the crowd. When they finally alight on the young man, they follow him as he weaves through the well-wishing throng to his mother.

Now, the ray of sunlight that picked out the young man envelops them both.

The mother notices the position of the suns, which draw inexorably nearer to their instant of union. "I must get back," she says, her voice an uneasy mix of sadness and anticipation.

"I know," he says, equally conflicted. "I must stay."

"You choose to stay."

He nods. "I do." He glances toward the dais. "I wish it did not have to be this way," he continues. "I wish you… I wish we—"

She touches his shoulder, aware not only of his height — he stands half a head taller than she — but, for the first time, of his stature. He has earned this honor, and more. Much more.

"This is your wish," she says. "Your deepest heart's wish. Or it would not be happening this way. It couldn't. You know that, don't you?"

The old man catches his eye.

"It's time," the young man says.

They step into each other's arms and hug fiercely, their eyes moist.

"I am so proud of you, Ben," the woman says. "I have never been more proud of anyone than I am of you right now."

"None of this makes any sense," he sighs.

"Nothing here ever has. Maybe that will change now. I pray that it will."

They separate. She holds Ben at arm's length, determined to absorb as much of him into her memory as she can.

"I, as well," he says.

"I love you, son." She steps away from the sunbeam. As in the earlier dream, everything around her washes out…fades out…dissolves.

"I love you too, Mother," she hears faintly. Then, even more faintly, a thunderous cheer. Then, nothing.

The nothingness spirals around her, slowly at first, in a silent whiteness blinding in its brightness. She shuts her eyes, but the same glare assaults her behind her eyelids. From the silence emerges a hum, hushed at first then louder, with increasing pitch and volume…grating pitch, deafening volume. She longs to cover her ears. Her arms refuse the command. She opens her mouth to scream, but she has no voice. Yet her throat is raw, as though she has been screaming without cease. Her heart pounds with painful urgency.

The vortex intensifies, whips color after color at her. Black. Blue. Red. Orange. Green. Colors joust amongst themselves then fuse into a dizzying kaleidoscope of images and scenes. These, too, lash at her, with such vehemence that she flinches…flinches again. Then again. The images confound her. The scenes make no sense. They hurtle forward in time, careen backward, loop and overlap. Some are familiar. Many are foreign. All feel real, as though all have happened…as though they are happening right now. All contradict each other…each controverts the next…until all coalesce into a cacophonous jumble.

Now, the percussive pulse of her heartbeat overpowers the discordant dissonance. It grows louder and more insistent, louder and more insistent, its relentless thudding thump driving everything else from her awareness…

two

"Ko'lar! You must get up. Ko'lar! Please! Now!"

Q'nta opened her eyes, squinting against the early morning brightness and clutching her head against the staccato banging inside of it, which somehow merged with the battering on her door and the hammering sound from outside her window.

The young man's voice gained in urgency. "There is no time to waste, Ko'lar. Please!"

"What is it, Samson?" she croaked.

Q'nta reached for her dressing gown. Her head felt as though it would explode.

"Ko'lar!"

The old man must not have heard her. She knew he was losing his hearing, but he was proud and he refused to admit it. He had served her father for more years than she could count. Now he served her. On more than one occasion, she had suggested that he retire. Then, hearing her perfectly, he pretended not to.

She staggered to her feet, clutching at the bedpost for support.

"Come in, Samson. Come in."

The door flew open and a young page charged into the room, his ginger hair askew and his freckles barely visible through the deep flush on his cheeks and forehead.

"You must come at once, Ko'lar." He made straight for the window and peered down to the courtyard below. He spun back to Q'nta, alarmed. "There is no time."

The old man must be losing his wits as well as his hearing, she thought. "Why do you keep calling me Ko'lar? It's premature." Q'nta squinted at the boy, now as agitated as she was. "You're not Samson. Where is Samson?" She stumbled to the window. "What is going on out there? Why all the noise? They were to have finished the preparations last night. Can they not let me sleep late on the morning of my Naming—?"

She flung open the window. The Castle Rose walls were chipped and splintering; little of their original pink hue was visible through the dirt and soot that encrusted them. Directly across from her window, two flags, bleached and tattered, hung limply from atop the two front towers: a silver moon against a midnight-blue background and a flying eagle emblazoned on a scarlet rose. Below, on a crude dais in the center of the courtyard, a gallows was taking form. A dozen soldiers dressed indistinguishably in black — shirts, pants, boots, eye masks — stared stonily at the five haggard workers who struggled with the heavy wooden beams. One workman, older than the others — older than Q'nta — noticed her at the window. He watched her for an instant then dropped his eyes. The soldier nearest to him stared up at Q'nta with sneering defiance before remembering his duty: He punched his charge so forcefully in the abdomen that the workman slumped to the ground, gasping for air.

"Get up! Get back to it," the soldier bellowed, kicking him repeatedly. "You'll see her down here soon enough."

Q'nta fell back from the window. The page caught her.

"Who are you?" she whispered. "Where is Samson?"

"I'm Simeon," the boy replied, his voice edged with panic. "Samson was my grandfather. He is dead, ma'am. You spoke at his funeral this past twelvemonth. You don't remember?"

Q'nta clutched her head with one hand, the curtain pull with the other. "I don't know what I remember, Sam— Simeon. Everything is so…so—"

Simeon pushed her from the window. "Never mind that now. You must get dressed, quickly, and come with me. If not…" He eyed the activity below. "I can wait in the study while you change. But hurry. You must hurry."

*   *   *

Simeon climbed the half-dozen well-worn stone steps to Q'nta's turret study. Behind him, the frenzied sound of armoire doors slamming blended with the more measured but menacing pounding that drifted up from the courtyard. He shut the study door to give Q'nta some privacy and began to explore the storied space. Barely into his teen years, Simeon had only been in this room once before, shortly

20

before Q'nta's father, Toshar, had died. Samson had wanted his young grandson to meet the man he had served for so many years, the man said to be Q'ntana's greatest Elderbard, the man who in his youth had initiated The MoonQuest, slain evil King Fvorag and driven Bo'Rà K'n from the land.

If Bo'Rà K'n had been defeated, Simeon wondered, why was Fvorag's grandson now on the throne? And why had King Gravel decided, only this morning, that Toshar's daughter must be killed? There had been no talk at all about it in court. If he hadn't just happened on two soldiers who were discussing the imminent hanging with undisguised glee, it might have been too late to save her. It might still be too late. But it might not be. With any luck, Gravel's legendary capriciousness and his army's well-known disarray would buy them enough time to escape from Castle Rose. After that...well, he hadn't thought that far ahead. The first and most important thing was to get out of the castle.

What Simeon hadn't counted on was the Ko'lar's muddled mind. How could she not know that she was already Elderbard? How could she not remember her own Naming? He remembered it as though it had been yesterday. In truth, three twelvemonths had passed. Even so, it remained among his most vivid memories: The courtyard overflowed with people singing and dancing until just before suns-merge. Then O'ric — that peculiar O'ric of so many legends and stories — passed the light-filled Nayr to Q'nta as the crowd chanted her name and old King Kyri watched proudly from his stretcher.

The Nayr. The ancient, polished-black chalice sat on Q'nta's writing table, the round, black-marble Kol Kolai, the Table of Prophecy that had figured so prominently in The MoonQuest. The table was cluttered with quills, inkwells, burnt-down candles and parchment in reams and rolls, just as he had seen it in Toshar's time. Simeon touched a finger to one of the table's lightly pulsing red veins. The throbbing intensified and the vein grew hot. He jerked his hand away and glanced guiltily back toward the door. Q'nta was still in her bedchamber. Next, he leaned over to peer into The Nayr, hoping to see the light that had filled it when Q'nta had drunk from it. It was empty but for a thin layer of dust. Did he dare pick it up? Yes, he did. As he reached for it, the door creaked open. He shoved his hands into his pockets as Q'nta entered, dressed in a simple, pale blue dress and matching sandals.

At first, she seemed to Simeon less dazed and more in control of her faculties. Then she noticed a large rectangular area on the wall, cleaner than its surroundings. Her face darkened. "My father's tapestry," she cried. "What have you done with it?"

"Ko'lar, ma'am. You must come with me. We have to go. Now."

"Why do you keep calling me Ko'lar, young man? It is not right. It is not time."

She touched her finger to the table as Simeon had. It seemed to soothe her, if only for a breath. She picked up The Nayr and clutched it to her chest.

"What have they done to Toshar's study?" she whispered, close to tears.

"This is your study now, Ko'lar," Simeon said. He took her arm and gently pulled her to the window. Here, curtains concealed them from the soldiers and workmen below. He pointed to the gallows, now nearing completion. "Don't you understand?" he asked. "They are building that for you. You must let me get you out of here."

Q'nta did not understand. All the conflicting scenes from her dream played out in her head, simultaneously: lives she remembered, lives she didn't...lives she had lived, lives she hadn't lived... Or had she lived them all? All at the same time? Her head throbbed. The pain was excruciating, blinding. She pressed her fingers to her temples and let the young man — Simeon? — guide her to the main door of her study and down the winding tower staircase. Why did nothing make any sense? How could this be at the same time her study and Toshar's? How could she be both Elderbard and not yet Elderbard? Why was Castle Rose in such disrepair? Why were the soldiers dressed so menacingly? Why did they act so cruelly? Where was Uncle Kyri? Who wanted to hang her? Why?

The thud of heavy boots clattered up toward them. Soldiers. At least three. Simeon dragged Q'nta back up the stairs. Perhaps they could escape through to the corridor on the far side of the bedroom.

"Where do these stairs go?" A soldier's voice rasped up the stairwell.

"Her study. The others are on their way there now from the bedroom side."

"We've got her."

"About time."

Then, from above them: more soldiers, in the bedroom and study.

"The maid said she was here, Captain. With that page, Simeon."

"The maid was wrong," Prak'kà retorted. "The maid is dead. The boy too…the page. As good as dead."

Simeon froze.

"What is happening?" Q'nta asked, her voice finally tinged with some awareness of danger.

"Someone will hang at suns-merge," Prak'ka barked from upstairs. "If it is not the Elderbard, it will be one of you. Do you understand?"

"Y-yes, sir," his subordinate stammered.

Simeon clapped his hand over Q'nta's mouth. "Shh," he hissed. He pressed her against the wall. Maybe they won't see us…maybe they'll run right past us, he thought…he prayed.

Forgetting its centuries-old solidity, the wall behind Q'nta shivered shimmeringly and, for an instant, lost its stone-and-mortar rigidness. In that instant, Q'nta fell backward through the wall and vanished.

The clatter of heavy boots grew louder, from upstairs and down. It converged and stopped where Simeon still stood, now alone.

three

"I still don't understand." Q'nta gripped the edge of the Table of Prophecy, now cleared of its bardly clutter and standing in the center of a circular stone chamber she had never seen before. She could not even be certain whether she was still inside the castle. The chamber was free of adornment, the bare table its only furnishing. Windowless, with no ceiling, the room opened to the sky, where the two suns, Aygra and B'na, neared their midday union. Across from her stood her father, Toshar, and her great-grandmother Eulisha, both looking as they had in their final years of life. O'ric stood apart, holding The Nayr and looking much as he always did.

"Understanding is not req—," O'ric began.

Eulisha interrupted him. "This one time, O'ric, I believe it is required." Although equal in height to the two men, Eulisha seemed to tower over them. She braced herself against her simple wooden staff and leaned into Q'nta. Her close-cropped white hair so caught the suns-light that it cast a halo around her.

O'ric nodded. He set The Nayr onto the table. Its veins throbbed with increasing insistence. "Perhaps you are right," he agreed, gazing up at the suns. "But time is short."

"You remember nothing?" Toshar asked. His voice trembled and his dark eyes were sad.

"It would be easier if I remembered nothing," Q'nta replied, still disoriented. "But I remember everything. I remember things that can't have happened as clearly as things that I know did happen. I remember too much, and not enough."

"Let me try to explain." Toshar tugged on his beard and cast a quick glance at O'ric.

O'ric nodded.

"Time has turned in on itself," Toshar said. "Your mind remembers all possible versions of many of your life's events, even as you appear to be living only one."

"Why am I not surprised that what you say makes no sense?"

"It is more peculiar still than that," Toshar replied. "Eulisha?"

"In this moment," the old woman continued, "your mind believes that no time has passed since you returned from your StarQuest." She paused. "You do remember your StarQuest?"

Q'nta nodded. "I remember that it succeeded, that it achieved Completion. Beyond that..." She looked unhappily from Eulisha to Toshar, desperate to understand. "Why do they want to kill me?"

"The king died," Toshar replied.

"Uncle Kyri? How? When?"

"There is no time for the 'how,'" Eulisha said, "or, frankly, for the 'when.' For now, all you must know is that he died. Childless. Gravel is now king."

"Gravel?"

"Fvorag's grandson."

Q'nta turned to Toshar. "You killed Fvorag."

Toshar stared dreamily into the distance. "Long ago. Once upon a time..."

"Toshar." Eulisha prodded him with her stick. He shook his head to clear it and refocused on his daughter.

"Yes, of course. I killed Fvorag. We all thought that his son had also been killed in the battle. What Kyri and I did not yet know was that Margolin managed to escape, to the southern lands beyond Q'ntana."

Eulisha pointed her stick to the south. "That is where Gravel came from, with his army. He had been preparing, all the time Kyri was ill."

Confusion, nearly erased from Q'nta's face, raced back. Her brow furrowed. "But... But if Kyri died childless, *I* am his heir. Aren't I?"

"Yes," O'ric said. He stepped forward to join the others. "You were queen, for a short time. The people named you their ruler when Kyri passed."

Toshar touched Q'nta's shoulder. "Gravel did not dare attack while the king still lived. Even after your coronation, he waited three moons before striking — just long enough to amass more troops and to secure Bo'Rà K'n's support."

"Bo'Rà K'n? He is behind this?"

"Of course," Toshar replied. "Always."

"You did your best to hold Q'ntana and Castle Rose against Gravel's forces," Eulisha said. "No one could have done more."

"I failed?"

"You failed," O'ric said.

"Gravel did not dare kill or exile you," Eulisha said. "Not at first. The people loved you too much."

"He agreed to let you live," Toshar said, "and permitted you to remain in Castle Rose as Elderbard."

Q'nta shook her head. "I couldn't have agreed to that. I wouldn't have. It makes no sense."

"Not in this moment, perhaps," Toshar said. "At the time, however, you rightfully saw yourself as the sole bulwark against Gravel's tyranny. That is why you agreed to abdicate. The alternative would have been death."

"Not only yours," Eulisha added. "Many, many more would have died."

"That doesn't explain why, now, Gravel suddenly wants me dead. What happened? Did I do something to anger him? What did I do?"

"The king is not entirely right in his head," Toshar explained. "To seek sense from the actions of such a man is a futile exercise." He hesitated before continuing. "Early this morning Gravel decided you were threat enough that you had to die. Immediately. There is no other sense to it than that." He looked into her eyes. "I am sorry."

Q'nta twisted her hair distractedly. If only she could remember one timeline, the right timeline, she would know what to do. But everything in her mind remained a muddled stew. She clutched her head. Her headache was returning. "What happens now?"

"That depends on you, my dear," Eulisha replied. "Do you remember your son?"

"Of course, I—"

"From father to daughter, mother to son," O'ric intoned. "The mantle passes. The balance is done."

"Ben? But he...but he is—" She glanced up at the suns. Aygra and B'na were now touching.

"Ben is ready to return," O'ric said.

"Here?" Q'nta asked. "What do you mean? That isn't possible. How can that be possible?"

O'ric's attention strayed to B'na before returning to Q'nta. "Everything is possible."

"But why? Why now?"

"To deal with Bo'Rà K'n once and for all," Toshar replied, "in all the ways I could not."

"It was not yet time, son of my son," Eulisha said.

Toshar tugged again on his beard and shook his head sadly. "Alas for us all, it was not." His eyes pierced his daughter's, black as his own. "It is now."

"The SunQuest," O'ric declared.

Q'nta groaned. "Another quest? Haven't there been quests enough?"

"This quest," O'ric replied, "is the final quest."

The *final* quest? Q'nta's face brightened. Perhaps she could manage one more, if it meant she would see her son again. Would she see Ben again? Was O'ric saying that the son she had twice lost was being returned to her? Of course! Just as they had begun The StarQuest together, she and Ben would now reunite to complete The SunQuest. Whatever had happened was worth it if this were true. She felt O'ric's intense gaze on her. He shook his head so slightly that it was barely noticeable. Everyone noticed. Q'nta, especially, noticed.

Toshar was the first to speak. "I am sorry, Q'nta. Unless—"

She swallowed hard. This could not be happening. "Unless I die, Ben cannot return. Unless he returns…"

"Bo'Rà K'n wins. This time for all time."

"It's not fair," Q'nta whispered.

"There is always a choice," Eulisha offered.

"I have never much liked your choices," Q'nta snapped. She turned to her father. "Is there no other way?"

No one replied.

"Will I be able to see him before…before…" Her voice trailed off.

Again, no reply.

"Can you at least promise me that he will succeed?"

Toshar could not meet her gaze. "I am sorry," he said softly.

four

The suns merged. Their brilliant light bleached out the scene in Q'nta's sky chamber, unveiling in its place the dingy Castle Rose courtyard.

The hangman released the trapdoor. "Death to the storyteller!" he cried.

Q'nta's body dropped.

It jerked, then swayed lifelessly in the suffocating heat of a breeze-less summer afternoon.

From a tower window high up above, a scrawny man barely older than Q'nta, wearing a heavy gold robe and jewel-encrusted gold crown, stretched his lips into a broad, sneering grin.

BEN'S RETURN

I returned the gold-crystal orb to the table. It had revealed enough of Q'ntana to me for the present. Instead, I cast my eyes around this space that had been my home through scores of generations.

"Too much gold," I had complained to O'ric when I first arrived here or, rather, when I first *became* here.

"What do you expect?" he had replied. "You are the sun."

Had I been a cleverer man while I still was a man, perhaps I would have deciphered the truth much earlier — not only about who I was and what I was destined to become but about Akila, my father, who had arrived from nowhere and had returned, mysteriously, to that same place just before I was born. Had I understood the full import of my journey, I would surely have allowed it to interfere with my life as Ben Ko'lar, first Elderbard of the newly rechristened land of Q'ntana. As it was, Prithi made certain that I knew no more than was necessary, even to the moment of my death.

At that moment, as the final breath left my body one autumn morning in the glimmer before dawn, I heard O'ric's voice, even though he was not present in my bedchamber. "It is time, Ko'lar," he whispered.

Still, I did not understand.

How I was removed from my deathbed and laid out in ceremonial gold on a funeral pyre, all before midday that same day, I never knew. Ever-accustomed to having his own way, O'ric saw to it. He also saw to it that the kingdom knew of my passing and that the Castle Rose courtyard was thick with mourners when I was borne in. At precisely noon, as Aygra hovered directly overhead, my body began to glow, more and more brightly.

"It is time, Ko'lar," O'ric repeated, now alone with me on the dais.

In that instant, my body dissolved into a swirl of golden light that whorled up into the sky, into the sun.

"Welcome home, son," Aygra said and, before I could respond, I too was a sun, separating from Aygra as B'na and traveling eastward across the Q'ntana sky.

Never did I expect to take Ben's body and name again. Never did I expect to return to Q'ntana. O'ric made certain that I would know nothing of this until, once again, it was time.

"It is best not to know too much too soon," he would always say — to me as he had said to Toshar and to so many others. "It is best to know only that the story continues and to follow where it takes you."

It had carried me to this moment. It had carried me to The SunQuest.

six

I had already taken Ben's form when O'ric appeared. Barely older than the Ben of The StarQuest, I was dressed in black books, dun pants and a green tunic, and I bore a pack filled with what I remembered to be the essentials of such a journey: meat, cheese, bread, a knife and a change of clothing.

"It is time, B'na…Ben…Ko'leya," O'ric said, eyeing my pack curiously.

I picked up the orb again. Now it displayed a soldier cutting down Q'nta's body from the gallows. A second soldier helped him lift it into a wobbly, wooden handcart. My mother's body lurched and jounced as the cart teetered over the uneven cobble and out of the courtyard.

"Was that necessary?" I asked.

"You know it was," he replied.

Again, I let my eyes wander around my golden-sphere home. There wasn't much to it. But, then, a sun needs little more than eternal fire to sustain it; eternal fire and the wisdom of detachment. Would I remember anything of this place? Would I carry any of B'na's knowingness down to Q'ntana as Ben?

"Even if you do," O'ric said, reading my mind as he so often did, "it will not help you."

"Meaning?"

"You will be human again."

I glanced at the orb one last time. It had clouded over. My sun-vision had left me. I was human already.

"Nearly," O'ric corrected me. "But you are also a bard and an Elderbard. All the gifts of that legacy remain with you always: wisdom, story and a vision that, while not B'na's, is Ben's — and singularly potent for all that." He pressed a claw finger into my forehead. "One more thing, Ben."

"Yes?"

"Astel Elohia. The Ring of Unity. You still carry it within you."

I touched my hand to the spot O'ric had. Astel Elohia. The Ring of Unity. The Ben I had once been had received it in the same breath that Q'nta had received the Heart of the Star so pivotal for her StarQuest. I had often wondered, during my previous lifetime, whether anything of equal significance would occur for me around Astel Elohia. Nothing had.

"Now is its time," O'ric said. "The SunQuest is its time." He moved closer until we stood nose-to-nose, then stared so piercingly into me that I could barely hold his gaze. I wanted to turn away but didn't dare. For the briefest of instants, I saw the entire SunQuest play out in his eyes. Then, just as quickly, I forgot it all.

O'ric lifted the orb from my hands. "It will be waiting here for your return," he said.

Then I would be back.

"One way or another," he said.

He unhitched the pack from my back and let it fall to the ground. "This will be waiting for you too."

"If I'm human," I argued, "I will need—"

"You have all you need." He poked at my chest. "You should know that."

I grunted.

"Are you ready?"

I laughed. "Has *anyone* ever been ready for one of your quests?"

O'ric's mouth twitched, displaying the nearest thing to a smile I had ever seen from him. He raised an eyebrow in silent repetition of his question.

I sighed and nodded.

seven

I am falling…a leisurely, slow-motion tumble designed to convey me away from one home and toward another. As B'na, I have no emotion about this journey. Like the sun I have been, I go where I must without thought or feeling. Until now, my human history has been so far distant that it might almost never have been. Almost. Now, though, I am as much Ben as B'na, and this earthward journey begins to reawaken passions long ago suspended. Questions too. How will this life as Ben differ from my last? Where will this SunQuest carry me? Who will I be when it is complete?

As B'na, I would never think to question how the sun-me could still shine in the sky while the Ben-me floats toward land. As Ben, I struggle to make sense of an occurrence that inherently has none. But as my mother so often pointed out, little in Q'ntana has ever made sense. It made no sense that Aygra continued to shine when she and Akila were twined together in marriage. It made no sense that I hung suspended in a void through all of my first childhood, emerging fully grown in M'ranna to meet her. It makes no sense now that I am a similar age at the start of The SunQuest as I was at the start of The StarQuest. It certainly makes no sense that instead of watching the Q'ntana of my past and future rush up toward me as I fall through the sky, I see instead into Gravel's throne room in Castle Rose.

I swear to Prithi that I will never again complain about the gilding in my sun-home after having seen this most ostentatious of chambers. As long as a corridor, yet broad as a castle apartment, its gold-encrusted walls are hung with gold-framed portraits of Gravel, but for one of a scowling Fvorag. Gold chandeliers hang from its sculpted-gold ceiling, gold inlays crisscross its ebony floor and gold gewgaws are scattered everywhere throughout. It barely seems conceivable that anything could exceed the rest of the room in gaudiness. Gravel's throne does. The only seat in the room, it rests on a raised dais (solid gold, of course) at the far end of the chamber, its massive gold bulk fussily carved with spheres, spires, seraphs and sundry other expressions of his grandiosity. Its back, seat and arm are plumply upholstered in gold silk. Behind the throne is the chamber's only window. Uncurtained and east-facing, it lets in the afternoon sun — my sun — which renders the space blindingly bright and intemperately hot...which it is as someone pounds on the chamber's colossal gold double doors.

"Who goes there?" calls one of the pair of soldiers flanking the throne-room side of the entry.

"Prak'kà," responds one of the pair flanking the corridor side. "He bears news for the king."

The king nods and the soldiers fling open the doors. Captain Prak'kà, clad in the same anonymous black as all soldiers in the kingdom, rushes in, shoving the door sentries aside. When he reaches the dais, he drops to his knees. Even the most senior of Gravel's officers must grovel before their liege lord.

Prak'kà's face is hard; his eyes are harder. A deep slash scars his right cheek. "She is dead, Your Grace."

Gravel glowers imperiously. His crown slides down over his brow. "I know," he barks. "I saw it all. What about the body?"

"Left by the river for the vulture ants, as you ordered, sire."

Gravel nudges his crown back into place, smoothes his gold tunic.

"Better than she deserves. She should have died a long time ago." He turns to one of the assorted obsequious advisors clustered on either side of the dais. "Why did she not die before now, Grizz'm? Why?"

Grizz'm, Gravel's portly first minister, his white beard waxed to a point, his face glistening with sweat, stammers a reply. "You ordered her kept alive, sire."

"Did not," Gravel retorts. He turns his attention back to Prak'kà, still kneeling. "You!"

"Your Majesty?"

"What about that boy, that page of hers?"

"The same, sire."

Gravel nods, pleased. An instant later, his face reddens with rage. He leaps to his feet, springs over the five steps from throne to floor and kicks the soldier hard in the ribs. Prak'kà falls over, rights himself. Gravel kicks him again. He stays down.

"The same? The same? I ordered him beheaded. Her too. I did."

Prak'kà opens his mouth to object. Grizz'm, behind the king and unseen by his master, shakes his head warningly at the soldier.

"Don't argue with me, soldier," Gravel snarls. "Are you arguing with me?"

"No, sire."

"I want heads. Do you hear me? Heads. Heads. Lots of heads."

He spins back to Grizz'm. "A Wall of Traitors. That's what we need. Yes. A Wall of Traitors. It if it was good enough for Grandpa Fvorag, it's good enough for me. Better, even."

He glares down at Prak'kà. "You," he snarls.

"Sire?"

"I think… Yes." His face breaks out into a ghoulish grin. "I will inaugurate it with you." He boots Prak'kà savagely in the head then hollers to another soldier, "Seize him!"

The soldier grabs Prak'kà, a little too eagerly.

"You will regret this, Korb'at," Prak'kà hisses.

"Maybe," Korb'at retorts, dragging his former superior officer toward the door. "Likely not."

"But Your Grace," Prak'kà calls back to the king. "You said— You ordered—"

Gravel ignores Prak'kà, stares out the window at the vast expanse of brown, brittle lawn that rolls unevenly from the castle wall to the partly stripped forest beyond.

"Yes. A Wall of Traitors." His head bobs briskly. "Grizz'm?"

"Sire?"

"A wall. Build it today. Now. Down in the village square. And fill it by suns-down. I don't care how, or who's up there. Just make sure she is."

"The Elderbard, sire?"

"Elderbard, Grizz'm?" Gravel's eyes blaze. "You forget yourself. What is an Elderbard? There is no Elderbard."

"Y-yes, sire. I mean, no sire."

"I want her staked right at the top, so that when I ride into the village I can watch the vulture ants playing with her. See to it, Grizz'm."

"Of course."

"Now!"

Grizz'm bows low and backs toward the door. "Your Majesty."

Gravel pivots around. "Wait."

Grizz'm stops, bows again. "Your Grace?"

"Send couriers to all the villages. I want a Wall of Traitors in every village square in Q'ntana. Every one. Do you hear?"

"Yes, sire. Right away, sire." He bows again, turns and hurries to the door.

"By suns-down," Gravel shouts after him. "By suns-down. Do you hear? Or I will see yours up there too."

The throne room fades.

"Right at the top. Instead of hers."

My tumble is no longer leisurely. I plummet earthward and, with a crashing splash, drop deep into the ocean.

eight

When I surfaced, I was alone in the middle of a vast, endless sea, empty but for the dazzling reflections of two soon-to-be setting suns and a fog that rolled toward me in between them. No land jutted up from any horizon. No seabirds screeched through the cloudless sky. The only sound in this infinite watery wasteland was the faint plash of tiny wavelets and my hacking cough as I spit up all the brine I had swallowed.

"O'ric!" I shouted into the sky, half-angry, half-bemused.

To no great surprise, O'ric did not reply.

With no shore to swim to, I treaded water and waited. And waited. And waited.

The suns sunk lower into the sky, darkening from white-yellow to fiery gold. The fog rolled and billowed. Still, I waited.

Finally, when both daylight and my stamina were nearly depleted, a distant sculling sound broke through the plashing. As it drew nearer, a swish-swash-swish joined its gentle rhythm. Not long after, a giant tartaruca paddled toward me from out of the fog, muttering loudly, nonstop.

"Here and there, hither and yon. Little more than an errand boy, don't you know."

The tartaruca stopped in front of me, his single eye squinting short-sightedly from the center of his fleshy, mud-colored head.

"Is that you, Pryma?" I asked.

"Is that you, your bardship? My eyesight is not what it once was. Not at all." He pushed his face into mine. "It must be. Who else would it be? Who else could it be? Well, right on time, I suppose. Climb up, now. Don't be dilly-dallying. I do enough of that for the both of us. Don't dilly-dally, they always tell me. I don't, don't you know. But nor am I as young as once I was. Not like you, your bardship. You, sir, are as young as ever you were."

I struggled to climb up onto Pryma's slick, scaly back. We were both too wet. Whenever I half-managed, I lost my grip and slid back into the water.

"This always happens, don't you know. I keep asking for a rope ladder. No one listens. No one. Not one. Not ever." He sank slowly into the water, still talking. "Don't you be going anywhere," he burbled.

"Where would I go?" I grumbled.

A long breath later, Pryma rose up underneath me, still talking. I grabbed onto his neck before I could slide off again, and away we swam.

"An errand-boy, that's all I am. Fetch this one. Fetch that one. Go here. Go there. Nothing against you, your bardship. Nothing at all. I know it is important work you are here to do. That's what they tell me. Important work. Mind you, they would say that, wouldn't they. Are you all right up there? Please say. I want you to be comfortable, don't you know. Yes, important work…"

As the suns dropped into the sea, Pryma's nonstop chatter lulled me into a daze and, before M'nor luminescence could brighten the velvet sky, I was asleep and in the dreamwalkers' realm.

I hover just outside the village square. The afternoon is bright. The village is not. Its squalid buildings lean precariously into one another as shabby villagers stumble dispiritedly along its sewage-streaked roads. A whip cracks, a familiar sound not only in Castle Rose Village, but in every Q'ntana village in these times. The townsfolk push and shove each other to clear the road for the King's Men, muscular, black-clad soldiers on sleek black stallions. One elderly man cannot shuffle out of the way quickly enough. The lead soldier strikes him down, where he is trampled to death by the soldier's mounted companions.

Flanked and followed by more lash-bearing King's Men, weary, malnourished horses drag rickety wagons laden with wood, stone, rope and spikes toward the town center. Laborers, bony and ragged, trudge behind. At the village square, a second group of haggard men, supervised with equal brutality by a second group of soldiers, has finished preparing the ground for the Wall of Traitors that Gravel has ordered to be built here.

High overhead, a massive black cloud scuds toward Castle Rose from the west, borne by an icy gust and a clap of thunder. A horse on the village road rears. Its wagon tips, scattering rocks and planks. A soldier drives his saber through the wagon driver's chest, slaughters the horse. Death and debris are left behind as the King's Men press their surviving charges forward to the village square. There, one anxious eye on the storm nearing the castle and another on their savage masters, the laborers begin work on the wall.

The only storm ushered in by the cloud is a storm of terror. Accompanied by more claps of thunder, the cloud smashes through an upper-story window and disappears into Castle Rose.

Now as before, I see into Gravel's throne room. Little has changed. A self-satisfied grin pasted on his face, Gravel is unruffled by the cloud's incursion into his castle. The same cannot be said for his courtiers and advisors. Pale with fear, they dare say nothing — to each other or to the king. Even the soldiers who guard the entry squirm anxiously.

With a whooshing roar, the cloud rams the double doors. The doors shudder, only for a breath, then surrender, disintegrating into dust. Soldiers and courtiers scatter. Gravel turns as the cloud eddies into a sooty column that, in an instant, becomes Bo'Rà K'n. He is an imposing figure cloaked in black, a swirling mass of dusky mist largely masking his face.

Gravel seems unafraid. He is either courageous beyond words or foolish beyond reason. "I killed your bard for you," he says, in an almost offhand way. "What do you want from me now?"

Bo'Rà K'n towers over the king. "You killed the bard," he says icily.

"That's what I said, isn't it? And now she will sit right at the top of my Wall of Traitors." Gravel reclines into his throne. "It will be just like Grandpa Fvorag's, only better. He only had bards. I have an Elderbard. Grandpa never had an Elderbard."

Bo'Rà K'n leans into him. "Do you realize what it is that you have unleashed?"

Gravels crosses his legs casually, studies his highly buffed fingernails. "Not my problem, is it?"

Bo'Rà K'n steps back, spreads his cloak. "No?" He stares past the throne to the window. It shatters.

"What did you do that for?"

"First Fvorag, then S'kyaga," Bo'Rà K'n says, as much to himself as to the king. He glares down at Gravel. "No more!" he roars.

Gravel shrinks back, for the first time displaying a tinge of fear. "You can't do anything to me," he whines. "You wouldn't dare. I am king."

Without moving, Bo'Rà K'n dissolves back into mist.

Emboldened, Gravel sits up and pokes a finger into the mist. "See?" he sneers.

The mist that is Bo'Rà K'n eddies savagely around king and throne,

*engulfing them both. Gravel chokes, coughs. "I am king," he wails, gagging…
then cries no more…for he is no more.*

*Another roaring whoosh. The mist swells back into a cloud, expands to fill
the room then pushes back out through the doorway. The throne room is now
empty of king, soldiers and courtiers, its gold dulled and tarnished.*

*The cloud whips through the castle, its greedy tendrils leaving no room
untouched. Strangled cries echo through the sprawling network of halls, cor-
ridors and chambers. The cloud then pushes out of all windows at once and
coils stranglingly around the castle, merging with the stone and mortar. The
ancient fortress trembles, quakes…refuses to fall. Enraged, the cloud tightens
even more, sucking all color and substance from the once-mighty redoubt. Its
mission complete, the cloud rises and gusts back to the west.*

All that remains of Castle Rose is a spectral hull, reeking of despair.

All is silent.

All is dark.

When I opened my eyes, Aygra and B'na were peeking up over the
horizon, on either side of the fog that still sat atop the water. The suns
shot darts of orange, yellow and white into the lightening sky. Moments
later, dawn's illumination began to pick out a silvery slip of beach strewn
with giant, misshapen boulders in singles and clusters. A tree-fringed
dirt path wound up from the beach through a flower-studded meadow
to a giant stone circle. A dense, dark forest of gurja trees stretched up
into the gently rolling hills beyond it.

And Pryma was still talking.

nine

"**A**h, the shore. We're nearly there. Are you? There, I mean." Pryma twisted his head but couldn't turn it quite far enough to see me. "You haven't fallen off, have you? Your bardship? Are you there? I will be in trouble if you have. Big trouble. Hallo? Hallo? Are you there? Hallo?"

"I'm here. I'm here," I managed to interject before Pryma started up again. "Don't you ever stop talking?"

Pryma harrumphed. "They said you might be headstrong. Never said you would be rude. No call for rudeness, don't you know. No call at all."

With both suns having crested the horizon, the sky was a clear, unblemished azure. The sole cloud was a dusky scar in the far distance, well beyond the forest.

"Bo'Rà K'n," I whispered.

"Bo'Rà K'n, indeed." Although Pryma continued to swim forward, the beach grew no nearer. "He was expected, don't you know. Just as you were." He nodded his head at the cloud. "That is what you will be needing to attend to, I'll wager. Not that smudge, of course. That unpleasant Tikkan dreamwalker fellow who is always conjuring it up. Not that it is any of my concern. None at all.

"Rev'Àn, he was, when I knew him as a lad. That was a long time ago. Once upon a time, you might say, your bardship. He was a strange one, even in those days. Not like his sister. No, not like Na'an at all. Although she has an edge about her, she does. All those Tikkan do. That's their way. Young Rev'Àn? He was just mean. For no reason. None at all. Kept getting meaner too. And now? Well, look at him."

The cloud eddied angrily higher into the sky then disappeared.

"I am," I said.

"What are you going to do about him? Hmm? What are you going to do? Whatever it is, better you than me. I have no time for that one.

None at all. Last time I saw him, he bit my tail. Hard. He has teeth, that one. Why did he bite my tail, you ask? Because I would not swim any faster for him. I go as I go, I told him. That was not good enough. Not for that Rev'Àn. So he bit my tail. Did I mention that?" His tail swished defiantly.

"I—"

Pryma jerked to a stop, his tail still swishing. For all his huffing and plashing, the tartaruca had carried me no closer to the beach, which remained the same distance from us as it had always been. Once again he tried, unsuccessfully, to twist his head around to see me. "You can swim, can't you?" he asked, still stretching his neck. "They said you could swim. There would be no reason to say so if it were otherwise. Still, I like to check…not that there is anything I could do if you couldn't. Nothing at all, don't you know. Can you? You didn't say."

Without waiting for an answer, he began to sink into the ocean.

"This is as far as the story will let me go. Did I mention that?" Only Pryma's head remained exposed. It, too, dropped from view, and his remaining words were an incomprehensible gurgle. Sighing, I swam toward shore.

At first, as I had experienced on Pryma's back, the distance between me and the beach never compressed. I made no progress, as hard as I paddled. Then, just as I feared that I lacked the strength to continue, the shore raced toward me with a sudden surge. An instant later, my mouth full of sand, I lay on my stomach staring at two giant hairy feet.

"You look terrible," a deep gravelly voice called down to me from a great height.

An oversize hand, equally hairy, pulled me to standing and fussily brushed the sand from my face and clothes.

"Stop that." I punched his hands away. "Who are you?"

Panesh — I did not yet know his name — was two heads taller than I was and stocky. Although hairier than anyone I had ever seen, his face was clean-shaven. He wore coarse cotton trousers that stopped at his calves and a bright, shimmery-green sleeveless vest. His thick, wavy red-brown hair fell midway down his back and was tied neatly into a ponytail. He circled me, flicking sand from my shoulders.

"If only…" He tsked and shook his head. "You will have to do."

"I said stop it!" I backed away angrily. "I will have to do what? Who are you?"

Panesh tilted his head to the left and sniffed the air. He tilted it to the right, sniffed again, then nodded knowingly. Almost immediately, the fog seethed toward us from the ocean, blocking the sky and obscuring everything in the mid-distance.

"Time to go," he declared and loped off down the beach. The fog crawled closer. "Are you coming?" he called back.

"No." I ground my bare heels into the sand. "Not until you tell me who you are and where you want to take me."

Panesh halted and spun around. "That Pryma," he muttered. "For all his talking, talking, talking, did he not tell you anything?"

"You know Pryma?"

"Everyone knows Pryma. More's the pity." He tapped a hairy foot impatiently. "Well, are you coming?" He took off again.

I scrambled to catch up. What else was there to do.

"Hurry."

"Where are we going?"

He stopped again and turned. His eyes gaped in astonishment, and his bushy eyebrows shot up to meet his hairline. "Where are we going? Where are we going? Back to the start of the story, of course. Where else would we be going?"

ten

Just ahead, through billows of swirling fog, sat Na'an, a much younger Na'an than I had ever experienced. Like the Na'an of Toshar's MoonQuest, she was ethereal with milky skin and long silver hair. Here, though, she was in her late teen years and sat at a loom that was at once solidly wooden and airily unreal. As, humming softly, she turned the wheel, dreams, each bearing a likeness of its sleeping dreamer, spun from it and floated off into the fog. If she knew of our presence, she gave no sign of it.

"What is this place? Why are we here?" I whispered.

"Shh," Panesh replied. "Look."

A young man marched out of the mist and up to Na'an. A few seasons her senior, he towered over her. His blond hair was of medium length and he wore an elegant suit of gray and blue that showed off his taut, fit body. His face was hard, distorting handsome, chiseled features, and his mouth twisted into a contemptuous sneer. He gripped Na'an's loom tightly, preventing its wheel from turning. She pushed his hand away, resumed her spinning.

"This is a waste of time," he snarled. "Don't I keep telling you that?"

"You do," she responded evenly.

"Why, then? You know I am right."

"Do I?"

He paced in front of her in increasing agitation. "You send them dreams. They ignore them. You send them more dreams. They ignore those. How long must this go on before you see the futility of it all? Why do you bother?"

"What makes you suppose that it is a bother?"

He snorted contemptuously. "I have a better idea."

"You always have a better idea," she said, not glancing up from her loom. "What is it this time?"

He raised his arm as if to strike her or knock her loom over, then thought better of it. "No one will ignore *my* dreams. Not anymore."

As he dropped his arm, his clothing blackened and a broad, coal-colored cloak unfurled behind him. His hair, too, darkened to jet, as did the fog seething angrily around him.

"Join me, sister."

Na'an suspended her spinning and silently watched her brother's transformation. Her face remained impassive and calm.

"There can be no together in this, Rev'Àn," she replied at last.

"Then I will find a way to destroy you," he growled. The dusky fog twisted up his body to his face, veiling most of its features.

Na'an lowered her gaze and resumed her dream-spinning. "You will do what you must, brother. That is your role. I know mine."

"Your role will come to naught, sister. I will prevail." With that, the dark fog enveloped him fully and he was gone.

"You may show yourself now, Panesh." Na'an rose from her loom and, in a breath, aged into the timeless Tikkan dreamwalker I had always known her to be.

Panesh stepped forward, pushing me out in front of him. Na'an studied me closely.

"The youngest of the old, who is also the oldest of the young. Just like your grandfather. Just like Toshar...or was he just like you, I wonder? No matter. That is Time's concern, not mine. You are here now. That is the important thing." She paused, noticing my condition. "You are wet and dirty. That will not do."

Panesh looked downcast. "I am sorry, Na'an. I tried to clean him up."

"No matter."

In that moment, a green-and-scarlet bird flew out of the fog to perch on her shoulder. "Caaa-ooo-eee," the bird shrieked. "Pa-REE-ka, caaa-ooo-eee! Pa-REE-ka. Pa-REE-ka. Pa-REE-ka."

"Is that Parika? How can that be Parika?" I was confused. Parika had perished on Toshar's journey, incinerated by the fire-breathing serpent S'kala.

The bird flapped his wings excitedly at hearing his name. He circled my head three times, then disappeared back into the fog, screeching his signature call. "Pa-REE-ka. Pa-REE-ka. Pa-REEEEE-ka."

"Parika is a creature of the Dream Realms. He can no more die than I can. Nor can Nya." Na'an whistled a short melody and a furry black-and-white k'nrah, another of Toshar's companions, leapt into her arms from the fog, purring. "Nor can my brother."

Nya scampered up Na'an's dress and draped herself around the dreamwalker's shoulders. Stroking the k'nrah, Na'an touched my arm. "But you can. Again. Because you are human. Again. My brother cannot take your life. Not directly. Not yet. Until he gains that power, he will conjure up all he can to thwart you. Should the day arrive when it is possible for him to kill you, he will — without a minim's hesitation or regret. You can be absolutely certain of that."

"He will not succeed," I replied with a confidence I wasn't sure I felt. I was human again. "He cannot."

"I admire your self-assurance, Ko'leya. But remember that who you have been as B'na cannot help you here. Here you are Ben: fully human and fully mortal. You would be foolish to underestimate my brother's power, cunning and determination. This is Bo'Rà K'n's final chance at eternal dominion. He will stop at nothing to achieve it. He will destroy anything that might stop him. He will destroy you, if he can."

She sighed and returned to her loom. She spun out a few more dreams then spoke again. "Bo'Rà K'n has failed twice before, once because of your grandfather and once because of your mother. He does not take well to failure, as most in Q'ntana could testify if they dared. Nor does he look kindly on you, as son of Q'nta and grandson of Toshar. Yet your greatest gift and strength is something he will dismiss as your greatest weakness."

"What is that, Na'an?"

Her eyes bore deeply into mine. "Your humanity, Ben. Your humanness."

I stared blankly back at her.

"Embrace that and he will not know how to fight you."

"I don't understand."

"You will, when the time is right," she said. "For now...The SunQuest."

"That is why I'm here. But what is it? O'ric has told me nothing. Pryma told me less. All Panesh did was bring me here, to you. Where must I go? What must I do?"

"Discover your destiny and fulfill it."

"Which is?"

Na'an laughed softly. "Even as Ben you should know better than to ask me that question." She spun one more dream then rose. "Come," she said.

Her hand was soft and delicate as a rose petal as she pulled me deeper into the fog. Her grip, almost masculine in its firmness, was at the same time so ethereal that it felt as though she might merge in an instant with the mist. Panesh followed at a respectful distance. Unlike most fog, there was no dampness to this one. Nor was it entirely dry. If anything, it felt like the most filmy of gauze, rubbing gently against my skin as we passed through it. Na'an said nothing as we walked, her pace measured but purposeful. Although I had many questions, I knew she would answer none of them. The only sound was Nya's purring, which reverberated loudly through the stillness.

I cannot say how long we walked. It felt like days, yet, also, as though no time had passed. It felt, too, as though we had traveled nowhere at all, for our destination appeared no different from our starting point. When we reached it, Na'an released my hand and reached into the fog. Satisfied with something I could not perceive, she dropped her arms to her side and stood in silence, waiting. After a time, Nya dropped to the ground and rubbed her head against my leg, purring even more resonantly.

"She likes you," Panesh said, breaking the wordlessness.

I knelt down and scratched under the k'nrah's chin. She leapt into my arms and kneaded my bare skin with her front paws, a low throaty growl causing her entire body to vibrate. From there, she climbed onto my shoulder, licking my face sloppily on her way up. Then she promptly fell asleep, snoring gurglingly.

"That is good," Na'an pronounced. "Very good." She stroked the k'nrah's head. Nya moaned softly and resumed her snoring.

"Because?" I asked.

"Nya will lead you to the Maya Ko," she replied. "She would have led you there regardless, because I have asked her to. That she likes you will make the journey more pleasant for you, and her return more pleasant for me."

"The Maya Ko?" Panesh whispered reverently.

"What is the Maya Ko?" I asked.

"You do not know the Maya Ko?" Panesh gaped at me as though I were a halfwit.

"Panesh!" Na'an snapped. She turned to me. "The doorway of destiny. The first of the p'rtulles you must pass through on your SunQuest."

Panesh raised his eyebrows at the uncomprehending look on my face, holding back the trenchant comment so clearly at the tip of his tongue. Finally, his incredulity exploded. "How can you not know about p'rtulles?" he sputtered. "Especially the Maya Ko."

Na'an glared at him but said nothing.

"Maybe I did once…upon a time," I said. I shook my head.

Not only was it peculiar to be human again after so long, it was even more peculiar to be aware that whatever knowingness I still carried as B'na was hidden in increasingly inaccessible places within me. Adding to the oddness were my memories from the last time I was in Q'ntana as Ben. Some of those memories felt impossibly fresh. Others were so distant I could barely touch them.

Na'an patted my hand. "That is what it means to be human. You remember less and less…until you remember more and more."

"Then you start all over again," I sighed. "Tell me what it is I have forgotten."

"There is not nearly time enough for that." Na'an laughed. "You will remember what needs remembering when that need is most pressing."

"And a p'rtulle?" I asked with a sharp look at Panesh.

"A gateway to other realms. You must pass through three if your SunQuest is to achieve Crowning."

"Crowning?"

Na'an said nothing.

"How do I find them, these p'rtulles?" I sensed Na'an's reply before she spoke it.

"They are not yours to find," she replied. "They will find you…in their time, not yours."

"How will I know them?" This was most likely another pointless question, but I had to ask.

"They will know you," she said simply.

I groaned, deeply frustrated. "You are as bad O'ric. The two of you speak only in riddles. How am I to embark on this SunQuest, let alone Crown it, whatever that means, if no one will tell me what it is?"

The fog began to lift, though the one in my mind remained discomfitingly intact.

"It is for you to find your own way, Ben Ko'leya," Na'an said. "That is why you are here."

I thought I detected the faint ebb of the surf and the slight salty tickle of the sea's tang, and I hoped that I was not about to be dropped, once more, into the middle of an ocean.

"It is for Panesh to help you," she continued. "That is why he is here. It is for me to guide you as dreams would guide you. That is why I am here. The initial p'rtulle—"

"When it finds me," I interjected.

Na'an ignored my interruption. Panesh regarded me peevishly.

"The initial p'rtulle will carry you back to Castle Rose…back to the old home I have already sent you in dream."

"Gravel's Castle Rose."

She nodded. "What you need to know next you will discover there…and beyond."

As the fog continued to fade, Na'an faded with it, until Panesh and I stood back on the rocky beach under a cloudless cerulean sky. My dry clothes and sandals, along with a sleeping Nya draped on my shoulder, were the only clues that Panesh and I had ever strayed from this spot.

eleven

"I have food for you…for us," Panesh said. He retrieved a large woven basket from a hollow in one of the boulders. When he opened it, I instantly remembered what it was to be human and ravenous. How many generations had it been since I had last eaten?

Panesh spread a gold- and silver-checked cloth on the sand and laid out more food from the basket than it could possibly have held: joints of meat, slices of fowl, wheels of cheese, many varieties of bread loaves and a vibrant array of fruits in all shapes and sizes. From somewhere deep in the wicker, he pulled out a large flagon of wine, two water skins, large plates for each of us, a smaller dish for Nya and all the requisite utensils. Once he had arranged and rearranged the feast to his satisfaction, Panesh grabbed my hand and shook it solemnly.

"I am Panesh," he said. "It seems that we are to be traveling companions."

I laughed and shook it back, heartily. "Good to know you, Panesh. And thank you," I said, indicating the generous repast, "for all this."

"I am sorry if I—" he began. "I may not have made the best impression when we first—"

"No, no," I said. "I understand. When you are about Na'an's business…"

Panesh eyed me soberly. Had I offended him? Then he exploded into gales of laughter, guffawing so hard, so loud and for so long that I thought he might explode. "You are all right," he said, pumping my hand again. "I could not be certain about you at first. But you *are* all right."

*   *   *

The earth trembled, so subtly at first that I assumed it to have been my imagination. Nya's head jerked up. Her eyes darted warily in all directions then snapped shut again when she could identify no imminent danger. Within a breath, she had dropped back into her postprandial nap and I had returned to my dreamless dozing, still uncomfortably full from our substantial meal. Panesh lay across the picnic cloth from me, his eyes twitching in dream, unaware of any disturbance. Between us, the ground was littered with bones, cheese rinds and other detritus, as well as with enough leftover to keep us well-fed through several more days.

There was no mistaking the second tremor, alarmingly more powerful than the first. Nya sprung to her feet, barking. Panesh leapt up after her.

"We must get moving," he said with quiet urgency just before a third tremor struck, then a fourth.

We had barely finished packing the two travel satchels that Panesh had snatched from the basket when the lightning-scarred sky turned black, winds squalled in from all directions at once, massive breakers crashed onto the beach and the thundering heavens hurled cascades of water at us. Through it all, the earth continued to shudder and quake, and the elements boomed deafeningly around us.

I gestured toward a nearby cluster of boulders that offered the possibility of shelter. Panesh shook his head and pointed farther along the beach.

"Too far," I mouthed. It was futile even to shout. I pointed instead back to the boulders.

Panesh shook his head again, even more adamantly. With one giant hand, he gripped my waist and heaved me up, determined to haul me down the beach. I wriggled free, cursing.

While Panesh and I mimed our argument, Nya raced around us, yapping loudly and pecking at our heels. When we ignored her, she bolted up toward the meadow path, dashing back when we failed to follow. Barking shrilly, she bounced up and down on her hind legs, her front claws scoring my trousers and Panesh's shins. Panesh scooped her up angrily. Struggling against his forceful grip, she snarled at him and bit his nose. He howled in pain, flinging her to the ground.

"Come, Nya," I bellowed and made for the rocks.

She followed at a distance, barking and whining, her belly dragging through the rain-soaked sand.

The ground beneath me pitched, catapulting me across the beach. From my landing spot, my face coated with drenched grit, I watched the earth split open. Those sheltering boulders that were to have been my destination cracked, crumbled and collapsed into a newly formed chasm. Had I made it there, I would have been crushed, possibly killed.

Nya slithered toward me, gripped my shirtsleeve between her teeth and yanked. The fabric ripped and she took off up the path. This time, Panesh and I sprinted after her, along the path, past the stone circle and into the gurja forest.

As heavy as the rain had been on the beach, the forest canopy was so thick that only a light trickle managed to drizzle down through the trees. That helped our progress. What hindered it was jungly ground cover so dense with tangles of knotted vines and roots that keeping pace with Nya's circuitous scampering would have been impossible had her nonstop barking not clearly communicated her route.

Panesh was panting heavily and I could barely breathe by the time we caught up with Nya, next to a vast, sunken clearing. If the forest was still dark and drizzly, within the clearing the suns shone warmly on tall, breeze-rippled grasses.

"Don't you ever do that again," I wheezed at Panesh.

"What?"

"Next time you try to force me to go somewhere or do something… the way you did back on the beach? If you do anything like that again, I will not have you on this SunQuest with me. I don't care what Na'an says. Do you understand?"

Panesh fidgeted with the middle button on his vest. He stared first at his feet then, refusing to meet my eyes, watched Nya.

"I know you were trying to help, but… You must promise."

"I—" He regarded at me uneasily. "You will not say anything to Na'an?"

"Of course not. As long as you promise."

A relieved smile broke out on his face. "I was afraid for your safety, Ko'leya. But you are right. I am sorry. It will not happen again."

For her part, Nya paid no attention to us. She was too intent on sniffing a tiny patch of ground at the very edge of the clearing. Satisfied that she had located the spot she sought, she pawed at the ground, turned to make sure we were watching, purred softly, pawed at the ground again and leapt into the clearing.

"Nya?" I called anxiously.

She had disappeared in mid-jump, never landing in the clearing… or anywhere else.

"Nya!" I called again. There was no sign of her.

"Now what?" I asked Panesh.

Mimicking Nya, Panesh dropped to his hands and knees and sniffed the same ground. Then he sniffed the air above it. Then he sniffed the ground again.

"Well?"

"Shh." He pressed his ear to the ground.

"What do you hear?"

"Shh!" He turned his head to listen with his other ear then stood up, dried leaves and twigs sticking to his pants and poking into his hair. "I say we follow."

"Follow? Where? She's gone."

Panesh pointed into the clearing. "In there. Jumping. The way Nya did."

"Are you sure?"

"No," Panesh replied. "I am not at all sure. But Na'an said that Nya would lead us to the first p'rtulle, to the Maya Ko."

I stared into the clearing, hoping for a glimpse of the k'nrah or of anything that might hint at what had happened to her…or for confirmation that we ought to follow her.

"What do you know about the Maya Ko? Other than what Na'an said."

Panesh shrugged. "Very little. That it is sacred. So sacred that it only permits those it deems worthy to pass through it."

"Do you think this is the Maya Ko?"

"I doubt it. It must be the way to get there, I think. Maybe." He paused. "There is only one way to find out."

"Unfortunately."

"I should go first, in case—"

"No. Together." If we were going to disappear as Nya had, I wanted us to disappear together, preferably to the same place. I grabbed his hand. We jumped.

*   *   *

Panesh and I stood on a dry, dusty plain that stretched endlessly and desolately in all directions. Forest and clearing had vanished. There was no sign of Nya, and the emptiness of the place swallowed my voice as I called her name.

Panesh looked up and pointed.

"What?" I didn't see anything.

"The suns."

"What about the suns?"

"They are not there. The color of the sky. Look at that too."

He was right. The sky was empty of suns, yet its light was as bright as if it were midday. And the color *was* off, diffusing a greenish cast that resembled more the hue of sea than sky. As if to underline its ocean-like character, the green tint slowly deepened to turquoise and wavelike patterns rippled silently through it from horizon to horizon. While most waves matched the color of the sky, some repainted themselves in shades of crimson, orange and pink. Those waves streaked earthward like sunbeams. Where they converged, fifty paces ahead of us, the earth steamed, smoked, smoldered, then…

CRA-A-A-CK!!

A massive leafless tree thrust itself out of the earth. As it settled quiveringly into place, arthritic roots thicker than one of Panesh's legs shot out from it in all directions. We hopped and danced around the assertive roots to avoid being knocked over.

"The Maya Ko," Panesh breathed.

A broad, weather-worn door, a wrought-iron ring at its center, trembled into view in the middle of the tree's gray, furrowed trunk. Panesh moved toward it as though entranced, his right arm outstretched longingly. Before he could touch the door, it blended back into the trunk.

"No," he moaned. A single tear rolled down his cheek as he backed away.

"What is it?" I asked.

"You." He pushed me toward the tree. "It has come for you, not me." The door re-formed as I drew nearer. I reached for it then pulled back.

"No," Panesh insisted. "You must."

A gust of wind blustered through the plain. It should have raised dust and dirt, but it didn't. Instead, everything around us rippled in and out of focus. A second gust held the blur longer. A third held it longer still. Shards of the forest we had left behind sliced through the tree.

Panesh shoved me harder. "You must pass through," he shouted over the wind. "You must. Now."

I took his hand. "You mean 'we,'" I yelled back.

"If it will let me." Panesh shook his hand free and pushed me again. "Go!"

I pulled on the ring. The door would not budge. I pushed. Still nothing. I felt a drop of rain and saw wavery shadows of the forest canopy. The wind blew harder now. The drizzle fell more steadily.

"Hurry," Panesh cried. "It will not wait."

"It won't open. I don't know what to do!"

An icy blast slapped my face and whooshed stingingly past my ears.

Elo-heeeeee-ia. Astel Elo-heeeeee-ia. Elo-heeeeee-ia.

Of course. The Ring of Unity. I touched my forehead with my left index finger and the door with my right hand. The door shuddered, but still would not open.

"What are you doing?" Panesh shouted. The wind whipped his ponytail into his mouth.

"Astel Elohia. The Ring of Unity," I shouted back. "It's in here." I tapped my forehead.

Panesh stood motionless, impervious to the wind's lashing. Then in a single movement too quick for me to resist, he picked me up and began to heave me, head first, into the door.

"What are you doing? Are you crazy? I told you not to do— Put me down!" I struggled to free myself, but Panesh was too strong. I clenched my teeth and braced myself against the coming impact. It never came. Instead, when my face was a hair's breadth from the iron ring, Panesh halted my trajectory and, gently, touched my forehead to the door.

The wind stopped. The blur faded. Forest and rain vanished. The cracks in the scene sealed. The door dissolved.

Panesh put me down and brushed me off. "I am sorry," he said.

"We will talk about this later," I said, teeth still clenched.

"I know I said I would not. I did not know what else to do."

"You could have—" I began, then stopped when I noticed what lay on the other side of the p'rtulle: Castle Rose on a rise overlooking the serpentine River Alanda, its wooden ferry dock almost right in front of us. In the early light of dawn, the castle's aspect was as it had been when I had lived in it, when it was still new: pink stones glinting against the lightening sky as the morning suns rose on either side of it.

Without thinking, I ran through the opening in the tree. I couldn't help myself. In my other life as Ben, Castle Rose was the only home I had known and, seeing it in front of me, both castle and my humanness beckoned to me more loudly than I could have thought possible.

"Are you coming?" I called over my shoulder.

Panesh followed tentatively, not sure the Maya Ko would let him through. It did. The instant both his feet landed on the Castle Rose side, the tree shattered into shards of light that merged with the dawning light.

As dawn brightened, I realized that the castle was not the Castle Rose of my previous lifetime. Its crumbling stone walls were encrusted with dirt. Many window frames bore cracked glass, shattered glass or no glass at all. And the flags, Castle Rose's ancient, glorious standards, had shredded into limp, filthy rags. It was every bit Gravel's Castle Rose.

"I thought Bo'Rà K'n destroyed all this," I said. "I saw it happen. In a dream."

"He did destroy it...or will," Panesh replied. "Na'an showed me the same dream."

"Then how— What do you mean?"

"The Maya Ko. It sends you wherever you need to go to start your story. Or finish it."

"Into the past?" I should not have been surprised at that possibility. Twists of time had long been hallmarks of my peculiar life. Lives.

"That is what a p'rtulle does. It carries you into the past or the future...or into other realms altogether."

"Which is this?"

"I do not know."

Studying the castle again, I tried to picture it as I had first seen it, when Reesa Kam'ana, the Heart of the Star restored to her care at the conclusion of The StarQuest, snapped it into existence in place of S'kryssna S'kyaga's malevolent Castle Do'am. At that time and for generations after, it had been a place of laughter and story, a place of vision, a place of promise. Even during its darkest years, when with Bo'Rà K'n's help King Fvorag had tyrannized Q'ntana, Castle Rose had managed to elude his control. Now, still the capital of Q'ntana, it was also the headquarters for Gravel's demonic madness.

However insidious, Fvorag's objectives had carried their own cruel logic. He had desired absolute control and brutal dominion over all Q'ntana, a goal shared with and carried out for Bo'Rà K'n, his master.

Gravel had no such goals. His sole interests involved random, mindless persecution and his own enrichment. In his twisted mind, anything was worth doing, regardless of cost or consequence, if it was viciously entertaining or would multiply the gold in his treasury. If there was truth in the Castle Rose dream that Na'an had sent me, Gravel was about to pay the ultimate cost and face the ultimate consequence.

twelve

Morning sounds drifted down toward us as we climbed the winding road from the ferry dock. If I closed my eyes to the castle's disrepair and pushed its deranged master from my mind, the blend of grunts and shouts, chirps and crows, clatter and clamor, could have seemed normal. It was anything but that, as we experienced with heart-rending clarity.

The road we walked, for example, was pitted and overgrown with weeds, slicing through a Great Lawn that was "great" only in its breadth. Its grasses were patchy, brown and uneven, and the horses and gita'as that grazed discontentedly on them were scrawny and ill-groomed. Upriver, the village, new since my time, was as shabby and unkempt as it had been in my vision. Its drab, ramshackle buildings listed disconsolately, as though some underground force was intent on uprooting them.

No, nothing here was "normal," and nothing displayed any sign of hope…or joy. The dawning suns-light only heightened the anguish I saw and felt around me, even as it brightened the sky.

Moments later, five girls in their early teen years sprinted across the Great Lawn from the direction of the riverbank village, challenging my despair. They giggled, taunting the five boys who chased after them. I smiled. Maybe Q'ntana wasn't as bad as it looked.

Although Panesh and I stood directly in the girls' path, they didn't notice us. We stepped aside, but regardless of how we danced, a collision was inevitable.

"Excuse me," I began, but then the girls ran not into us but through us. It was as though the girls were winds that whipped through and disheveled my insides. I wanted to shake myself all over to put everything back to rights. Then it happened again, with the boys.

"They don't see us?" I asked Panesh.

He shrugged. "It is possible."

The girls looped back and headed for the river, the boys close behind. When they reached the ferry dock, they dove into the river, laughing, shrieking and splashing.

"At least someone is happy," I noted.

"Perhaps," Panesh offered, "in this moment. As for the next..."

We continued up toward the castle.

"Wait." I stopped. "If we go into the castle and Bo'Rà K'n comes, like in the dream, won't the same thing happen to us as will happen to everyone else?"

Panesh scratched his chin and stared up at the decaying battlements. "You were not hurt in the dream, were you?"

I shook my head.

"Nor I."

"Does that mean that it's safe for us to go in?"

He considered my question. "I do not know."

"Even if it is safe, do we go inside or wait out here for something to happen? And if we go in, where do we go and what do we do?"

He pondered some more. "I cannot know. This is your SunQuest, Ko'leya."

It was, and Na'an had been clear that we would find the next answers we needed here at the castle. We pressed on toward the drawbridge. When we reached the moat, I stopped again. Once upon a time, the moat had been clean enough to drink from. An underwater channel had connected it to the River Alanda, which cycled and recycled its water. Sometimes, moku fish found their way up through the channel and into the moat. Their iridescent scales would shimmer a brilliant silver at suns-merge and an equally radiant gold at dusk. The groundskeepers would catch them before dark and cook them as a feast for visitors to the weekly market. There were no fish in the moat now. Nothing could survive in its slimy, stinking, mold-green sludge.

The drawbridge wobbled precariously, creaking and moaning as we crossed. Rust flaked from its corroded chains. We stepped over the gaps where planks were missing and passed under the unguarded archway into the courtyard. Where were we in time? Had my mother been killed or was her execution still to come? As uncomfortable as the wish made me feel, I hoped her hanging was already in the past. If it had yet to happen, I knew I would not be able to stop it. That would be worse than knowing she had already died.

The Castle Rose courtyard had once been a superb and grand space — elegant on state occasions, merry most other times. Even on market days, the bustling disarray was joyful, with merchants and customers equally animated and brightly dressed. Now, the courtyard was littered with rubbish and cluttered with scowling, ill-garbed, ill-mannered folk who could no more see us than the teens had been able to. I gazed up at the windows and arches that bound the cloister. Part of me wanted to climb the stairs to those upper chambers and reexplore what had once been my Elderbard's realm. Another part could not wait to be quit of here. A third was rooted in place, grimly fascinated by all that evil and madness had wrought on this once-beneficent citadel.

"Have you been here before?" I asked Panesh as we continued our aimless wandering.

He shook his head.

"I wish you could have seen it…once upon a time."

"This was your home?" He reflected on the decay.

"When it was new."

"You must be sad to see it like this."

I had not known sadness as B'na. I did now.

We stopped at the north-wing entrance. My apartments had been here. My study too. I was not yet ready to go in. I signaled for Panesh to wait.

"What are you?" I asked him, as much to put off stepping inside as out of curiosity. "You're not a Tikkan dreamwalker like Na'an. Are you? And why are you here? Why did she send you with me? She never said, and you have not said anything…about anything."

Panesh laughed. "It is not always clear why Na'an does what she does, or says what she says. That is the nature of dreams, so it must also be the nature of dreamwalkers. If I were one, maybe I would better understand."

"But you're not."

"No. I am Angarusha. Do you know what that is?"

"As B'na, I must. As Ben…"

"Angarusha walk between the worlds. We have one foot," he stamped one hairy foot on the uneven pavement, "in your world, and the other," he touched his other foot down feather-lightly, "in the world of dream and story. Sometimes, we are messengers for the Tikkan. Sometimes, we are messengers to the Tikkan."

"Which are you here?"

"Neither and both. We are also quicker than our size would indicate, fiercer than our temperament would suggest and gentler than our voices imply. As such, we make ideal companions for questers." He laughed so boomingly at this that I thought he would take down Castle Rose before Bo'Rà K'n could. "The truth is, I do not know why I am here with you, other than to aid and protect you however I can. When Tikkan request anything of Angarusha, we comply unquestioningly. The 'why' is not ever a concern or consideration. That is our nature. Na'an asked me to travel with you, so I do. There is nothing more I can tell you. Are you good with that, Ko'leya?"

"I am more than good with that, Panesh. I am grateful for it."

Panesh nodded, satisfied. "Now, what? Do we go inside?"

"I don't know." Scrutinizing each brick and stone for a clue as to what to do next, I walked to the center of the courtyard, doing my imperfect best to dodge those people who would unknowingly pass through me. I found no answers and returned to the north-wing doorway. The carvings of M'nor in all her lunar phases that had once adorned the lintel had been chipped away. Only crudely pocked stone remained. I touched the door. It rasped open, revealing a darkened, musty corridor. A chill shivered through me, immediately followed by an ominous foreboding. I grabbed Panesh's hand and tugged him back toward the castle's main gate.

"We can't stay in here," I whispered.

thirteen

The teens still cavorted in the river when we crossed back over the moat, their squealing laughter the only sign of cheer anywhere nearby. Once Bo'Rà K'n passed through, would anything resembling that kind of innocent delight ever visit this castle again? Gravel deserved what would befall him. But what of the innocent victims of his madness? They did not deserve the fate suggested by my dream.

"I have to stop it."

"What?"

"Everything. Gravel. Bo'Rà K'n. Whatever it is that is going to happen here." I turned back toward the castle. I would go inside and confront the king. I would kill him if that's what it took.

"No," Panesh said, softly but firmly. He gripped my arm tightly. "You must not."

"Why not? We have to do something. That why we're here. Isn't it?"

He pulled me away from the stink of the moat and partway down the road. "Your SunQuest is bigger than one king and one castle. I may not know a lot, but I know that. I say take care of your SunQuest, and king and castle will take care of themselves."

"What about them?" I pointed to the splashing youths.

"I wish I could give you an answer. I cannot. I do not know about them. I know only that Castle Rose has not spoken to you yet. You must at least wait for that."

I sighed. "You're right. But I feel so helpless." I clutched my chest. "And pain. I had forgotten what that felt like. I don't like it."

Your humanness. I heard Na'an's voice. *Embrace that and Bo'Rà K'n will not know how to fight you.*

"Did you hear that?" I asked Panesh.

"What?"

"Na'an."

He shook his head. "But I hear something else. A song. Listen."

The minor-key melody was familiar, though I knew I could never have heard it before. Even more baffling was that I recognized the comely woman who ambled toward us, distractedly humming it. Perhaps I had not yet lost all B'na's knowingness? I could only hope. The woman was slightly shorter and a few seasons older than I, with dark mahogany hair that made a pale complexion pierced by perceptive blue-green eyes seem even paler. As she approached, two red-headed twins, a young boy and girl, barreled toward her. They held hands and giggled loudly. The woman paused her singing at their approach and smiled warmly. The twins unlinked hands just long enough to race by either side of her. She ruffled their hair as they flew by.

"It's almost time for lessons," she called after them. "Don't be late again." She laughed when they pretended not to hear and resumed her song, singing more softly as she drew nearer to the castle.

My'leen. Her name is My'leen. I still do not know how I know her, but I do. I see her, not here on the Great Lawn. I see her in the clean but rundown village hovel where she lives with her younger sister, B'tha. Her parents are dead. Her grandparents too.

Her patron, if you can call him that, is Grizz'm, the king's elderly first minister. He owns her one-room shack and has only permitted My'leen and B'tha to remain living in it after their parents died because My'leen has agreed to teach the youngsters in the castle school. The curriculum, designed by Gravel himself, is vile and pernicious, and My'leen despises it. Still, she loves the children, and the alternative, agreeing to wed Grizz'm, would be considerably worse. Grizz'm has not abandoned the notion of taking My'leen as his wife. But he has not found a threat potent enough to force her into it. Not yet. He will. He has no doubt of that. For now, he is able keep a watchful eye on her during her daily duties in the castle.

As for My'leen, if she could conjure up a way to escape Grizz'm, Gravel and Castle Rose, she and B'tha would be gone quicker than lightning. But King's Men possess even fewer scruples than do their masters. Black Riders, those soldiers who have gone rogue, possess fewer still. Two young women traveling alone through Q'ntana can never be safe from either.

She will marry Grizz'm if she must. It is the least unpalatable in a vast catalogue of unpalatable choices.

How did I know all this about My'leen? And why did it matter? I never discovered an answer to the first question. The second answered itself almost immediately.

"Good day to you, sirs." My'leen tipped her head at us and continued on toward the castle.

Startled, I glanced around. Whom had she greeted? There was no one. We had been the only ones in her path.

"She saw us," I exclaimed.

"It would appear so."

I started after her. Panesh pulled me back.

"If she is able to see us when no one else can, we must to talk to her." In as few words as possible, I told Panesh what I had "seen" of her.

"Wait," he urged.

"For what? She will soon be inside the castle, in her classroom not long after that."

"For what is to be. For what already has been." It was Panesh's lips that moved; the voice that issued from them was O'ric's.

"More riddles," I muttered, shaking him off.

Before I could move toward My'leen, an elderly gentleman appeared twenty paces in front of her. When I say "appeared," I mean it literally. One moment the road was empty. The next, there he was: a thick mane of snowy hair falling past his shoulders to frame a deeply lined face that was at once kindly and intense. His eyes were close-set, chocolate-brown ovals flecked with orange. His nose was long and beak-like. A long cottony beard fluttered halfway down his chest. Barely My'leen's height, he leaned heavily on a simple walking staff of rough-hewn woods. For all the weight he placed on his staff, there was an ethereal quality to him, as though his very physicality was tentative. My'leen appeared to know him. She raised a hand in greeting.

"Yzythq'a," Panesh said. "I thought he might well turn up here. Interesting that you know My'leen. Interesting that My'leen knows him."

"Yzy—?

"Yzythq'a."

"Who is Yzythq'a?" I asked.

"Shh. Watch. You will see."

A massive, angry cloud whipped in from the far west on a gust of chill air, unnoticed by My'leen.

"Bo'Rà K'n," I said. "The dream."

Panesh nodded. "Wait."

As My'leen reached the old man, Yzythq'a raised his staff to the heavens. All sound and motion ceased. Birds hung motionless in the sky. The young swimmers were caught in mid-dive, drops of water suspended around their frozen bodies. The air was eerily still. Only Yzythq'a and My'leen were exempt, as were Panesh and I. As was Bo'Rà K'n. If anything, Yzythq'a's action accelerated his approach.

A deafening thunderclap shattered the silence, then another, over-powering Yzythq'a's words. My'leen pointed to her ears and shook her head. Yzythq'a repeated himself, nodded toward us. My'leen turned. Before she could acknowledge us, she saw Bo'Rà K'n's cloud and screamed. Even that could not be heard over the thunder. When the cloud narrowed and smashed through a castle window, she fell into Yzythq'a's arms and buried her head in his chest. With his free hand, he stroked her hair. A moment later, he lowered his staff. Time, sound and motion resumed.

Panicked cries assaulted us from all directions — from within the castle, from the village and from the river, where the young men and women paddled to the opposite shore and fled.

Another crack of thunder, this time from within the castle as Bo'Rà K'n's cloud punched out every castle window at once. The sound was chilling. Even more chilling was what happened next. As in my dream, the cloud swirled around Castle Rose, spiraling more and more tightly until the entire structure was enveloped. All sound from within ceased. When the castle was released, all that remained was a pale, insubstantial specter and scattered wisps of black mist. The cloud hovered menacingly over the village, where more weeping and cries of alarm greeted it, then sped back whence it had come.

Yzythq'a motioned for us to join him. "I was not certain he would leave you untouched," he said to us. "I suppose, though," he added to himself, "he had no choice."

My'leen wept softly.

"How do I stop that?" I asked as the cloud disappeared into the distance. "How can anyone stop that?"

"You will know what you need to know when you need to know it, Ben Ko'leya," Yzythq'a replied. "Panesh will help you. My'leen, as well."

"What happened?" My'leen whispered. "Is everyone...? Is anyone...?" She pulled herself free. "I must go."

"There will be no one there, child."

"No one? But—"

"They will be with Bo'Rà K'n now."

"With Bo'Rà K'n?" My'leen asked shakily. "Even B'tha?"

Yzythq'a nodded.

"And the children? B'tha was in the classroom with the children. They were waiting…for me."

"The children too."

"Why B'tha?" She burst into tears. *"Why?"* She fell back into Yzythq'a's arms. "Why was I spared?"

Yzythq'a held her until she had cried herself out.

"What happens now?" she whispered.

"Ben," he said.

"Ben? What is Ben? Who is Ben?"

"Meet the next king of Q'ntana."

She squinted up at Panesh. "You?" she asked.

Panesh tapped my shoulder. "Him."

"Me?" The next king of Q'ntana? That was absurd. How was I to be king? And why? That I was here to succeed my mother as Elderbard made as much sense as was possible in Q'ntana. But king?

Yzythq'a tapped a bony finger on my forehead. "You carry Astel Elohia, the Ring of Unity, yes?"

I nodded. "How do you know—?"

"Never mind that. Do you?"

"But—"

"It is a crown, yes?"

"Yes, but—"

"You are the son of Q'nta Ko'lar and great-nephew of the Kano'ha Kyri?"

"I don't see what—"

"There exists no other rightful heir to the throne of Q'ntana. You, Ben Ko'leya, are sole heir, as much to your great-uncle's legacy as to your mother's. King and Elderbard as one. Ko'lar and Kano'ha as one. That is what Astel Elohia is about. That is the new Law of Balance. That is your path. That is your destiny."

"No." Not after what had happened to my mother when she tried to succeed Kyri.

"You speak as though you believe you have a choice," Yzythq'a said.

"Of course I have a choice," I countered with more certainty than I felt.

"You made your choice already," he said. "The moment you agreed to return to Q'ntana, you made this choice too."

I stared up the hill at the ghostly remains of the home that had once been so dear, that had been ruled so wisely for so long…until Kyri's death.

"How can I be king? I'm a bard, a storyteller. I'm no king."

"You are also Ko'leya…and B'na."

My'leen eyed me quizzically, then looked up at the sky.

"You are not king yet," Yzythq'a continued. "But you will be. Once you prevail over Bo'Rà K'n."

I immediately felt better. I still wasn't sure about being king. But I would thwart Bo'Rà K'n? My SunQuest would succeed?

"I will destroy him?" I asked.

"I did not say that. A dreamwalker, as you know, cannot die. And Bo'Rà K'n is still Tikkan. But you will meet your destiny. Just as your grandfather did." He stared into the distance, then up toward the castle turret that had housed the Elderbard's study since my time. "I met Toshar once," he said dreamily. "Here in Castle Rose. He was not much older than you are now. He had not yet grown into the fullness of his wisdom. You have. You have already lived it once. Now that you live it again, will you remember it all, I wonder…" He shook his head and turned his attention back to My'leen.

"I had hoped to reach you earlier," he said to her. "I had hoped to warn you. It would have changed nothing, of course. It never does. Nothing at all."

"What is to become of me?" My'leen asked quietly. "You have not said."

"Haven't I? I was certain I had. Why, you must travel with Ben, my dear. That is your path, your destiny."

"I am to leave?"

"There is nothing here for you anymore, My'leen. Not yet. You are part of this SunQuest now. You and Ben and Panesh and— Well, never mind that."

"SunQuest?" she asked. "What is a SunQuest?"

Ignoring her, Yzythq'a turned to me. "What do you know of The SunQuest, Ben Ko'leya?"

"Nothing. Nearly nothing. That I am to stop Bo'Rà K'n. That's all."

Yzythq'a waited, watching me intently as though expecting me to say more.

"I don't know any more than that."

He leaned into his staff, gazed off into the distance again, then up at the suns — first at Aygra, then for a few breaths longer at B'na. Finally, he closed his eyes, muttered a few inaudible words and sang, to My'leen's melody.

When Son of Sun in tireless quest
In fearless journey beyond the west
Does touch the point where earth meets sky
Where Tikkan's dreams are born and die
There, darkness lifts and light returns
There, Rev'Àn's soul still fiercely burns
O, Son of Sun
O, young king wise
Restore the dreams to Rev'Àn's eyes
Pass on the ring
Pass on the crown
Let bright then merge with shadow's frown
A king and bard he then will see
And Rev'Àn's soul at last be free.

The final line of the song echoed around us. When it had faded to silence, Yzythq'a handed me his staff.

"You will be wanting this," he said.

The moment I touched it, it transformed into the staff all Elderbards in Q'ntana carried…the staff I had carried as Elderbard once…once upon a time: a braid of light and dark woods topped with a creamy, moonlike orb and carved with sacred symbols.

"It will point you to the next p'rtulle," Yzythq'a said. He gestured toward the river. "You will be wanting those too."

Rising from the waters of the River Alanda by the ferry dock were two horses: one, pale blue, the color of dawn; the other, the smoky-plum color of dusk. Toshar's horses, Rykka and Ta'ar. As they leapt onto the dock and charged toward us in a blur of color, saddles took shape on their backs, along with packs and saddlebags of food, plates, mugs, clothing and blankets.

When we turned back to Yzythq'a, he was gone.

A New Beginning

I was not sorry to leave Castle Rose behind. Solid or spectral, it had already poisoned too many joyful memories of my old life and ancient home. Yet, what we rode toward would surely be no better. Under Fvorag, no one who believed in the old ways had been safe. "Believers," they had styled themselves. If you managed to keep your beliefs to yourself, were not a bard and refrained from storytelling, you might be spared. Gravel's Q'ntana offered no such subtleties. The controlled tyranny of Fvorag's Q'ntana had given way in these times to indiscriminate violence. If a court official wanted your wife, he sent a soldier to kill you. The rest of your family — and village — might also die…or not. If Gravel coveted your spouse, your daughter, your house, your land or your best mare, a similar fate awaited you. Where under Fvorag's rule, fact was the only legal tender, as Toshar had put it in his MoonQuest, under his grandson the sole currency in the land was power. The more arbitrarily you exercised it, the more you terrorized the populace. The more terror you could inflict, the greater your ultimate power.

Though a fool and not much of a king, Gravel had managed to maintain nominal control over his army, known, as in Fvorag's time, as the King's Men. Yes, many had gone rogue as Black Riders. But because Gravel freed his soldiers to rape, steal and plunder at will, as long as they first did his bidding, his army remained mostly loyal and somewhat obedient. With Gravel gone, there would be no sovereign's rule for these thugs to follow. They would all become Black Riders. As terrifyingly chaotic as Q'ntana had been under Gravel, what lay ahead could only be worse, for all but the strongest or most malevolent.

Rykka and Ta'ar had come to us fully provisioned. We had all the food and supplies we would need for several days ahead. What we lacked were weapons. No swords, clubs or knives. Our wits — and

Panesh's size — would have to be our only protection against the Black Riders. I wondered silently whether that would be enough.

*   *   *

From Castle Rose we journeyed due west, mostly through forestland, with Rykka and Ta'ar as our navigators and guides. Bridles and reins, we discovered in the first moments of our travels, served only to give us something to hold onto. They played no role in steering the horses. Rykka and Ta'ar steered themselves, making their own decisions about speed, direction and rest stops.

I took Rykka, just as Toshar had done, and My'leen rode Ta'ar behind me. That was the only arrangement the horses would accept. Panesh would have preferred for us to travel side-by-side-by-side, but the trails were generally too narrow. Nor did it make sense for him to ride, either behind me on Rykka or in front of My'leen on Ta'ar. Although the horses did not flinch at the extra weight, their backs were not broad enough to accommodate both Panesh's bulk and a regular-size adult. Fortunately, with his long legs and lengthy stride, Panesh easily kept pace. Or perhaps it was Rykka and Ta'ar who kept pace with Panesh. From what I recalled of The MoonQuest, I was certain that at full gallop they would have left him far behind.

We stopped once at suns-merge, only briefly. We had barely laid out a meal when Rykka whinnied, tossed her head and nudged the back of my neck. It was time to move on. It would be dusk before the horses stopped again, this time by a brook in a pocket-size woodland clearing. While Panesh hied off in search of firewood and My'leen set up our tiny encampment, I bathed in the icy stream. Rykka drank thirstily nearby, pausing every now and again to eye me from the mossy bank. As soon as I was dry and dressed, she pawed the ground then stomped her right foot three times.

"What is it Rykka?" I whispered, stroking the white bolts that flashed from her forehead to her muzzle. "What are you trying to tell me?"

She nickered softly and rubbed her nose against my cheek. Above us, M'nor rose in her fullness above the trees, bathing our campsite in a silvery, otherworldly glow. I hadn't noticed before, but My'leen was humming, that same melody I had first heard her sing, that same tune to which Yzythq'a had sung his tale.

"What is that song?" I asked Rykka. "Why do I know it?" Rykka nudged my forehead and the top of my head. Then she pushed me away, toward the nascent campfire, where Panesh and My'leen waited for me.

As I dropped to the ground between my two companions, sparks shot into the air from the fire, dispersing into the sky like stars. Panesh laid my staff on my lap and we all three watched the flames' mesmerizing dance as My'leen continued to hum.

"Around your head," My'leen said. "What is that?" Her words startled me. I must have journeyed to another realm because I hadn't realized that she had stopped singing. I touched my head but felt nothing.

"What?" I asked.

"A light," she said. "Like a crown."

I touched my head again. "Like a crown?"

She nodded.

"Do you see it too?" I asked Panesh.

"I have seen it all along," he replied. "Astel Elohia. You did not know it was there?"

"Inside, yes. But not visible to everyone."

"Not everyone," he said.

I jumped up and ran to the brook. Even in the dim, moon-dappled light, a halo-like crown around my head shimmered back at me from the water. The Ring of Unity. Rykka whinnied and tossed her head. Ta'ar joined in.

"What is this Astel Elohia?" My'leen asked, when I returned. "Yzythq'a mentioned it too. Why did he call you B'na? That's the name of the sun."

I touched my forehead again, stared into the fire and began my story. Panesh knew some of it and accepted the rest with equanimity. My'leen, however, was dumbfounded when I recounted how I had been born of a mysterious father who, I would learn much later, was the embodiment of Aygra, the larger of Q'ntana's suns. I told them how I had disappeared from my mother's arms as an infant and how Bo'Rà K'n had cast me into a limbo-like void until I had found myself, fully grown and many generations earlier, in M'ranna, the land that predated Q'ntana. I told them how my mother had turned up there too, in defiance of Bo'Rà K'n, whose plan had been to separate us in time and place and thus thwart The MoonQuest. And I told them of my mother's StarQuest and of my minor role in it.

"It was in the Stone People's cave under Ko'Ba Rock that we found Astel Lev, the Heart of the Star, and Astel Elohia, the Ring of Unity," I said. "Q'nta took Astel Lev into her heart and I took Astel Elohia into my brow. Astel Lev had been taken from Reesa Kam'ana, the Star Chantress and—"

"What about Astel Elohia?" My'leen interrupted, staring at the halo, still visible to her. "Where did that come from?"

Until then, it had not occurred to me that I had never known. I waited, hoping for a flash of insight. None came. I shrugged and continued.

"Restoring Astel Lev to Reesa Kam'ana was Q'nta's purpose in The StarQuest. Once she succeeded, she came back here, to Q'ntana, and was...was—" My voice broke.

"Murdered," Panesh said.

My'leen nodded. "I know. I am sorry...although I could not know she was your mother."

All of a sudden, I was sorry too. I was more than sorry. I was heartbroken. I tried to swallow my tears, but I couldn't. As B'na, I had possessed the gift of perspective. Nothing that occurred on the earth below me was either good or bad. It just was. Q'nta had died because she had to, because Prithi had written it so. That was the way it was. Now, fully human in a way I had not been for many, many generations, my heart had been wrenched open. It felt as though every part of me had been peeled raw. I had barely known my mother. I was imprisoned during most of her StarQuest and we were separated again once it was complete. Yet what I did know I had come to respect, to cherish...to love. That she had been cruelly slain and her body abused was not new. That the pain of it now stabbed at me unbearably was. I wept. I wept as hard and long as I had done when I had first known us to be mother and son, all those lifetimes ago. Then I wept still more. Through it all, Panesh pressed his hand on my back and My'leen sang softly.

By the time I was spent, the moon had vanished behind the trees and fire was our only light. I sipped some wine and completed my story. "When The StarQuest achieved Completion, Q'nta returned to her right time in Q'ntana and I stayed behind."

"He became the very first Elderbard," Panesh added proudly, as if I were his son and he was boasting of my exploits. "It was he who established the line of Elderbards that would ultimately produce Eulisha, Toshar and Q'nta—"

"And," I added, "in a strange twist of time, me." If Yzythq'a was right, this time I would be king as well as Elderbard. That part I chose not to speak aloud. I pondered it for a while before continuing.

"Even if I don't know where the Ring of Unity comes from, Yzythq'a's song made it sound as though it will end up with Bo'Rà K'n." I paused. "That does not make any sense to me." I turned to Panesh. "Does it make any sense to you?"

"Your mother gave the Heart of the Star to S'kryssna S'kyaga…"

"True. But only so that S'kryssna S'kyaga could then return it to Reesa Kam'ana. There is no one for Bo'Rà K'n to give it back to. Not that I know about. If Bo'Rà K'n keeps it… I don't see how it can be a good thing. Can it?" I fingered my staff and stared pensively into the flames. "Can it?" I asked again.

"I do not know, Ko'leya," Panesh said. My'leen said nothing.

It was late and we had not yet eaten. We wolfed down the food that My'leen had set out for us long before, then sat quietly, watching the fire's final embers blink out one by one. When the last one died, My'leen started to sing again, the same melody.

"What is that song?" I asked. "I feel as though I know it, but I don't know how…or how I could."

My'leen continued for a while before answering. "I don't know. Melodies just come to me. They always have, since I was a girl. As far back as I can remember, really. I don't know what they are or why they come. Until now, they have never had words, and I have never sung the same one twice. This one is different. The first time I sang it was when I saw you at the—" She swallowed hard. "At the castle. Ever since, I cannot get it out of my head. Yzythq'a says that my songs are a special gift. I wish he would tell me what that means. He always talks in riddles."

I laughed. "He isn't the only one." I poked at what remained of the coals. A single spark ignited then fizzled. "I did not know that about you," I said cautiously, "but I may already know more of your story than you may be comfortable revealing."

"What do you mean?" she asked warily.

I told her what I had seen in my vision.

"All of it is true." She gazed sadly into some distant world. "I'm not sorry you saw it. It saves me from having to tell it."

Panesh threw a handful of twigs onto the coals, struck a flint on a rock and rekindled the fire. When it was blazing again, he turned to My'leen. "May I ask what happened to your parents? If you do not mind the question."

My'leen sighed heavily. "I don't mind. I have no secrets. Not anymore." She drew abstract figures in the dirt by her feet. "The king's captain, Prak'kà, saw my mother at the market one day and decided he must have her. She was very beautiful." She paused. "He killed my father. Right in front of us. In front of my mother and in front of me and B'tha. B'tha doesn't remember. Didn't remember." She stifled a sob. "But she was there."

"What about your mother?" I asked

"She grabbed a cleaver from a meat merchant's stall and tried to kill Prak'kà. He was too strong for her." She started to cry. "He raped her. Right in the market. In front of everyone. In front of us. In front of me and B'tha. Then he threw her onto his horse — she was still half-naked — and rode away. I never saw her again. Prak'kà probably killed her when he was finished with her."

I put my arm around her. "I am sorry," I said. "So sorry."

She nodded and wiped her eyes. "It was horrible. Worse than horrible." She steadied her voice. "It was worse for B'tha. B'tha was... is younger. I already knew what King's Men were capable of. She did not." Her voice grew steely. "That is why I am here, with you."

I looked at her inquiringly.

"Not because Yzythq'a said it was my destiny. I suppose it must be or I would not be here. But that isn't why I agreed to come. And it isn't because there was no place else to go. Maybe there wasn't. But I would have found something. No." She stood and slowly circled the firepit. "What happened to my family happened because of the king. As bad as it was, even worse things have happened to other people in Q'ntana. Whatever they were, Gravel let them happen. All of them. And it was Bo'Rà K'n who let Gravel happen. It's because of him. All the evil. It's all because of him. When I heard Yzythq'a's song...when I heard the words, to *my* melody...when he sang about somehow stopping Bo'Rà K'n— That's Rev'Àn, right?"

I nodded.

She hurled a rock into the darkness. "If Bo'Rà K'n can be stopped... if I can help with that... Well, I have to. After what happened, I have to. I have no choice. Whatever it takes."

She stared westward into the night. "Is that where he lives?"

"What do you mean?" I asked.

"Beyond the west. Is that where he lives?"

"Maybe," I said. "I don't know." And then I did. I stood and joined her. "The west," I said slowly, understanding coming to me as I spoke, "is where B'na wakens and Aygra goes to sleep. Somehow, we must get past the place where the suns rise and set. I don't know how or what is there. I don't know if that is where we will find Bo'Rà K'n, or Rev'Àn. I don't know anything, except that we will find out when we get there…however we get there." I shut my eyes, trying to recall my B'na self, the self that might know more. It didn't work. Whatever that part of me knew, it revealed nothing.

fifteen

A brooding, dusky cloud, Bo'Rà K'n's cloud, looms forbiddingly over a vast, gray churning sea. Sheets of rain slash down from it into the icy water, veiling anything but this immediate view. The cloud seethes and swells, its shape constantly rearranging into abstract whorls of gloom.

Within the cloud is a chamber, its indistinct walls, floor and ceiling barely visible through snaky tendrils of mist. Its furniture is hulking and heavy, massive pieces crafted from giant slabs of timber bolted together with iron pegs the size of my fist. In one corner stands a long dining table, bare but for a thick coat of dust and a tarnished candelabra, its nine tapers melted down to ossified nubs. A single chair, equally dusty, sits at an awkward angle at its head. Cluttering a workbench on the opposite side of the room are slivers of wood, strips of metal, strange tools and scraps of parchment upon which are scrawled indecipherable words, numbers and drawings. All are caked with dirt and grime. Beyond the workbench, a partly closed door leads to a second chamber. I cannot see into it, but I hear mechanical clunks, thunks, squeaks and squeals clamoring from within it. Another doorway, this one open, leads down a dim hallway. No furniture rests on the stained lattice-patterned, wine-red carpet laid between dining table and workbench. But a few steps from the carpet's fringe, facing away from me and toward a fireplace more than large enough for a man to stand inside with his arms outstretched, sits a hefty, plum-cushioned high-back chair. Three dull-silver candlesticks, each holding fresh tapers, all unlit, rest on the chair's otherwise-empty side table. The chamber's only light is cast by the fireplace, which burns an eerie shade of red.

"Janq'a!" The grating, not-quite-human voice blaring from the chair is repugnantly familiar. Bo'Rà K'n. "My food, Janq'a!"

A stocky, dwarf-like man waddles in from the gloomy corridor, as quickly as his stumpy legs will allow. He carries a tray laden with food…if you can call it that. Whatever it is is greasy, moldy and barely fit for the slimiest of *ghoraks. Janq'a doesn't look much better. His long, brown hair is dirty and stringy, his teeth are broken and yellow, and his sallow complexion is pocked and pitted. He knocks the candlesticks to the floor with his elbow and drops the tray onto the table with a noisy clatter. One of the candles rolls to the exact center of the carpet, where all the lattice pieces meet in a large, ornate circle that, itself, encloses a faded spiral. When it touches the spiral, the candle falls through and disappears, as though there were an opening in both carpet and floor.*

"What is this?" Bo'Rà K'n picks up a dark green drumstick with thumb and forefinger, sniffs it, grimaces and pitches it into the fire.

"Your dinner, your nastiness." Janq'a bows with mock obsequiousness.

"I do not know why I keep you around, Janq'a," Bo'Rà K'n growls. "You either cannot cook or will not. You cannot clean. Or will not. On top of that, you are filthy, and you stink. Have you bathed any time in the last few seasons? Your smell is worse than usual. Or is that the food?"

Janq'a bows again, lower. "A perfect manservant for the likes of you, I would say." He smiles an ugly, toothy grin.

"You go too far, Janq'a," Bo'Rà K'n retorts. "I should have you killed."

"You should. It would put us both out of our misery."

Bo'Rà K'n stares into the fire. A blurred, shadowy image forms in the flames: of me, My'leen and Panesh, asleep at our campsite.

"Just kill them," Janq'a says. "You know you want to."

Bo'Rà K'n heaves the tray, food and all, into the fire. The image vanishes. "You stupid little man," he snaps. "You know it is not in my power to kill, anyone. Not yet. If it were, you would be the first on my list."

Janq'a kicks bits of stray food onto the hearth. "It does not make any sense to me. It never has. You should be able to kill whoever you want. You are Bo'Rà K'n, after all."

"And Tikkan. Still. Dreamwalkers cannot kill. Not directly. Not yet." He smashes his fist onto the table and I am certain he glares at me. "That will change. Soon. Count on it."

*   *   *

I said nothing about my dream when we set off the next morning. It was too chillingly fresh. Had Bo'Rà K'n known I was watching? How could he have? I was dreaming. Yet his final warning seemed to have been aimed at me. I shuddered, clutched Rykka's reins more tightly and urged her forward. She continued at her own pace.

It was reassuring to have Bo'Rà K'n confirm what Na'an had told me: He could not kill us directly. Even so, the unremitting evil I had felt in his presence, even in a dream, left me feeling powerless and anxious.

He will destroy anything that might stop him. He will destroy you, if he can.

Rykka whickered. Ta'ar snorted a reply.

I heard Na'an's voice again: *Your greatest gift and strength is something he will dismiss as your greatest weakness. Your humanness. Embrace it and he will not know how to fight you.*

I still did not understand what she meant. I was not at all sure I wanted to.

We rode uneventfully for the next five days and camped easily each of those nights, even though food was growing scarce and there was little opportunity to add to our provisions. On the rare occasions that Rykka and Ta'ar permitted us more than a brief rest stop, there were either no fruits, nuts or game to be had or no opportunity to seek them out. Even the brooks were surprisingly devoid of fish, not that we were given the time to cook anything we might have been able to catch.

As we traveled, forest gave way to meadowland, which, in turn climbed into rolling hill country. Gauging by the suns' progress, we still traveled west, if in a vague, meandering sort of way. Whatever their other reasons for our path, Rykka and Ta'ar seemed determined to bypass all farms and villages, for we saw no one, not even in the far distance. Panesh, to my amazement, kept up with the horses, regardless of their pace, and never tired. He spoke little, as well. None of us had much to say. We had already shared our stories and we had no itinerary to debate.

On the morning of the sixth day, we climbed through the hills to a broad, barren plateau dotted with spindly trees, prickly scrub and, on the far horizon, a wall of palisade-like boulders. From a distance, the wall of sheer crags seemed impenetrable. Drawing nearer, we could see the labyrinth of cramped passes toward which the horses cantered.

The path Rykka unhesitatingly selected was cool and breezy, a refreshing contrast to the hot suns of the mesa. It turned, twisted, climbed, dropped, then climbed again. Any sense of direction we might have thought we had when we entered the maze was gone, and we wondered how this could be our best path. Still, our only choice was to continue forward. Rykka and Ta'ar would not have permitted a retreat. I tried not to question Rykka's wisdom. After all, this was the horse that had led Toshar into battle against Fvorag. She had to be wiser and more knowing than my increasingly human self. Still, I couldn't help but doubt as our path felt increasingly ominous.

*　*　*

As silently as wild cats, two Black Riders leapt down from the boulder's crown to block our path. Another two checked us from behind. Three more, these on horseback, flew up behind the infantrymen, two in front, another in the rear.

Before I could curse Rykka, Panesh let out a blood-freezing roar, lifted up the nearest highwayman as though he were weightless and slammed him into the rock. He crumpled to the ground like a rag doll.

Still thundering, Panesh grabbed onto the collar of the dead man's trembling companion, set to do the same with him.

"Do what you like with him. I can easily find plenty more just like him." Clearly the leader, this man was smoother than his brutish colleagues. Where they were unshaven, ill-groomed and spoke roughly, he was polished and, likely, well-educated. He had pushed past his colleagues and now held a saber to my neck. Another of his men threatened My'leen similarly.

Panesh exploded with rage. He hoisted the Black Rider over his head, ready to fling him against the rocks.

"Before you do that," the leader continued calmly, "consider the consequences." He gave his blade a gentle nudge. It drew a drop of blood from my neck.

Panesh growled, hesitated, then released his grip. The Black Rider dropped to the ground and crawled away.

"What do you want?" I asked.

"Whatever you have," he retorted. He whipped a sword from a scabbard strapped to his stallion's saddle and prodded My'leen's breast. "And her."

"Take anything we have," I replied, more bravely than I felt. "But leave her."

He snickered and poked his sword at My'leen's groin. The others joined in, making crude remarks and hand gestures.

The foot soldiers rummaged through our packs.

"Just food and blankets," one of them grumbled. He uncorked My'leen's wineskin and tilted his head back.

"Empty," he spat and kicked it away.

"Gold?" the leader asked.

"None."

"Can't buy your lives, then?" the leader scoffed.

Another of the men grabbed my staff. It had fallen to the ground when he had sliced my saddlebag free. "What about this? Maybe it be val'yable. Or magic." He twisted at the orb, trying to wrench it from the head. When it would not come free, he smashed it against a rock. It incurred no damage. "Piece o' crap," he muttered and tried to snap it in two over his knee. The staff wouldn't break. Perhaps his knee did. He yowled in pain. Enraged, he lashed first me then Rykka with the staff.

"Kill the men," the leader ordered quietly. "Leave the girl and the fancy horses. I want those."

Rykka and Ta'ar had stood stock-still throughout the ambush, unconcerned by the threat. Now, as one, they reared. In a single motion, they kicked away the foot soldiers and knocked the leader and his nearest colleague off their mounts. Panesh grabbed the two remaining soldiers at the rear, one in each hand, knocked their heads together and tossed them up into the rocks. He scooped up my staff, awkwardly mounted one of the stallions and followed Rykka and Ta'ar as they sprinted ahead through the pass.

JANQ'A

A real bed! A straw mattress, a feather pillow and a blanket that was not coarse and scratchy. A bath…hot and steaming, with soap. A roof for once not open to the vagaries of the weather. Hot meals *not* cooked over an open fire. If this manner of luxury constituted what it would be like to be king, I was all for it.

"You *are* human now," Panesh joked after I shared my contentment with our rare indoor comforts. Everything except the king part. I still preferred not to talk about that, even to Panesh and My'leen. We dined together at an immense, wood-plank farm table weighted down with steaming, home-cooked delicacies to suit every taste: roasts and stews, soups and fricassees, vegetables of all shapes and sizes. And the desserts! More pies and puddings, fruits and compotes, than we could begin to consume.

Our hosts, Yeerg'a and Ra'ina, kept placing more mouthwatering delights in front of us, continuously entreating us to keep eating long after we were too stuffed to lift ourselves from our seats at their table. Longtime friends of Panesh's, they had welcomed us enthusiastically when we arrived on their doorstep the previous night, still shaken from our encounter with the Black Riders.

Where Yeerg'a was stocky and built like a barn, Ra'ina was short and slight. Her build suggested that the weakest of breezes could knock her over. Yet she was as strong as her husband — in both body and will. Yeerg'a's family had farmed this land for many generations, all the way back to Q'ntana's early days, he said, bragging that he could trace his family tree back to the time of Queen Karenna Kihanna and the first Elderbard, Ben Ko'leya.

"Funny, you having the same name as he did," Yeerg'a said, eyeing me curiously. We had told them that we were on a quest to restore peace and stability to Q'ntana and that it somehow involved finding

Bo'Rà K'n. Still, my story was so implausible that I urged Panesh not to share the details of it, especially the king part, with his friends.

This was our second evening under their roof, and we could have stayed on until we were as old and gray-haired as they were, had that been our wish. But two nights in one place was an extravagance on this SunQuest. I had already advised our hosts that we would need to depart next morning.

"Of course," Yeerg'a said. "Yours is an important journey. For all of us."

"A dangerous one too," Ra'ina added soberly.

"We know all about the King's Men," Yeerg'a said. "Too well."

"Did we tell you that Panesh saved our Miggy?" Ra'ina asked. She squeezed Panesh's hand as best she could, given its size — and hers.

Multiple times. I acted as though it was the first.

"That is why any friend of this Angarusha's is a friend of ours," Yeerg'a added.

"Miggy is our granddaughter," Ra'ina explained. "Her real name is Mig'lanta, but we have always called her Miggy."

Yeerg'a took her hand. "A band of King's Men tried to kidnap her, for the king," he said. "That was when we still had a king. If you can call him that."

"A poor excuse for a king," Ra'ina spat.

"Well, there is no king now, thank Prithi." Yeerg'a bobbed his head once for emphasis.

"True, my love," Ra'ina said. "But those Black Riders are even worse." She put one arm around me and the other around My'leen, hugging us so tightly that I could barely breathe. "Are you sure you will not eat more?" she asked.

I laughed. "If we eat any more, our horses will refuse to carry us."

"Not to worry," she said. "I will pack up as much as I can in the morning for your journey. Yeerg'a has already stitched up your saddlebags and readied extra packs for you." She looked at each of us with concern. "Maybe you should stay an extra night? To build your strength back up?"

I smiled and shook my head. "I wish we could, Ra'ina."

"You will stay longer on your way back, then," she insisted in a tone that brooked no argument.

"On our way back," I agreed, even as I doubted that there would be a way back, at least not the kind Ra'ina meant.

*   *   *

That night, I dreamed again of Bo'Rà K'n and Janq'a. This time they silently watched our battle with the Black Riders play out in Bo'Rà K'n's massive fireplace.

"And?" Janq'a asks.

The scene lingers on the dead and injured highwaymen after we have ridden off.

"And what?" Bo'Rà K'n sits in his chair, nursing a goblet of wine. Janq'a stands next him, resting his chin on the chair's cushioned arm.

"That wasn't how you planned for it to end, is it?"

"You are even more insolent today than usual, Janq'a."

"Yes, master." He grins.

"You do not know your place."

"No, master."

Bo'Rà K'n stares into the fire until the ambush scene fades. He drains the goblet. Janq'a refills it.

"Gravel's soldiers were of little use with a king to command them. With no king, they are nothing but mindless bandits who cannot be counted on to follow simple orders. Not so different from someone else I could name."

He finishes one glass of wine, then two more, and returns his goblet to the table, still staring at the fire.

"You are going down there," he says to Janq'a at last.

The manservant edges away from Bo'Rà K'n's chair. "Me? What do you mean?"

"What I said. It is time you did something useful for me."

Janq'a refills the wine glass and gulps it down before Bo'Rà K'n notices. "Who will cook for you?"

"Someone who knows cookery and is not practiced in the art of poison." He drums his fingers on the arm of the chair, then reaches for his goblet as Janq'a is pouring wine into it. It spills on Bo'Rà K'n. Bo'Rà K'n turns slowly to face Janq'a. He is furious.

"I-I'm sorry, master."

"Clean it up," Bo'Rà K'n says icily.

"Yes, master." Janq'a races down the hallway, quickly returning with an armful of rags and a fresh cloak, identical to the wine-soaked one that Bo'Rà K'n wears.

Bo'Rà K'n paces along the carpet's fringe, staring contemplatively at the lattice pattern. He ignores Janq'a as the servant wipes up chair, table and floor. Janq'a does not ignore his master. He glances anxiously up at him every time Bo'Rà K'n pauses to peer at the carpet's central circle. When he hands his master the dry cloak, Bo'Rà K'n waves him away, then changes his mind. He grabs Janq'a by the collar and jerks him up to eye level.

"You are going down there." He steps toward the center of the carpet. "Yes. Definitely."

"Wh-what will I do?" Janq'a stammers. He drops the cloak. It vanishes through the spiral.

"Whatever I tell you, when I tell you." Bo'Rà K'n releases Janq'a. He follows the cloak and disappears. "For a change."

Bo'Rà K'n wipes his hands on his trousers and returns to his chair. He refills his goblet, picks it up and stares through the liquid at the fire. He then takes a sip as he watches Janq'a in the flames, hurtling somersaultingly toward earth.

Next morning, although tempted to share what I had seen, I said nothing to my companions. This dream had come from Na'an, with instructions that I keep it to myself.

"I hope we have not put you in danger by stopping here," I said to Yeerg'a as we prepared to leave, stuffed from another royal feast of a meal. Ra'ina was cramming food into every available crevice in our packs and saddlebags. All three horses were freshly groomed and fed.

Yeerg'a shook both my hands warmly. "Remember. You are welcome here any time."

Rai'na hugged My'leen then kissed me on both cheeks. "Take care of our Panesh," she said, sniffling. "Take care of yourself too, Ko'lar," she whispered in my ear. "Come back as Kano'ha, as king."

"No— How—?" I asked.

She pointed at Panesh then shook her head conspiratorially. "He doesn't know," she mouthed, pointing at Yeerg'a.

I threw Panesh a dirty look. He grinned sheepishly. "She guessed," he said when Yeerg'a was out of earshot, attending to the horses.

"She *guessed!* What kind of hints did you give her so she would make the right guess?"

"I…well— She…"

Before we could argue, Yeerg'a returned. Moments later, we were packed, in the saddle and ready to go.

"Ride through my fields," Yeerg'a offered after our final goodbyes.

"It cannot hurt to be off the road after what happened with the Black Riders."

"And pick any food that tempts you," Ra'ina added. "Much is ripe, more than we can harvest."

"Thank you, both. But the route is not up to me." I stroked Rykka's mane.

As it turned out, Rykka agreed with Yeerg'a, though for reasons all her own.

seventeen

Yeerg'a's farm was immense, stretching many leagues in all directions from the couple's simple frame-and-stucco house. To my surprise, Rykka chose not to travel through their largely open fields to the west. Instead, she carried us north through dense stands of mokìa trees. Three of the pies Ra'ina had served us had been baked with succulent mokìas, large, irregular-shaped magenta berries that hung in heavy, juice-soaked clusters from these green-limbed trees. Many, overripe, had already fallen to the ground where, still sweet-smelling, they rotted.

"The farm is too big for Yeerg'a now," Panesh explained. "These days, too much of his harvest goes to waste."

"What about Miggy?" My'leen asked. "Can't she help?"

"Her husband has his own farm, five days' ride away." He pointed south. "It is not as ambitious as this one. But it has been in Vaareq's family nearly as long as this one has been in Yeerga's. They come out to help when they can. It is not enough."

"Can't Yeerg'a hire extra help?" I asked.

"Young men who do not join the Black Riders willingly are, more often than not, kidnapped and forced to join…or be killed."

"If they resist, the Black Riders kill their families too," My'leen added. "It has happened to friends of mine." She paused. "Maybe when you become king you can change that?"

I said nothing. Did embracing my humanness, as Na'an had said, mean that I also had to embrace my destiny as king? It still did not sit well with me. What did I know about kingmanship? I was a storyteller not a leader, an Elderbard not an elder statesman. Nothing had prepared me for this.

"What prepared you to be Elderbard?" Panesh asked quietly.

"I—" Nothing had.

"Yet you were a great Elderbard once. You will be again. A great king too."

I smiled. "A good king, at the very least. I hope. I know I will try... if that truly is what is to be."

A low moaning interrupted us. It came from off to the right, peppered with muttered curses.

"Someone is hurt!" My'leen exclaimed. She urged Ta'ar away from us, toward the sound. To my surprise, Ta'ar obeyed and she disappeared from view.

"Not by yourself," Panesh called after her. "Wait!" Ever awkward on his horse, he chased after her.

When we caught up with the others, My'leen was kneeling over a prone figure who now cursed more than he moaned. I couldn't see his face or body. Panesh could. He glared angrily at the injured man, who kicked at My'leen every time she tried to touch his ankle.

"Are you all right, My'leen?" I asked.

"Is *she* all right?" a familiar voice carped.

Janq'a.

"I'm the one who isn't anything like all right," he whined. "Me! I'm the one whose ankle must be broken in six or twelve or twenty-eight places. It's hurt so bad that I just know they are going to have to cut my leg off." He kicked at My'leen again with his good leg. "Get her off me. She's more harm than help."

I pulled My'leen off Janq'a, who tore his attention away from his swollen ankle to glower up at me. "Don't just stand there, boy. Do something. Can't you see I'm hurt. They will be cutting my leg off next. Mark my words."

"What are *you* doing here?" Panesh asked coldly.

Janq'a's mouth twitched nervously. He looked everywhere but at Panesh. Finally, he clutched his ankle, moaning loudly.

"You know each other?" I asked, not letting on that I knew already who Janq'a was.

"He is—" Panesh began.

"He threw me out!" Janq'a pointed up to the sky, still moaning. "He threw me down." He cursed, then began to cry.

Panesh turned to me. "Leave him here. He is—"

"We can't leave him," My'leen cried. "He's hurt. Look at him."

"Yeah. Look at me."

Panesh glared at Janq'a with undisguised contempt. "Do you

know who he is? That is Janq'a. Bo'Rà K'n's manservant."

My'leen leapt back in alarm.

"Was," Janq'a corrected.

"Is. Was. It is the same thing. He serves Bo'Rà K'n. What else is there to know?"

"*Served*. As his slave. I cooked and cleaned and attended to his every impossible whim." Janq'a pointed to his ankle. "This was the thanks I got. I will be hopping around on one leg for the rest of my life…after they chop this one off. You'll see."

"Janq'a is the closest thing to a friend Bo'Rà K'n has…or ever will have."

"Had. Had. *Had*. Didn't I just say? He threw me out. Down. All the way down. That's why my ankle is—" He propelled himself to standing, shrieked in pain and collapsed back to the ground.

Sympathetic in spite of herself, My'leen crouched next to Janq'a. "See how hurt he is? We can't leave him."

"He would leave us if he could," Panesh asserted. "Is that not right, Janq'a? Or you would do worse, whatever that might be. Wouldn't you? Ask him My'leen. Go ahead."

"He's right, Panesh is." Janq'a stared mournfully into My'leen's eyes. "I would have done worse. Truly, I would have. Not anymore, but. Not anymore at all. Now I see my master for what he is: evil. He's evil, evil, evil. A devil."

Of course, Janq'a was lying. I knew from my dream that he had been sent to spy on us. I also knew I was not to share that knowledge. Not yet.

"Bo'Rà K'n is your master," I said evenly.

"Was. Was. *Was*. Not now. No more. Nohow." Janq'a gazed up at me pleadingly.

What an actor! Even knowing what I knew, it was hard not to feel sorry for him, hard not to believe him.

"What if we carry him back to the house?" My'leen asked. She could not bring herself to turn away from someone in need, even someone as odious as Janq'a, even someone so recently linked to Bo'Rà K'n. "Wouldn't Yeerg'a and Ra'ina take him in?" She looked up at Panesh. "If you asked them?"

"I would not ask them. Not ever. Not for him. Yeerg'a and Ra'ina are good people. Janq'a is…worse than swamp slime." Panesh scowled at Janq'a with disgust. "I do not want him anywhere near them…or us. He is trouble, nothing but trouble, can only ever be trouble."

My'leen sighed. "If he cannot go to Yeerg'a and Ra'ina, then he must come with us. At least until his ankle heals and he can look after himself."

"Look after himself? That one? More like look out for himself." Panesh crouched next to Janq'a. "I should kill you right now and be done with it."

Janq'a nodded eagerly. "Yes, yes," he agreed. "Kill me. Now. What have I got to live for? Branded forever as Bo'Rà K'n's manservant. Yes. Kill me. That is more than I deserve. Do it. If you don't, someone else will. Someone else should." He leaned back, closed his eyes and laid his cheek on the ground. "I know I deserve to suffer…for what I have done…for who I have been. But I have already suffered so much, from Bo'Rà K'n's lash. If it's possible that I don't have to suffer anymore…" He whimpered. "Can you do it quickly?"

Panesh rolled his eyes. I stifled a snicker.

My'leen tugged on Panesh's sleeve. "You're not really going to kill him, are you? He hasn't done anything to us. Not like those Black Riders." She shuddered.

"He will," Panesh muttered.

"No one is going to kill anyone," I said. "You, Janq'a. Can you ride a horse?"

He opened one eye and nodded.

"With those stubby legs of yours?" Panesh sneered.

With melodramatic effort, Janq'a pushed himself to standing and hopped around on his uninjured foot. "I do all right," he whined.

"You can ride Panesh's horse," I said.

Panesh harrumphed. With one hand, he scooped Janq'a up and dropped him onto the stallion. Then he climbed on behind. "Not by himself, he won't."

eighteen

I lay awake long after the others had fallen asleep. Why was Janq'a with us? Knowing what I knew, why had I allowed it? Now that he was here, what were we to do with him? Surely, letting him continue with us on The SunQuest made no sense. Or did it? The fire crackled a response, though not in any language I knew. I turned over and tried to sleep, with no success.

Instead, I reflected back over our day. After leaving Yeerg'a and Ra'ina, we had ridden in uneasy silence. Yeerga's land had melted into a neighbor's and into another neighbor's after that. For a while, we followed a path alongside a river so straight it might have been a canal. After that, we meandered south through more woodland, before stopping in a grassy gully for the night. Through it all, Panesh barely unclenched his jaw. My'leen did her best to act as though nothing was wrong, but the strain of juggling anxiety and compassion, along with her discomfort at Panesh's displeasure, carved permanent creases on her forehead. Our nighttime meal was equally tense, and when we mumbled strained goodnights, we were all grateful for the solitude.

Our solitude was not to be complete. For the first time since returning to Q'ntana, I heard nayla howling in the distance. Quick, stealthy and vicious, these wild beasts hunted as much for pleasure as for food, and they were just as content to rip out the throat of their prey and race off to seek more sport as they were to remain by the corpse to devour it. Some said that a nayla's teeth were so sharp that they could grind bone as well as flesh. I did not know whether that was true, nor was I eager to find out. Let them stay far away, I prayed.

I pulled the blanket over my head, closed my eyes and curled up — as much for a false sense of protection from nayla as against the night chill. With another long day's ride ahead of us come morning, I could not afford a sleepless night. I tossed restlessly for a long time, cursing the cold, hard ground and Janq'a's snoring. When at last I fell asleep, I was awakened almost immediately by Janq'a surreptitiously pulling my staff from my side. I opened my eyes a crack and watched him hobble down the gully, my staff as his walking stick, the white cloth that bound his ankle bobbing up and down in the moonlight.

Panesh's eyes also opened. He had been sleeping on the other side of Janq'a. Either that or he had been feigning sleep to keep watch on the little man. He tilted his head for a better view.

At first, all I could see of Janq'a was his shadowy form, now still except for his arms, which waved around his head excitedly. He was either mad or up to no good. "Both," Panesh would probably say. I shut my eyes again. I would deal with this, whatever it was, in the morning. Right now, I needed sleep. But as soon as my eyes closed, it was as though I stood next to Janq'a, eavesdropping on the silent conversation he was having in his mind with Bo'Rà K'n.

"I am here, master. Are you there? Where are you?"

"It took you long enough, Janq'a."

"I snuck away as quickly as I could. That Panesh is always watching me. Always. He knows me. He knows who I am. You should have warned me. Really, you should have."

"It is up to me what I tell you, just as it is up to me what I do with you… and how I deal with you should you betray me."

"He would have killed me right there on the spot if the girl had not stopped him. He would kill me right now if he knew I was talking to you."

"That changes nothing."

"Maybe not for you."

"If you do not do what I say, you can be certain that you will crawl to me begging for a quick death."

"Can't you see that there is nothing I can do for you with that Panesh around?"

"You will do what I ask, Panesh or no Panesh. Or you will suffer the consequences. What have you found out?"

"Nothing…much."

"Be careful, Janq'a. Perhaps I cannot kill you with my own hands. Others can at my bidding…and they will if you do not serve me as you ought."

"Yes, master. All I know for sure is that we are heading west, sort of." Janq'a glances back toward the firepit, scrutinizes the scene for signs of movement. Convinced that no one is watching him, he continues. "What if I

just kill them all in their sleep? What about that? Then I could come home."

"It is not that simple."

"It never is," Janq'a mutters. "What do you mean?"

"I must have the Ring of Unity."

"You didn't tell me that part either."

"I did not."

"What is it? I haven't seen any ring."

"It is the key…to everything. It is with Ben."

"You must be mad. How—"

"Janq'a!"

The menace in that one word is so intense that I break into an icy sweat.

"I'm sorry, master. How am I supposed to get it? I haven't seen it. If you won't tell me what to look for, how can I steal it for you?"

"Stay with them. Make them like you. Summon me the instant the Ring shows itself. It will. It must. Only then will I know what is to be done."

"Make them like me? Even My'leen doesn't like me. She feels sorry for me, but she doesn't like me. Panesh despises me. Ben…I don't know about Ben. I'm pretty sure he doesn't like me either. How am I supposed to get them to like me? How?"

"That, Janq'a, is beyond even my power."

"Ha, ha. Funny. Please, can I come home?"

"Not yet. Not ever if you continue to whine and complain like this."

"I still don't understand why you need me down here. Why can't you watch them and everything from up there? Then, when the Ring shows itself, you can do whatever it is you need to do."

"I have already told you. It is not that simple. With the Heart of the Star, I always knew where it was. So I always knew where Q'nta was. The Ring of Unity is different. I do not know how or why it should be so, but I cannot easily keep track of it or of Ben. If I cannot keep track of one, I cannot keep track of the other. If I cannot keep track of either, you must do it for me."

"Something else the great Bo'Rà K'n cannot do?"

A fiery thunderbolt strikes Janq'a's injured ankle. He stuffs his fist into his mouth to stifle a scream.

"Watch your impudent tongue, Janq'a. You, I can always track — through your whining. If I cannot kill you, yet, I can make you sorry that you are alive."

A second thunderbolt. Janq'a bites down on his knuckles.

"More sorry than you have ever been or can ever imagine being. Am I clear?"

"Master," he gasps.

"Find a way."

"Yes, master."

When Janq'a returned to the fire, Panesh wrenched my staff from his hands and knocked him to the ground.

"What were you up to over there?" he growled.

"Can't a man go and, you know, without everyone knowing his business?"

"What does that have to do with waving your hands like some kind of madman?"

"How I go about my business is none of yours." He lay down with his back to Panesh and closed his eyes.

"I aim to know all your business, little man, even if I never sleep again."

"Yes, your bigness," Janq'a mumbled. "Do whatever you need to do. I need to sleep. Good night."

Panesh shook him. Janq'a ignored him.

"Maybe you can fool the others," he hissed. "You cannot fool me. I will be watching you…even when you think no one can see you."

"Watch me as much as you want, you bully. Like I said, I'm going to sleep." A moment later, he was snoring.

Panesh poked the fire back to life and stared into it for a long time. I fell asleep and woke up three times. Each time the light from the flames still danced on his expressionless face. If I could have thought up something reassuring to say, I would have. But Janq'a was a problem I did not yet know how to resolve, and I was not prepared to stay up all night trying. I turned over and went back to sleep.

When I woke a fourth time, the night still dark, I heard Na'an's voice. Panesh was staring even more intently at the fire. Na'an's face gazed back impassively at him from the flames.

"Why have you summoned me, Panesh? You know there is nothing I can do for you at this time. For any of you."

Panesh pointed to the sleeping Janq'a. "Him. What am I to do about him? You know who he is. He should not be here."

"Are you so certain?"

Panesh said nothing.

"I do what is mine to do, Panesh. The rest is up to Ben, My'leen and you…and Janq'a."

"Janq'a?" Panesh leapt to his feet angrily, then dropped back onto his haunches.

"Everyone in this story has a role to play, Janq'a no less than you. You should know that by now."

"I do, Na'an. Of course, I do. But *Janq'a?*"

"Yes, Panesh. Janq'a."

"Why is there nothing you can do? What about Toshar? You guided him in The MoonQuest. Why is it not possible for you to do the same for us here?"

"That was that story. This is this one. A single instant in this one. I cannot speak to what might happen in the next. But in this one…" Na'an shrugged. Her face melted into the flames.

"I will tell you one thing and one thing only," the fire spoke, in Na'an's voice.

"Yes, Na'an?"

"I promise you will not like it."

"There is little that I like right now." He turned away from the fire, embarrassed. "I am sorry to speak so impertinently, but there it is. You know I only speak truth to you."

"I know you do, Panesh. That is why I rely on you. Do you wish to hear what I have to say or not?"

Panesh nodded. "Please."

Na'an's face reversed its fade. It was now so solid and real it was almost as though I could reach into the flames and touch it.

"The SunQuest cannot succeed without Janq'a," she said.

"No." Panesh shook his head. "That cannot be. What do you mean?"

"As I said. The SunQuest cannot succeed without Janq'a, will not succeed without Janq'a." Her face dimmed again and was now barely visible. Her voice remained clear. "Watch Janq'a. That is your role. Protect Ben and My'leen. That is also your role. Let Janq'a play his. It is an important one."

Her face disappeared and the only remaining sound was the fire's crackle. Then, unseen, she spoke again. "In the final moments, his role will be a critical one."

The flames extinguished themselves and the night went black. In the distance, the nayla resumed their howling. I closed my eyes and, in a breath, was asleep.

nineteen

Dawn arrived too quickly, hastened for me by the sound of clanking dishes and snapping wood. I cracked my eyes open a slit and winced against the harsh light. My'leen was setting out our morning meal, while Janq'a fussed with the fire and Panesh led the horses down the gully to better grazing. My head throbbed with fatigue and my body ached from the hard, damp ground. I groaned, shut my eyes and turned over, hoping to sleep some more, knowing it was unlikely.

"I don't get it," Janq'a said to My'leen. "If those horses are magical like Ben says, why can't they take you where you need to go. Right now. Just like that." He snapped his fingers.

"I don't know, Janq'a," My'leen said with a brittleness born of mounting impatience. "I don't know any more than you do. All I know is that somehow we have to go 'beyond the west,' whatever that means. Maybe Rykka and Ta'ar know what it means. Maybe they're the only ones who do. Maybe they're the only ones who can get us there."

"Why do you have to go there? What's there?"

"I don't know that either. Bo'Rà K'n, maybe? I hope not."

"Oh, he's not so bad," Janq'a replied, "once you get to know him."

Panesh's heavy tread signaled his return. "If he is not so bad, as you say, why are you here? Why not return to your dear kind master."

I sat up creakily. "Panesh…"

"I am glad you are awake," he said. "We must talk."

I edged closer to the fire that Janq'a had finally managed to light. "Let me warm up first and eat something." I reached for the plate My'leen was passing to me. Panesh grabbed it and placed it on a rock.

"Now," he said. He pulled me up.

"I know what you are going to say—"

"Now."

With my blanket wrapped around me against the still-crisp air, I followed him back to where Rykka, Ta'ar and the stallion munched contentedly. They ignored us. I tried to tell Panesh that I had seen everything he had, and more. But he was so excitable that I could not get him to listen. In the end, I let him speak his piece without interruption. Only when he was done would he listen.

"If you knew who he was, why did you let him come? Why did you not say anything?"

"I'm not sure, Panesh. I think because I knew he needed to come with us, even though I did not much like the idea. Because I knew it was not the time to say what I knew."

"I still do not trust him," he grumbled.

"I am not saying I do."

"He is still loyal to Bo'Rà K'n. You heard him."

"And you heard Na'an, just as I did. Trust or not, Janq'a is part of this story. An important part. That is what Na'an said, and I trust her to know the story better than either of us does. Do you?"

Panesh muttered his assent.

"And I trust you to do your best to keep us safe, even with Janq'a along."

Panesh pulled up a clump of grass and fed it to Rykka. He pulled up a second for Ta'ar.

"I'm not asking to you like him," I said.

"That is good."

"I'm not even asking you to trust him."

"Even better."

"What I am asking is that you trust me…and Na'an. You must be able to do that. Can you?"

He nodded. "Do I have to like it?"

I laughed. "No more than I do." I stroked Rykka. "Wherever this one is taking us today, it's probably far, with few stops. Let's get back to the fire and eat. This may be our last chance for a big meal until nightfall."

*　*　*

"I don't know what your plans are," I said to Janq'a once we were ready to move on.

"I have none," he said. "I don't know anyone in Q'ntana. Only you."

"Then you are welcome to journey with us. All the way, if that is your choice."

Janq'a bowed. "You saved my life, master. I live only to serve you now."

Panesh groaned.

"It could be dangerous."

Janq'a shook his fist at the sky so melodramatically that My'leen stifled a giggle. "If I must die," he shouted to the heavens, "I do so willingly. As long as I first see vengeance done."

I lowered Janq'a's arm. "This is not about vengeance, or killing." I buckled my last pack to Rykka's saddle. "Something is out of balance in Q'ntana. It has been for a long time. Maybe since the beginning of time. This journey, this SunQuest, is about seeing that balance restored, whatever that means and however it must be done."

"As you say, master." He bowed again.

"I am not your master, Janq'a. If you choose to quest with us, it must be as an equal. No one here is greater or better than anyone else."

Janq'a shook his head vigorously. "Oh, but I couldn't. I could never be your equal."

Panesh bowed deeply and repeated, mockingly, "Oh, but I couldn't."

I ignored him, helped Janq'a onto the stallion and climbed onto Rykka. "Are we ready?"

Everyone nodded. "Then let's get going—" Rykka whinnied loudly. I looked at her, startled — both because I knew what she had communicated and because of what she was telling me.

"What is it, Ben?" My'leen asked.

"We need to get as far as we can today with Rykka and Ta'ar. They will be leaving us tonight."

Before anyone could ask for an explanation, Rykka leapt up to the top of the gully and sped off into the woodland.

*　*　*

It was a long day's ride, and a speedy one, almost too speedy for Panesh's stallion, which, swift though he was, was hard-pressed to keep up with Rykka and Ta'ar. The horses made little allowance for obstacles, following Aygra due west through fields and lakes, across rivers, over hills and walls and, in more than one case, through a bustling local market, whose alarmed shoppers and merchants flung themselves out of our way to avoid being trampled.

Although we encountered no Black Riders that day, we saw

111

unnerving evidence of their activity everywhere we traveled. Either the Riders had grown more active or they terrorized these western lands more than they did other parts of the country. Or both. As we journeyed on we saw limp bodies dangling from trees, gnawed-over human carcasses by the side of many roads, and villages emptied of all but women, young children, the aged and the infirm. Just about every village hosted its own grisly Wall of Traitors. These traitors had not betrayed the king, for there was none. They had defied the Black Riders — or supported the wrong group of Black Riders — and had paid the price.

In Q'oroq'i, a grim cluster of shacks we entered just after sunsmerge, My'leen recognized a head on the village square Wall of Traitors: Ro'gàn, a cousin to whom she had once been betrothed.

"We have to go back," she insisted, stopping in the next road.

Panesh, Janq'a and I huddled close to her, scrutinized with mounting suspicion by a half-dozen Black Riders who had just come out of the tavern at the bottom of the road.

"Are you crazy?" Janq'a struggled to keep his voice low. "We shouldn't be riding through a town at all. We can't go back. Do you want your head up there next to his?"

The Black Riders, still eyeing us, mounted their horses.

"We have to," My'leen insisted. "Ro'gàn didn't deserve that. He deserves a decent burial, not to have his face eaten away by vulture ants." She shuddered.

"I'm sorry, My'leen," I said, and I was. I thought about my mother. "It's just too dangerous."

"We could come back after dark. It wouldn't be so dangerous then. Could we, Ben?"

Janq'a tried to grab the reins from Panesh. "Not me. I just want to get out of here. Now." Panesh slapped his hands.

"I will do it," Panesh said.

"No, Panesh," I said.

"I will do it," he repeated.

"You're crazy," Janq'a muttered.

"Don't you see?" I explained. "You can't. It's not only about the danger to us. It's about the danger to these villagers. If a head disappears from the Wall, the Riders are certain to take revenge. On everyone."

"Oh," My'leen said softly. "I didn't think about that."

"She didn't think about that," Janq'a parroted. "Now can we go? Now? They're coming. Look!"

They were coming. The Black Riders moved up the road toward us, slowly but menacingly.

"I'm sorry," My'leen said, close to tears. "Janq'a's right. We had better leave."

Panesh dismounted and leaned in to me and My'leen.

"What are you doing?" Janq'a screeched.

Panesh ignored him. "Wait here," he instructed us, "I will take care of the Riders. If anything happens to me, get out of here."

"How about I get out of here right now?" Janq'a challenged, tugging on the reins.

"If you do and I find you, I will kill you," Panesh responded simply.

Panesh turned to face the Riders. He inhaled deeply, raised both his arms, and ran directly into their path, roaring loudly. The Riders' horses reared in fright. The Riders lost control, two tumbled to the ground. In the ensuing chaos, Panesh remounted his horse, and we flew down the road and out of town.

*　　*　　*

By mid-afternoon, we had left all settlements behind and rode along the unpopulated northern bank of a serpentine river whose increasingly dense scrub ripped both our skin and our clothes. In the distance, the rugged, snowcapped Xa'qìa Mountains scraped the cloudless, cerulean sky, forming a broad arc across a landscape that was otherwise largely barren. I tried to steer Rykka toward easier country. Neither she nor Ta'ar, both of whom plowed through the brush unscathed, would brook even the slightest detour.

When we cleared the scrub at a fork in the river, Rykka and Ta'ar stopped. We had been riding without cease since our Q'oroq'i stop and were grateful for a chance to stretch and move about on our own legs, even if only for a short while. We dismounted, washed up and shared an early evening meal. We had barely finished when Rykka nudged me, indicating that it was time to leave. Yet once we were packed and ready to go, she would not budge. She and Ta'ar stood statue-still, ignoring my promptings and the impatient snorting and foot-stamping of Panesh's stallion. What were they waiting for?

"For you," I heard from some ineffable place within me.

"For me?" I asked aloud.

The others eyed me strangely.

"Rykka tells me that it is now up to me to decide where we are to go next." One branch of the forked river pointed due north; the other meandered in a vague westerly direction. "West makes the most sense. It's our ultimate direction and there are no mountains in the way." I paused. "But I'm not sure. It doesn't feel right. Any ideas?"

Panesh and My'leen shrugged. Janq'a cleared his throat but said nothing.

"Do you know something, Janq'a?" I asked.

He shook his head.

"Are you sure?"

"Well," he said slowly, "if 'beyond the west' is your destination, like you say, doesn't it make sense to keep going west?"

"If Janq'a recommends it," Panesh mumbled, "that alone is reason enough to choose any other direction, even back the way we came."

"Now, Panesh," My'leen admonished. "Give him a chance."

"To betray us?"

"Why would I be doing that?" Janq'a retorted. "You know that I can't go home. Right now, you're all I've got."

"And you are all Bo'Ra K'n has got," Panesh shot back.

"What would Bo'Ra K'n do with me, anymore? What could he need me for?"

"You tell us."

"That is enough, both of you," I snapped. "It's getting late and we have to make a decision. Is that right, Rykka?" She tossed her head and whistled piercingly through her nose. The sound was so odd and unexpected that we all burst out laughing, shattering the tension.

"Your staff!" My'leen exclaimed.

"What about it?"

"Didn't Yzythq'a say something about it helping you to find the next p'rtulle?"

"What's a p'rtulle?" Janq'a asked.

"It's a— It's kind of like a door," My'leen explained. "Only it's not."

"Uh-huh. That's clear."

"It's a way through from one place or reality to another," I said. "We are supposed to pass through three."

"You already did one. Right?" My'leen asked. "Before you met me?"

I nodded. "The Maya Ko. That's how we got to Castle Rose, from… from wherever it was we were."

I pulled the staff free from Rykka's saddle. My'leen was right. I had forgotten that it was meant to point us to the next p'rtulle. Was now the time? I fingered its braid of woods and moonlike orb. I had spent most of my previous human life with this staff, as Elderbard. If it had possessed any magical powers in that time, they had never revealed themselves to me. I stroked the runes carved into it. Nothing happened. I stared at the orb. Again, nothing.

"Point it," Janq'a said.

"What?"

"This is probably a dumb idea…but maybe if you point it in different directions it will tell you which one is right?"

I gaped at Janq'a with astonishment. It was anything but dumb. It was inspired. Maybe we did need him with us, in spite of everything. With the orb facing away from me, I pointed the staff west, the logical direction. I sensed nothing unusual. North? The same.

When I pointed south, the staff began to vibrate, more and more insistently. When I aimed it at the center of the mountain range, it shook so powerfully that I had to grasp it with both hands. And when the tip of the staff accidentally grazed my forehead, the shaking grew almost violent.

"South it is, then," Panesh said. "To the mountains."

To be certain, I pointed the staff east and, when nothing happened, I repeated all the directions again. Only when the orb faced south, did the staff react.

"Okay, Rykka," I said. "Let's go."

She tossed her head again as though asking, "What took you so long?" and bounded off in a flash, flying so quickly that she and Ta'ar had to stop frequently for Panesh's horse to catch up. About halfway to the mountains, with Panesh and Janq'a far behind, I reined Rykka in. The suns were already casting a golden glow on the landscape. It would not be long before they set.

"Is it time?" I whispered to Rykka.

She whinnied. *Almost. Soon.*

*　　*　　*

When the stallion caught up with us, Rykka nuzzled his ear. He snorted and nodded. Then we forded the river and were off again, more quickly than ever. I knew Rykka would never let me fall. Still, I gripped not only the reins but her mane to keep from slipping.

Somehow, the stallion kept pace with us, even though it was an obvious strain. When we finally stopped, with the suns low on the horizon and the craggy Xa'qìa peaks scalloping the darkening sky, foam dripped from the stallion's mouth and he was soaked with sweat.

"What do we do now?" Panesh asked.

"We wait," I replied, though I didn't know yet for what.

"We wait?" Janq'a complained. "It's getting dark. We can't just stay here. We have to find some place for the night. Some place protected. Not out in the open like this, where nayla can get us. Or Black Riders."

He pointed ahead to a knot of single-story dwellings that stood a short distance away, flanked on three sides by Xa'qìa boulders and dwarfed by the looming rocky range. It was a barren settlement, with no trees, bushes, flowers or other adornment to break up the bland monotony of the place. Even the houses were dully similar: dun adobe walls, gray-plank roofs and the same pyramid-shape door to the left of a flat oval window blanked out by mud-colored shutters. In only one house, the nearest, were the shutters open. There, I could just make out two figures peering at us through the window.

"What about there?" Janq'a asked anxiously. "We could go there. We should go there. Let's go there."

Panesh jabbed Janq'a in the back. "We stay here until Ben says otherwise. Without whining."

"Yes, your majesty," Janq'a grumbled.

"Or your sarcasm."

Janq'a grunted.

There was no movement in the village. Even the figures in the window stood unnaturally still. I wasn't sure what to do next. Should we ride into the village or bypass it? Regardless, how were we to get through the mountains? My whispered questions to Rykka went unanswered. She stood motionless, once more waiting for me to make a decision I felt ill-equipped to handle.

Perhaps the staff could help me again? Vaguely recalling the gold-crystal sphere through which my B'na self had witnessed Q'nta's execution — most memories of that time had already faded — I gazed into the staff's orb, hoping for a vision. For a long while, I saw nothing. Then I noticed tiny black dots floating randomly inside the orb. Thinking it to be the result of eyestrain, I squeezed my eyes tightly shut and reopened them. The dots had multiplied. There were now a dozen, moving about with apparent purpose. I brought the orb closer to my face, resting it on the bridge of my nose so that my eyes could no longer focus. Perhaps that was the key, for the dots became people and I now saw into the main room of the nearest house.

It is a smallish room, decorated simply if shabbily with cane chairs and a few bare, wooden side tables. Thin, worn cushions cover the chairs. Thin, worn lace covers the tables. A thin, threadbare rug covers a tiny square of the worn, uneven floor. The sole embellishment is a small but brilliant sunburst painted on an otherwise bare, unfinished wooden wall, its golds, oranges, yellows and crimsons startlingly bright in the drab, ill-lit room.

The room is jammed with people — all of grandparenting age but for a pigtailed girl and a boy near enough in appearance to be her younger brother. The adults gesticulate histrionically and talk over each other so loudly that no single one can be understood. The only two who stand still and in stillness are the couple at the window. They stare out toward the curious-looking people on their curiously colored horses…toward us.

The man, Rolo'En, white hair and pinkish complexion, turns away from the window and from Maysha, his wife, to face his neighbors. He raises his hand. The hubbub dies to a tense hush.

"They are still there, and they are not moving — either toward us or away. They are like statues." He crouches, pulls aside the rug and jiggles a square plank free from the floor, revealing a narrow earthen staircase that disappears into a dank, dark cellar. "I say we hide from them. What say you?"

The neighbors reply at once, in a cacophony of shouting that again renders everyone incomprehensible. Rolo'En climbs onto a rickety chair and bellows over them.

"Friends! Neighbors! One at a time. Please!"

"Aye," says a skeletally thin man once silence is restored. His face is lined and drawn, his mouth turned down into a perpetual frown. "I be for the cellar. Too many queer happenings up here." He grabs onto an equally gaunt woman, either his sister or his wife, and pushes her toward the stairs. "Down with ye," he orders, and follows her into the darkness.

"Men on horseback means only one thing," the woman closest to Rolo'En says. She nods once, with firm certitude. "It i'n't a good thing."

"Aye," the woman next to her agrees. "Bad things. Uncommon bad things."

Quietly and without turning from the window, Maysha says, "They are not Black Riders."

Rolo'En rejoins her at the window. "One of the horses be black."

"But one," Maysha counters. "The others are colored."

Another man joins her. His name is Marq'O. He is slender with strong hands, a kind, unshaven face and ears that jut out from a stubble-haired head. "Like the Tale of the Colored Horses," he says, a touch of awe stealing into his voice.

Grassi, his wife, pulls him from the window toward the trapdoor. "One black's plenty bad enough for me," she snorts. Grassi is plump, with multiple chins and an enormous bosom. Her white hair is wound tightly into a braid atop her head. With difficulty, she lowers herself through the too-small opening in the floor, trying to pull Marq'O after her. He shakes her off.

"That were The MoonQuest," Rolo'En replies to Marq'O. "That were many long ago's ago."

"Those colored horses from the tale be long dead now, for surely," Grassi adds, only her braid now visible.

Another woman, Mo'Rée, hugs the girl and boy close to her. "The last time Black Riders came, they took the wee ones." She pushes the children down the stairs. "I don't care who these riders be." She wags her finger at Maysha. "Riders be bad. Right bad."

Nodding heads and a chorus of ayes respond, drowning out the handful of nays. Lantern lights flare up from the cellar. "No lamps," Rolo'En called down. The lights flicker out, followed by a thud and a muttered curse.

"Maysha?" he asks.

"No change," she replies. "It will be night soon."

"Then it be time," he pronounces to those still in the room. "Hiding or hospitality?"

The arguments resume, now accompanied by shoving as most everyone stampedes to the trap door and disappears into the cellar. A hand reaches up from the blackness and pulls the plank back over the opening. Only Maysha, Rolo'En and Marq'O remain, huddled at the window.

"What do you say, wife?" Rolo'En asks.

"I am not afraid."

He ponders that. "Maybe's you should be."

Maysha strains to get a better look at us through the dimming light of dusk. "What if they are bards?"

"What if they ern't? Strangers is strangers. It 'uz been too many seasons since we've lucked with strangers."

"Maysha is right," Marq'O says, nodding slowly. "They could be bards. The bard in The MoonQuest rode a colored horse."

"That be only story. Even if they be real stories, they happened long before any of us was borned. Go be with your wife, Marq'O. That be your place." He tries to push Marq'O toward the trapdoor. Marq'O resists.

"If you be staying, I be staying."

Maysha leans into the window, staring out us. She does not move. Rolo'En watches her anxiously. Suddenly, she stands up straight, brushes off her skirt, ties a shawl over her head and flings open the front door. Rolo'En grabs her arm. She shakes it off gently, then hugs him. He holds her tightly.

"Watch from here," she says, wriggling free. She steps over the threshold and touches her hand to her breast. "I have to know, Rolo'En. I have to. I cannot hide anymore. I have hidden too long. We all have." She gazes out toward us, then back at her husband and Marq'O. "If bad happens and you can save me, do it. If not..." She shrugs and strides out, leaving the door open behind her. Rolo'En tries to follow. Marq'O holds him back.

"You're a-feared, yes?" he asks his friend.

Rolo'En nods, barely perceptibly. Shame is clear in his face.

"Me, as well," he says. "It be best not to go out with fear. Your Maysha's not a-feared. That be the only way."

The vision faded. I looked up from the orb. Maysha walked toward us with resolute certainty. I dismounted and started out on foot to meet her.

"Not by yourself," Panesh exclaimed.

"Yes," I countered. "You wait here with the horses."

Panesh argued, but I ignored him and walked on. Without knowing why, I knew that Maysha and I were to meet alone.

twenty

"*B*en," Maysha pronounced when I reached her, halfway between our horses and her village. Her eyes were wet and shining. She lowered her shawl to her shoulders.

She knew me? This, I had not anticipated. She twisted her head to acknowledge B'na, now almost at eye level, then looked back at me.

"How?" I asked, now even more startled.

Then I looked into her eyes. What I saw there left me speechless. Reflected back at me was a giant, green-scaled dragon, four claws on its right foot, six on its left. It sat perched at the apex of a colossus of a mountain, breathing fire into the sky. It spread its massive, feathered wings and leapt off the summit. After circling the mountain three times, it flew off, out of sight.

Kumba.

The Great Dragon of Creation was the first living being that Prithi had caused to be created, at the very beginning of time. Kumba had been born of the earth under what was now Castle Rose and had appeared to Q'nta during her StarQuest. It was Kumba who had guided Toshar and his companions to the Arms of K'varr that helped them defeat Fvorag. It was Kumba who had planted trees in the Pergosà paradise that bore the first stars, and it was Kumba who had tossed those stars into the heavens in the first constellations.

"You're— You're not—," I stammered.

Maysha laughed. "No. Of course not."

"I don't understand. Who are you that you know more about me than most in Q'ntana? Who are you that you reveal Kumba to me?"

"He has been here," she replied simply.

"*Here?*" Kumba was never seen, anywhere, outside of dream or vision. Toshar had seen only his tracks in the sand. Q'nta had witnessed only a fiery representation.

"Here." Maysha touched her heart. "He spoke to me in here. He said you would come. From there." She indicated B'na, now at chest level. "They do not know any of this," she said, gesturing back to the village. "They are too frightened to see, too frightened to believe, too frightened to understand."

I squinted at the house. Sensing my scrutiny, Rolo'En and Marq'O stepped out of sight.

"Of what?"

"Of the Black Riders, of course. Of the king and his men before that. What they truly fear is not out here—" she waved her arm to take in everything around her "—however terrifying so much in this land may be in these times. Their true fears lie inside themselves." She shook her head. "I am sad to say that they are too willfully blind to seek within for their fears and their courage, and they are too willfully deaf to listen for Prithi's voice, which would guide them through and past those fears."

"You are not?"

"May I?" She reached for my staff. I let her take it. She ran her fingers over the runes and caressed the orb. "My father was a bard. He met your father once, when Toshar was a young man, newly Elderbard. My father was a boy, then…here in this village. He told me that Toshar and Dafna passed through here that one time on their wedding journey. They were traveling the length and breadth of Q'ntana, to meet the people, to remind them of their stories, to help heal the land he had saved. That's how my father told it to me. It was Toshar, he said, who inspired him to become a bard. A great bard he was."

She handed me back the staff. "I would have been a bard too…"

"What happened?"

"Gravel happened. The King's Men happened. What happened to my father is what happened to your mother." She paused, wiped a tear from her eye. "What happened to your mother is why you are here. Yes?"

"How do you know that?"

"Sometimes I just know things. Sometimes the dreamwalkers send them to me. Sometimes I feel them here." She touched her heart again.

When I looked back into her eyes, there was Kumba, again perched on the mountain peak.

He spreads his right wing, plucks a feather from it with giant gold teeth. The feather has a silver spine and a pattern that suggests a simple crown.

Now, I am on the mountaintop next to Kumba. I feel tiny next to his massive presence. The dragon leans down, the feather still in his teeth, and touches its tip to my forehead, between my eyes. The feather glows.

"Astel Elohia," Kumba says. He breathes out a plume of fire that fills the scene. When the fire clears, he and I are gone, as is the mountain. Only the feather remains.

I blinked. Maysha watched me searchingly but said nothing. Instead, she pulled the feather of my vision, Kumba's feather, from inside her blouse, by her heart. She touched it to my forehead. It glowed.

"I found it next to my face when I woke this morning. It tickled my nose. That's what woke me. I knew what it was as soon as I saw it."

"How?"

"What you just saw in my eyes?"

I nodded.

"I dreamed the same thing last night. In the dream I saw Kumba touch the feather to your brow, just as I did now. The feather woke me before Rolo'En was up, so I was able to hide it. He would not have understood." She shook her head sadly. "None of them would." She glanced back toward the village. Marq'O and Rolo'En were no longer at the window. They stood just outside the open door.

"I must get back," she said.

"Come with us. I know you have the heart and vision for it."

Maysha sighed. "If your quest were my quest, I would. Without a breath's hesitation. I am sorry to say that it is not. My place is here. Perhaps when you are done, I can be a bard, here, for my village. Perhaps, then, I can carry on my father's legacy, as you do yours."

"I hope so. I will help you in any way that I can."

"I know you will." She handed me the feather. "This will help open the p'rtulle through the Xa'qìa Mountains…and more beyond that. It will save you much time…once upon a time."

"I cannot. Kumba gave it to you."

"He gave it to me that I might give it to you." She closed my fist over it. "That was clear in my dream. In your vision too. Use it tonight. I know it will help you." She hugged me and turned to go. "Take the northwest path around the village. It is the longer way, but you are certain to encounter no one. In these times, the emptiest path is always the best path."

Before I could thank her, she had hurried off, her shawl once again covering her head. When she reached the house, Rolo'En hustled her inside. The door slammed shut behind them. A quick flash of eyes at the window, Maysha's, then she stepped back as Rolo'En drew the shutters. I stared at the house, half-expecting Maysha to change her mind. When she didn't, I tucked the feather into my waistband and walked slowly back to the others.

*　*　*

"It's time," I said to Panesh and Janq'a, after sharing what had happened with Maysha. "We must leave your horse behind."

Panesh nodded and transferred his packs to Ta'ar.

"You ride with me, My'leen. Panesh and Janq'a can ride Ta'ar."

"You should have let Maysha take the horse," My'leen chided. "What will happen to him?"

"The horse belonged to a Black Rider," I replied. "If it were discovered in Maysha's possession, she would be killed. The whole village would be killed."

"We can't just leave him here."

As if to answer her concern, Rykka whinnied at the stallion. He snorted loudly in reply, reared and galloped off to the north. We watched until he disappeared into the failing light, then we began to make our way toward the mountain. I continued to seek out signs of life from Maysha's cottage. I saw none.

Prithi's Garden

twenty-one

The mountain soared up into the darkening sky with relentless verticality, sheer and indomitable. No path had ever been hacked through its unremitting solidity. No hand-grips scarred its blank perpendicularity. The only break in its unremitting featurelessness was a red-rock archway that yawned into a cave high above us.

A-whooo. A-whoo. A-whoo-eee. A-whoo-eee-ai. Aie-EEE.

First one nayla howled, then a second, then a chorus of countless others. They were nearby, somewhere in these foothills, and edging nearer, rapidly from all directions.

A-whooo. A-whoo. A-whoo-eee. A-whoo-eee-ai. Aie-eee. Aie-EEE!

I craned my neck up at the cave and stroked Kumba's feather. It glowed faintly. The others followed my gaze with little enthusiasm, all the while casting nervous glances in the direction of the howling. As terrifying — and terrifyingly close — as the nayla were, I did my best to ignore them. I focused instead on the arch. It also glowed, so subtly that it could have been a trick of the moonlight, for M'nor, full, plump and radiantly silver, now shone directly onto the rock face. No, there *was* something unusual about that cave. I was certain. Could it be our next p'rtulle? Clearly, there was no ordinary way through these mountains. Were we to pass through the cave? If so, how were we to reach it? If not, what other extraordinary path might reveal itself?

Ta'ar whinnied, breaking my focus. I turned to the horses. They stood just behind us, still packed with our gear. Rykka stomped her foot, shook her torso and snorted. The nayla fell silent. Ta'ar stared up at the moon.

"I don't know why you're all gawking up at that cave," Janq'a huffed. "There's no way to get up there. None. I don't see one. Do you see one?" He stabbed Panesh's leg with his finger. "It's even too high up for you to reach, and you're bigger than anyone has a right to be."

He eyed Ta'ar for a possible escape, but she shook him off every time he reached for her. Even had she not, Janq'a was too short to climb onto the horse by himself. He cursed and jerked his head dismissively in the direction of the cave. "Maybe you will find a way up there. Don't matter. Not to me. You won't be getting me into a dark cave like that. Not at night. Not with nayla around."

As if on cue, the nayla resumed their wailing.

A-whooo. A-whoo. A-whoo-eee. A-whoo-eee-ai. Aie-EEE. Aie-EEE. Aie-EEE.

I could almost hear their talons on the rock, could almost imagine the sound of flesh ripping under their razor-sharp incisors. My'leen and Janq'a crept closer to Panesh, the only one of us who with even a chance to survive an encounter with those savage creatures.

"That suits me," Panesh snarled at Janq'a. "Stay here. The nayla are hunting for their dinner. You are just about the right size, if a little tough."

"You'd like that, wouldn't you, to see me eaten alive by a nayla."

"I might. It would be better than waiting for you to betray us to Bo'Ra K'n."

"I told you. I'm not—"

"Stop it," My'leen cried. "Both of you." She glared at Janq'a. "Either you're coming with us or you aren't. If you aren't, maybe Maysha will take you in. Probably not, if you whine at her the way you whine at us. If you do choose to come with us, for Prithi's sake, stop complaining."

Panesh grinned. "Like I said."

"And you." She turned her wrath on Panesh. "You're just a bully. Always baiting him. I don't care who Janq'a is or who he knows. I don't care right now if he is Bo'Rà K'n himself. If Ben says he can travel with us, that is good enough for me. It should be good enough for you too."

Stunned by My'leen's outburst, Panesh and Janq'a glowered defiantly at each other then looked sheepishly back at her.

"Now what?" Janq'a asked, in a voice so tiny I could barely hear him.

Rykka stomped her foot again and neighed loudly, first at me then at the moon.

"Rykka and Ta'ar are ready to go home," I said. "Panesh, please unpack them. Help him, My'leen?" As soon as they were done, the horses glowed and flickered, then dissolved into the moonlight. Now, it was just us and the mountain…and too many packs to carry.

A-whooo. A-whoo. A-whoo-eee. A-whoo-eee-ai. Aie-EEE!

"Now what?" Janq'a asked again.

"I don't know." I stared back up at the cave. M'nor had passed behind a cloud and the archway was barely visible in the filtered light. What was I supposed to do? How was I supposed to get us to safety? I fidgeted distractedly with my staff, hoping for an answer. As I did, my thumb rubbed over something I hadn't felt before. A tiny hole. At the top of the orb. Had that opening always been there? Had I carried this staff through an entire lifetime without noticing it? It didn't matter. Without knowing how, I knew the hole was for Kumba's feather. The stem slotted in perfectly.

"What are you doing?" Panesh asked.

"I don't know." I pulled at the feather. It refused to budge.

A-whooo. A-whoo. A-whoo-eee. A-whoo-eee-ai. Aie-EEE. Aie-EEE. Aie-EEEEE!

"Please," Janq'a said, his voice trembling, "do something." His voice dropped to a whisper. "Before they kill us."

The feather was supposed to help us. But how?

It will save you much time...once upon a time...

I touched the tip of the feather to my forehead and the tip of the staff to the rock.

Once upon a time...

This time it seemed to be the staff that was speaking to me. Or the feather. Or both.

My'leen gasped. Her hand shot to her mouth. The halo she had seen around my head after we had left Castle Rose was now *in* my head. It whizzed around and around, illuminating the night around us and so startling the nayla a few paces away that they fled, yowling in fear. The light focused sharply where the feather tip touched my skin then shot through feather and staff into the rock. In that same moment, the cloud masking the moon disintegrated, freeing M'nor to glow even more brilliantly than she had before.

"Once upon a time," the staff began, in a voice that was neither male nor female, young nor old, "in the time that lies beyond time, lived a young dreamwalker. His name was Rev'Àn..."

Thunder growled angrily through the now-clear sky. The ground quaked and shuddered. Chunks of rock calved from the mountain, hurtling to earth around us, crushing our packs and satchels. Janq'a, My'leen and Panesh pressed their back against the cliff to avoid being struck. Panesh tugged at my arm to join them. I was barely aware of him or of the danger. I was aware only of the staff and the story it had begun, a story now mine to complete.

"His name," I repeated, taking over the storytelling and still holding the tip of the staff to the rock, "was Rev'Àn." Hairline cracks formed where staff met rock. The cracks spidered up the cliff face toward the cave.

The thunder boomed louder. Bolts of dry lightning slashed the sky, randomly stabbing the ground. One hit a stand of dry scrub. It exploded into flame. Another struck the mountain. An avalanche of rock cascaded crashingly to the ground. None of that mattered. All that mattered was the story. All I could do was continue.

"Rev'Àn was a carefree child, a joy-filled boy who frolicked among the clouds and danced through the people's most pleasing dreams. He sang too, in a voice so sonorously bell-like that people wept with joy when they heard him." Light continued to course through the staff. The hairline cracks swelled into narrow fissures. "If ever he felt called to send down a distressing dream, as at times all dreamwalkers must, he did his best to weave into it threads of gold and silver that would help the dreamer see the good in even the grimmest of nightmares.

"Then one day, once upon a time, Prithi saw fit to bring him a sister. The girl was called Na'an. If Rev'Àn's hair seemed to have been spun from the finest gold of the sun, hers must have been woven from moonlight, so luminescently silver was it. If his face could only have been carved from an angelic mold, hers was even more delicate and cherubic. If his singing left joyful weeping in its wake, hers awakened within her dreamers heartful depths that they never imagined they could possess."

Thunder echoed more fiercely. Lightening thrashed more frequently. Angry gusts flung churning clouds across the sky, forcing M'nor into a cruel game of hide-and-seek. Still, the story continued. As it did, the staff drilled more deeply into the rock.

"Where Rev'Àn had once been the only dream child," I continued in the same altered state, "there was now another. Where Prithi's smile had once brightened Rev'Àn's countenance alone, it now lit on another as well. On the new dream child, Na'an."

The outline of a staircase began to show itself in the rock, slowly carving its way down to us from the cave.

"Where Rev'Àn had once been destined to rule the Dream Realms alone, his future grew uncertain. As his future grew uncertain, his present grew unbearable. His voice hardened. His features hardened. His dreams hardened. He ceased weaving silver and gold threads through his nightmares, and most of the dreams he spun now were nightmares…nightmares that grew ever more dark, angry, menacing.

"Once upon a time, Rev'Àn had wept for those dreamers who awoke in the icy sweat of dread. Now, not only did his eyes remain dry, his heart remained cold. At first, the terrors he induced left him impassive. Soon, however, grim smiles cracked through his stoniness. Soon after that, those grim smiles distended into grinning sneers. It was not much longer after that his sneer at the misery of one tormented dreamer exploded into laughter so loud and long that the heavens shook with his malevolent mirth.

"Where, you might ask, was Prithi in all of this? Prithi was present, as Prithi always is. But Prithi does not meddle in the doings of dreamwalkers or in the lives of men. Prithi watched. Prithi listened. Prithi waited."

A spear of lightning thrust itself at M'nor. Its only effect was to brighten her glow. It attacked the moon again, with no effect. A third thunderbolt struck my staff. It shattered, its light fragmenting into a million sparks that flared brilliantly, for an instant turning night into day. As one, they extinguished, plunging us back into darkness. The feather dropped to the ground, undamaged. But it was too late for Bo'Rà K'n to hold us back: Our stairway to the cave was complete.

The story was not.

"Now, all Rev'Àn spun were nightmares, and dreamers knew only terror. Rev'Àn had secured his power, the power to control Q'ntana through the fear of its people. He reveled in that power and determined never to surrender it. He would, instead, expand and amplify it. In that moment, Rev'Àn was no longer Rev'Àn. Rev'Àn had become Bo'Rà K'n."

I stepped onto the staircase, clutching Kumba's feather. The ground beneath me rumbled and cracked. I ignored it and climbed up through the darkness to the cave. The others followed. The moment we stepped inside, lightning smashed into the cliff with an earsplitting crash. Boulders erupted all around us. A massive one exploded onto the cave opening, its mountain of rubble extinguishing all light and sound from the outside world.

We were trapped.

twenty-two

A hand grabbed onto my wrist. My'leen's. "Is-is there more to the story?" she asked.

"There is always more. To every story," I replied.

"What about to this one?" Janq'a squeaked. "Please let there be more to this one."

We stood in a cavern so vast that no walls were visible, other than the one that now blocked our entrance. All we could see ahead of us were arthritically twisted rock pillars that glowed faintly and cast malefic shadows all around us. Next to me, Panesh slung a protective arm around My'leen, who still gripped my wrist. He clamped his other hand onto Janq'a, who clung tremblingly to the giant's leg.

"This story? It's not over yet," I replied. "Whatever Bo'Rà K'n might prefer."

"We've been buried alive."

"I do not think so, Janq'a," Panesh replied with uncharacteristic tenderness. "You heard Ben. The story is not over. Not yet. Not for any of us."

"We're going to die," he moaned.

"Kumba's feather got us in here. It will get us out too," I said with as much conviction as I could muster. "I know it will." I moved deeper into the cave, the others close behind. "It has to," I added under my breath.

*   *   *

As we traveled through the cave, our path malevolently illuminated by the stone pillars, it felt as though we walked through one of Bo'Rà K'n's nightmares. The air in the cave was close — still but not quite stifling, and heavy with menace. The pillars, although set solidly into the stone floor, almost pulsated with hostility. At first, it was easy to avoid them, as they were widely and randomly scattered. However, the deeper we pushed into the cave, the more tightly they clustered, the more fiendishly alive they seemed and the harder it became to avoid brushing against them.

For the longest time, little changed on our level, stone-slab path. We slipped by the pillars without incident. Janq'a grumbled unceasingly, ignored after a time by the rest of us. Even when the rock-solid floor fractured into a rutted, uneven aggregate of slippery gravel and sandal-slicing shards, we managed to continue without incident.

Then My'leen tripped.

Two stony arms thrust out from the pillar to seize her. She screamed. She was still screaming after Panesh pulled her to safety.

"Wh-what was that?" she whimpered when her screams died into sobs.

I studied the pillar, from a safe distance. It appeared as stonily immobile as it had moments earlier, its neighbors equally so. I didn't know what had just happened. Whatever it was, we would now have to proceed even more cautiously than before. There was no way back, and the way forward could prove even more perilous than we thought.

"Why did we ever come in here?" Janq'a exploded into wails. "We're going to die. I know we are. What did I do to deserve this? I want to go home. Please, Bo'Rà K'n. Let me come home. *Please!*"

Panesh's jaw tensed. His temples throbbed. He clenched his fists.

I sympathized. It was all I could do not to throttle Janq'a myself. Instead, I swallowed my ill temper and lightly touched Panesh's arm. "There is a reason," I said softly, as much to convince myself as to convince him. "If there weren't, Janq'a would not be here with us. I'm certain of it." I was, even if I was far from happy about it.

"Can we make that reason be an early death?" Panesh responded through gritted teeth. "His?"

"That's right," Janq'a blubbered. "Kill me. Do it now. Please!"

"No one is going to kill you," I snapped. "But you have to pull yourself together, Janq'a. That is the only way we are going to make it out of here."

"What if there's no way out? What if this is a trap?"

"Set by your friend Bo'Rà K'n?"

"Panesh!"

"What if we walk and walk and walk…forever. Or what if we walk and walk and walk and end up at a blank wall? I know we're going to die. It's not fair."

I had no answer. I believed in Kumba and in the feather that had brought us here, but... Were we trapped? Had Bo'Rà K'n been behind the stone pillar's attack? Even if he hadn't been, were the pillars somehow alive? Were they trying to stop us? Could we make it past them? Or had our SunQuest already failed?

I clutched the feather more tightly. *Please, Kumba, don't let us down. Don't let Q'ntana down...*

My'leen rested her hand on Janq'a's shoulder. "It's going to be all right," she crooned, over and over again until he composed himself. It helped me too.

*   *   *

The cavern floor was no longer much of a floor. It was mostly loose rubble, some of it barely masking small but treacherous sinkholes. More than once, I nearly slid into one, only to be rescued by Panesh, who now dogged my heels. My'leen walked behind him, tightly gripping the tail of his vest. After My'leen's incident Janq'a insisted on being last in our single file. He argued with undisguised self-importance that at least one of the three people in front of him would succumb to any hazards before he was put at risk.

Panesh was glad to have Janq'a at the back. Likely, he secretly hoped that the ground would open up and swallow the little man before any of us noticed. I knew that Janq'a would have been more safely placed behind me or My'leen, with Panesh in the rear. Yet I was too weary of Janq'a's carping to do anything but surrender to his selfishness.

That is not what a king would have done. A king would have never let Janq'a have his own way. Gravel would have threatened him into silent acquiescence.

Gravel was not a king. He was a thug. Anyhow, that is not the kind of king I want to be. I want to rule with an Elderbard's wisdom and compassion. Wait! I don't want to rule at all. I don't want to be king...any kind of king. Do I? Do I even have a choice? Or is it the kind of choice Eulisha and O'ric always seemed to be offering: a choice that is really no choice at all...

A bone-chilling shriek shattered my introspection.

Janq'a! I spun around. Stone arms from the nearest pillar had caught him in a sinister embrace that tightened the more he struggled.

"My feet," he wailed. "I can't move my feet."

The pillar's stone had spread to his shoes, anchoring them to the ground. His arms, still free, waved hysterically. My'leen tried to pull him free.

"Now I can't *feel* my feet. Help! Do something. Please. I don't want to die. Not like this!"

The stone crept up his pant legs, crusting them in unyielding gray.

"Leave him," Panesh said quietly.

"Leave me? Oh, no. Don't leave me. I'll do anything if you don't leave me."

My'leen glared at Panesh. "What is wrong with you? I know you hate him. But we can't leave him like that. How can you even say that?"

"Panesh just wants me dead. He's always wanted me dead." Janq'a wept uncontrollably. "Now you get to have your wish, don't you."

"Janq'a! That is not at all what I wish."

"It is. It is." Janq'a thrashed against the tightening grip. "It is."

"Don't you see?" Panesh said. "The more you fight it, the worse it gets."

"Oh," he whimpered, still flailing.

My'leen dropped Janq'a's arm. Still in a frenzy, his arms still swinging wildly, he inadvertently pushed her into an adjacent pillar. In an instant, she was trapped too.

"Try to relax," Panesh said.

"You want her to relax?" Janq'a retorted. "Are you crazy?"

"I have a plan," he said.

"He has a plan," Janq'a mimicked, still struggling as best he could. Stone now encased his legs and had begun on My'leen's sandal-clad feet.

"I have a plan," Panesh repeated. "Stand back," he said to me.

I did. Too far. Two stone arms reached out for me from a nearby pillar. They shattered the instant they touched me. I stepped away, shaking.

"Astel Elohia," Panesh said.

"What?"

"You are protected. By the Ring of Unity."

I touched my forehead and almost thought I felt the braided coronet that had been infused into me all those lifetimes ago.

"Is there some way I can use it to help them?" The stone had reached Janq'a's waist and My'leen's knees. They both sobbed noisily.

"Perhaps," Panesh replied, "but I do not know how."

"What do we do? We have to do something."

"I know. I have a plan, remember? Block your ears."

"Block my ears?" Janq'a cried. "How? I can't even move my arms anymore."

"Be quiet, Janq'a, for once in your life. Not everything is about you. I was talking to Ben." Panesh took a deep breath. "I cannot promise that this will work…"

"Whatever it is, just do it,"My'leen shouted. "Please!" Her arms, too, were entombed. Stone crawled up Janq'a's neck.

"It could have unintended consequences."

"Just do it!" Janq'a's petrifying jaw distorted his words. It sounded like "Ja daw ate."

Panesh inhaled deeply again, holding his breath for an inhumanly long time. When he released it, it was with a piercing, off-key screech that grew progressively shriller and lasted far longer than any normal exhalation. Janq'a grimaced at the sound just as the stone reached his mouth, freezing his pained expression in place. Despite her terror, My'leen began to sing with Panesh, her melody weaving in and out of his increasingly dissonant and disagreeable tones. When I thought I could stand the sound no more, the stone encasing My'leen and Janq'a shattered, the arms enclosing them fractured, and the pillars them-selves splintered into fragments.

Panesh and My'leen no longer sang, but their notes hung in the air and their music continued its destruction. Pillars exploded. Jagged chunks of rock pelted down from the distant ceiling. The ground roiled and crumpled. A crevasse opened beneath us. Before we could scramble to safety, we plunged into a yawning blackness that never seemed to end. For a long time, the clamor of the destruction far above followed us. Then it subsided into spectral silence. Still we tumbled, the faint, flickering glow from Kumba's feather too weak to illuminate anything other than my trembling hand.

twenty-three

With a violent splash, we slammed into a giant underground loch that shimmered with blue-green luminescence. Distant rough-stone walls, glimmering with the water's reflection, encircled most of the pool, whose eddying current purposefully herded us together at its center point. We had barely caught our breath when the current shifted, propelling us swiftly ahead. There was no point trying to swim. The water supported us from below, even as it pushed us from behind. There was no point trying talk. A dissonant boom bounced at us off the rock, rendering conversation impossible. All we could do was surrender to the current and let ourselves be carried forward as the pool narrowed then narrowed some more, until it was little wider than our four flailing bodies. Moments later, it flung us over a ledge, down a waterfall and into a rushing stream that almost immediately calmed into a shallow, subterranean creek.

Although barely thigh height for me and My'leen, the creek was chest-high for Janq'a, who struggled to keep pace with us as we waded in the only direction possible, toward a tiny, glinting patch of daylight in the far distance. Here, although the water had no natural luminescence, twinkling starlike stones fixed into the arched tunnel's slickly smooth walls radiated just enough light to guide us. Panesh, forced to walk with a bowed head because of the low ceiling, said nothing as Janq'a complained loudly and vociferously about how hard it was for him to slog through the creek. We all did our best to ignore him. Finally, Panesh scooped Janq'a up and wedged him under his arm. Janq'a squirmed and fussed until Panesh threatened to smack his head against the wall if that was the only way to silence him. It worked. For a time.

"That story you told about Bo'Rà K'n and Na'an," My'leen asked. "Is it true?"

"I don't know… It must be. It came from Kumba's feather and from an Elderbard's staff."

"It came from an Elderbard who carries the Ring of Unity," Panesh corrected me.

"That too," I said.

"Janq'a would know all about it," Panesh said. "Wouldn't you?" He squeezed Janq'a.

"Ouch! Stop that. You're hurting me!" Janq'a tried to twist free. Panesh squeezed him more tightly.

"Is it true, Janq'a?" My'leen asked. "Do you know?"

"How would I know?" he muttered.

"He is your master," Panesh retorted.

"And I'm his servant. *Was* his servant. How many times do I have to tell you? Was. Was. *Was*. It was 'Janq'a, fetch this.' Or 'Janq'a, where is my food?' Or 'Janq'a, don't be insolent.' Do you really think that he talked to the likes of me about the likes of that?"

"You tell me," Panesh said.

Janq'a wriggled free and dropped into the water. It was deeper now, nearly up to his neck when he regained his footing.

"You think I want to be here?" Janq'a hollered up at him. He shook his fist at Panesh, blocking his way. "You think I want to have to listen to you haranguing me all the time? You think I want to be on this miserable quest? You should have just left me where you found me."

"You are right for once, Janq'a. That is exactly what we should have done. If it had been up to me—"

My'leen smashed her fist into the water. Her eyes blazed. "Stop it! I don't care what you think of each other. If you can't get along, pretend to get along. If you can't even do that, I don't see how we will ever make it to…to wherever it is we're going." She sloshed on ahead, splashing loudly.

"She's right," I said, trying to keep exasperation out of my voice. "This is our SunQuest. All four of us. Together. If either one of you doesn't think you can get along with the other for the rest of the journey, then maybe you ought to make your own way once we are out of this tunnel." It would not be long before we were. The patch of daylight was larger and nearer, its glare so bright that it was impossible to see what we were heading into. "Until then, if you can't at least be respectful, just be quiet. Please."

Panesh and Janq'a murmured their assent and muttered barely

audible apologies. I let Janq'a climb onto my back, and we continued forward in strained but welcome silence.

*   *   *

It was not until we reached the mouth of the tunnel that we could clearly see what lay beyond it: a tropical paradise of unparalleled luxuriance. Shockingly vivid flowers in every imaginable color and blend of colors, some taller than Janq'a, arrayed in front of us against a backdrop of lush verdancy. Thick vines, their scalloped, triangular leaves mottled with crimson and yellow splotches, coiled tightly around the barely visible trunks of sinewy, titanic trees. Thick clusters of purple-and-gold fruit dangled down temptingly from gracefully curving boughs that were too tall for even Panesh to reach. High above the canopy of trees, puffed snowy clouds scudded across a sunless, pale purple sky that speared shafts of brilliant dewy light down to a jungle floor carpeted in a pastel rainbow of ground cover. The sounds were equally spellbinding: a symphony of melodic birdsong that came at us from every direction at once. When My'leen began to hum an accompaniment, an explosion of color burst from deep within the foliage and fluttered fearlessly around her. Even Janq'a appeared uncharacteristically awed by the sound and spectacle.

We crossed the threshold from tunnel to jungle, still thigh-deep in the stream. The air was thick and moist, redolent with sweet scents. As My'leen continued to sing, more birds joined the avian chorus, trilling even more mellifluously. An instant later, tunnel and stream folded into the surrounding greenery as though they had never existed. We no longer waded in a stream in drenched clothing. We stood on a thick, loamy carpet, embarrassed by our sudden nakedness. All that remained of our previous world was Kumba's feather, clenched tightly in my fist.

"Kea Kana," I whispered without thinking, before I even knew what I had said.

"Prithi's Garden?" Panesh asked, his voice trembling.

My'leen blanched. "You mean we…we're…"

I glanced around. "We can't be."

"Can't be what?" Janq'a asked. "What's a Kea Kana?"

"Dead," Panesh said.

"Dead!? But— But—" Janq'a stammered. He crumpled to the ground in tears. "I don't want to be dead. I'm not ready to be dead. Didn't I already say that? Please don't let me be dead."

How could this be Kea Kana? Kea Kana was where the souls of the newly dead came to rest before being assigned a new life and body. Exceptionally, I had not experienced Prithi's Garden when I last died as Ben because my soul had immediately ascended to form B'na. If I had traveled to Kea Kana before that, I had no memory of it. Still, Kea Kana was a place for souls, not bodies, and these were definitely bodies we were walking around in — disturbingly naked bodies. Bodies, plus one dragon's feather.

We can't be dead, I decided. There must be something else going on, some other reason why we were here. I stared at the feather.

"Maysha said the quill would open a p'rtulle for us," I said slowly, thinking aloud. "No, wait. It did that already...into the mountain." I shook my head. "I don't know..."

"I know! I know," Janq'a exclaimed. "Didn't she also say that the feather would save us time? Is that why we're here? Is this some sort of shortcut?"

"Time..." I examined the feather more closely. Nothing about it offered any clues. Its silver spine still shone, and the crown pattern in its iridescent vane was unchanged. Or was it? As I stared, a faint roll of parchment wavered into view. It unscrolled up out of the crown, flickered, then vanished. "Once upon a time?" I whispered. "Is that possible?"

"What do you mean?" My'leen asked.

"A story. We must be in a story. It can't be anything else."

"That doesn't make any sense," Janq'a countered.

"Does this?" I gestured around the garden paradise. "Does anything about this SunQuest make any sense? You're right. Somehow being in the middle of a story makes no sense. Still, it makes as much sense as anything else we have experienced." I was certain now, or at least as certain as I could be. "This is a story we are in, here in Kea Kana. The only way out is to tell our way out of it."

"I don't understand," Janq'a said, a tinge of whine creeping back into his voice.

"Understanding is not required." I smiled when I realized what I had said. I had quoted O'ric.

Janq'a squinted up at the sky. "Where are the suns? We have to go west. How can we go west without suns to guide us?"

I looked up. No, there would be no suns in Kea Kana. "It doesn't matter. Not here. What matters is the story."

"I don't want to be in a story," Janq'a grumbled

"Maybe all we ever are is in a story," I said, "Prithi's story."

"Which story is this?" My'leen asked.

"I don't know it." I gazed around, seeking inspiration. "Not yet."

I also did not know how to find it. I hoped it would find me. Without knowing where I was going but trusting that, somehow, I did, I led Janq'a, My'leen and Panesh deeper into the jungle. The birds didn't follow us, but giant insects did. Green, orange or turquoise — never black — they buzzed harmlessly around our heads, briefly curious about these strange creatures who had invaded their garden. Bored, they flew off in a cloud of color.

The only sound now was the soft pad of our feet on the mercifully spongy ground and our breathing, increasingly labored in the musky humidity. When Janq'a's panting rasped into a phlegmy cough, Panesh picked him up, gently and silently, and set him on his shoulder. Janq'a said nothing, even after his breathing returned to normal.

Everything was so still that when a flock of long-necked blue-and-yellow birds poked screechingly through the underbrush, a startled Panesh stopped abruptly and Janq'a toppled to the ground. The birds waddled over, pecked at the air around Janq'a, then flapped their wings noisily and sprung into the sky. After collecting ourselves, we continued on. We encountered no further wildlife and stopped only once, to bathe in a cool spring that burbled tinklingly from a rocky creek bed. I was grateful that Panesh and My'leen — even Janq'a — said little and complained not at all. So we carried on. What else could we do?

The answer came soon after. From behind a thick stand of ivy-wrapped trees, a hissing creature pounced out toward us. Sleek and black with lustrous gold spots, silver whiskers, green eyes and a long, swishing gold tail, it halted in front of me, rose up on its hind legs and rested its giant, sharply clawed front paws gently on my shoulders.

twenty-four

The creature sniffed my face then licked it. "Your Highness," he said in a voice that was somewhere between a growl and a purr.

"What?" I said, too alarmed and disconcerted to say or do anything else.

The creature dropped to the ground. He slunk around us, sniffing at each of us in turn. When he returned to me, he stared into my eyes, snarling softly. "You are the Ko'leya Ben, are you not?"

If, back at the mountain, I had been too steeped in my story about Rev'Àn to react to the nayla, I had no such distraction here. I did not dare back away, even as, in my terror, that's all I wanted to do.

"What are you?" I managed to utter. "How do you know me?"

"What I am is not important," he replied. "You are what is important. You are the Ko'leya Ben, are you not?" he asked again.

I swallowed hard. "I am."

"As I thought." The creature knelt before me and bowed his head. "How would I not know my own king?"

Panesh shot me an "I told you so" look. I ignored it.

"Please get up. Who are you?"

"I am Da'nay, my lord. I am here to serve you."

"Thank you, Da'nay, but I am not king. Not yet."

Da'nay rose, his head still lowered. "Here in Kea Kana, you are already both king and Elderbard, Ben Ko'leya. You are already Kano'ha and Ko'lar, my lord, and have long been."

Janq'a's eyes bulged. He gaped from Da'nay to me and back again. Then he cocked his head as if he had just recalled something. "If this is Kea Kana, sir, are we dead?"

Da'nay bared his fangs and sprang at Janq'a, who ducked between Panesh's legs and tried to disappear. The creature licked his thin black-purple lips and returned his focus to me.

"You speak true," he said, nodding. "In order to move forward, you must leave this story and rejoin the other, the one you left. Then both stories can merge in a single time, once upon a time."

"I'm sorry, Da'nay. I don't understand. What would you have us do?"

"It is I who must beg forgiveness, my lord, for not being clear. If you will honor me by allowing me to be your guide, I will lead you to the Scriving Rock. There, you will be able to write the story that will continue your story."

"The Scriving Rock?" If all dreams were born of a dreamwalker's loom, the Scriving Rock, according to legend, was the place where all stories were conceived. "It…it's real?"

"Yes," Da'nay replied, "the Scriving Rock is more than a simple story. It is the ultimate story." He stretched his tensile body, extended his razor-keen claws and distended his mouth into long, lazy yawn, revealing a chilling mouth filled with knifepoint teeth. Then he slunk forward, stopping after a few paces to stare back at me. "Come," he said. "I will take you there."

There is no time in Kea Kana, so our journey felt at the same time endlessly lengthy and lightning quick. Nor is it a human realm, so we felt neither fatigue nor hunger. For however long we walked, the light never changed. The terrain did. Flat and dense at the outset, it gradually thinned until we came upon a sizable clearing ringed by pole-like trees so tall that we could barely make out their tops. Just within the border of trees, a narrow, moat-like rill encircled a massive, smooth, flat-gray rock, its jagged edges blackened with touches of umber, as though they had been burnt. A small spring burbled up from its center point.

"The Scriving Rock," Da'nay said. He leapt over the rill, which was so limpid that it almost seemed empty. We followed.

I don't know what Da'nay did next. I don't know where Panesh, Janq'a and My'leen went, what they did or, if they spoke, what they said. All I could do was walk the perimeter of the rock, slowly but purposefully, my eyes open the barest of slits. Even the rock itself was not present for me. All I knew were voices only I could hear. Men's voices, women's voices, children's voices. Voices of every age and timbre. Storytelling voices. Storyteller voices. It was as though all the stories ever told by all the storytellers who had ever told them were speaking to me, all at one time. Oddly, it was not the incomprehensible cacophony

I would have expected. It was a symphony, a tapestry that wove all stories into one story, that merged all time into one time, that blended all storytellers into one storyteller. That one storyteller was me.

"I surrender to the story," I repeated again and again as I walked. "I surrender to the story. I surrender to the story." Tears coursed down my cheeks, scoring the rock where they fell. "I surrender to the story."

I no longer followed the perimeter. Now, again with minimal awareness, I traced a spiral, coiling closer and closer to the center spring, to the well of stories, to that place that just by my being there, explained *my* story — who I was, the sun I was, the bard I was, the Eldberbard I had been and would be again…the king I would soon be. When I reached the spring, I collapsed in front of it, sobbing uncontrollably, still clutching Kumba's feather. Da'nay stood next to me on all fours, alert, his whiskers twitching and his fur crackling with some sort of charge.

"I couldn't know… I never imagined."

"No other Elderbard has ever set foot here," Da'nay said. He touched a paw to my heart. "But all Elderbards know it, even if they do not know they know it…even if they do not know that it is real."

"I was Elderbard," I said. "A very long time ago. Once upon a time…"

"In this place, once upon a time is this time…and all time. Do you understand?"

"I did as B'na. As Ben, I'm not sure…"

"Do you know what to do?"

I stood up shakily. "I think so."

"You must know so, my lord. The SunQuest demands it of you. Your SunQuest requires it of you. Your quill?"

I opened my fist. The feather was tousled but intact.

Da'nay touched the tip of his right front paw into the well. "This is your ink."

I dipped my quill into the well and waited.

"Now, Ko'lar, your story." Da'nay herded Panesh, My'leen and Janq'a away to clear space for me. Writing space. Scriving space. They sat a short distance away, watching in awed silence.

"Where do I begin?" I asked.

"Where all stories begin," I heard. Na'an's voice, not Da'nay's. "Once upon a time…"

With a shaky hand, I scratched "Once upon a time" onto the rock.

Although my ink was water, what emerged from the quill was black, and once on the rock, the letters and words swirled, reforming and recoloring themselves into images that illustrated the story as I wrote and spoke it. I dipped the quill back into the well and continued.

"Once upon a time…in a dream…the world was dark. The suns shone and the moon glowed. But still the world was dark…so inky black that naught was visible, only a velvet pall that cloaked everything in the grim gloom of a single dreamwalker who spun only nightmares on his loom of the night."

Through the absolute blackness initially formed by the words flowing onto the rock, vague contours could be detected. As the words continued, the contours became outlines and the outlines became Bo'Rà K'n himself, seated at a menacing mechanical contraption that soared high up above the cloud upon which it rested. As Bo'Rà K'n turned its giant wooden crank, the machine's wheels, gears and sprockets groaned and creaked, sparked, squealed and squeaked, grinding out a noxious black cloud filled with indistinct images of gruesome horror. These traveled through a wooden tube that ran from somewhere in the heart of the device to a funnel-like spout that pointed downward, out through a break in the floor.

Somewhere beyond my consciousness, I heard a gasp and was vaguely aware of Panesh's hand reaching across My'leen to cover Janq'a's mouth.

"Although stilled in lighter times," I continued, "Bo'Rà K'n had never been fully silenced. Nor had he been destroyed, for a dreamwalker never can be destroyed, even as he destroys the dreams of his long-forgotten heart."

Bo'Rà K'n cranked more quickly. The poison mist disgorged from the tube and rained down over the village below, partially shrouding moon and stars on its way.

"Bo'Rà K'n cranked more quickly, then more quickly still. Down in the village, the black gas sweated through window frames and oozed under the doors of every house. None was spared. It bled up through floorboards and seeped in through wooden slats. Not even the whitewash could hold it back. Once inside, it surged into every bedroom and soaked through every pillow. Children wept. Their parents wept too, for their children and for themselves. And nayla howled through the night, feasting slaveringly on the nocturnal horrors that surrounded them."

I heard crying too — and not only the weeping rising from the image on the Scriving Rock. My'leen cried. Even Janq'a cried.

"Then the crying ebbed as fingers of light sliced through the malevolent darkness and dawn forced its way into the village, as well as into Bo'Rà K'n's chamber of nightmares. Even as daylight finally brightened the land below when Bo'Rà K'n first slowed then ceased his cranking, daylight never reached Bo'Rà K'n's aerie. There, the best the suns could achieve was to dim the shadows surrounding the prince of shadows."

The image faded from the rock. If there was more to the story, it was not yet time, for no other words came through me to the quill. There would be more. I knew it.

My'leen leapt up, tears streaming down her face. "That was worse than I ever thought, worse than I ever imagined. If Bo'Rà K'n cannot be destroyed, what are we supposed to do?"

Da'nay padded over to her and licked away her tears. "There is no heart that does not yearn to be remembered," he said. "There is no heart that does not long to open."

"Even Bo'Rà K'n's?" Janq'a asked in a disbelieving whisper.

"Even Bo'Rà K'n's." Da'nay turned to me. "Write that story, Ko'lar."

At other times, I might have questioned my ability, especially with regard to the story Da'nay was asking of me. Now, the Scriving Rock erased all my doubts. I dipped Kumba's quill back into the well, held it suspended, then again touched it to the rock. "Once upon a—" I stopped, crossed it out and began again. "Now, in the time that is all time," I wrote.

"Now, in the time that is all time, broken dreams are mended, broken hearts are repaired, broken souls are made whole. Now, in the time that is all time, is this story told."

Once again, the words came to life on the Scriving Rock, flowing into animated images that illustrated the story.

Back in Bo'Rà K'n's loom chamber, the scene was radically different from what we had just seen. The morning suns, which had previously been powerless to penetrate the dark clouds that surrounded his aerie, now burst through, blanching the clouds and freeing the chamber from its shadowy pall. Bo'Rà K'n, his back to us, stood before his nightmare loom, which, in the dawning light of day, presented itself as at once more massive and less threatening.

"Wheel by wheel, gear by gear, sprocket by sprocket, Bo'Rà K'n disassembled and dismantled his machine," I spoke as I wrote. "With each piece removed, three things happened. First, whatever the piece was, it turned to dust the instant it was separated from the machine. Second, as each piece disintegrated, the chamber's dark mists lightened to white and the chamber itself grew brighter. Third and most astounding was the transformation in Bo'Rà K'n himself. As, bit by bit, the nightmare loom shrunk, his black cloak and clothing, which had so long hidden him from the world, turned silver, gold and white, revealing a handsome physique and delicacy of movement that belonged not to Bo'Rà K'n but to Rev'Àn.

"Once the final piece of his loom had passed from sight, Bo'Rà K'n was no more."

"It-it's not possible," Janq'a stammered at the fringes of my consciousness.

Panesh shushed him.

Bo'Rà K'n was no more? Was I seeing what Yzythq'a had sung to us what now seemed so long ago?

O, Son of Sun

O, young king wise

Restore the dreams to Rev'Àn's eyes

Was Rev'Àn's soul now truly free?

My mind trespassed on the Scriving Rock's storytelling space with the same skepticism Janq'a had just expressed. How was it possible that after all this time, Bo'Rà K'n could cease to be? Would he willingly deconstruct his nightmare apparatus and his nightmare being? Were we seeing something that had already taken place? If so, how had it happened? Or were we seeing what would be or could be? If it were the latter, what would it take to guarantee the success that O'ric had been unwilling to promise Q'nta that I would achieve? Which was it?

"In this place," Da'nay spoke into my mind, "all of them."

"And beyond this place?" I asked silently.

"That will depend on you, Ben Ko'leya, and on your companions on this SunQuest."

I held my quill over the Scriving Rock, not knowing whether there was more to write and if there was, what it might be. Could I write our conclusion here and thus know it in advance? Or was this our conclusion? My mind clamored for answers even as it refused to listen to what my heart yearned to say.

"There is more," Da'nay said aloud. "Your story is not done, nor is this one. Listen for it. Listen for it as only the Elderbard you have already been and will be again can. Listen for it as only the king that it is your destiny to be can. Close your eyes, empty your mind…and listen."

I shut my eyes to the now-blank Scriving Rock and shut my ears to everything except the faint burbling of the well. After a time, even the water-sound stilled for me and I listened to the silence. Then, from deep within the silence, I knew to open my eyes, once more dip my quill into the well of stories and begin again as I had previously begun.

"Now," I wrote, "in the time that is all time, Tikkan together weave the visions that guide man to live his dreams and together weave the dreams that enrich his life."

From those words an image took shape on the rock, of Na'an at her loom, singing softly as she spun out dream after dream for the people of Q'ntana. Someone sang with her. It was My'leen. Yet whether she sang in the story within the rock or here with me upon the rock, I could not say. As before, Na'an's dreams floated into the mist and down to Q'ntana, an image of its dreamer attached to each.

"In the midst of Na'an's spinning," I continued, "Rev'Àn entered her dream space, his blonde hair shimmering in the light. He waited in patient silence until Na'an had finished her sequence of weaving then stepped toward her, his arms outstretched.

"'Sister,' he said humbly.

"'Brother,' she replied warmly. She stood, her arms open to him. For the first time in more time than any human could measure, Tikkan brother and sister embraced. As they held each other in the renewal of a love and unity thought to have been lost for all time, the light in Na'an's dream space brightened and brightened some more, until Na'an and Rev'Àn melted into a shimmering radiance that was all that could be seen."

I paused and took a long breath, then I again dipped my quill in the well to conclude this story.

"Now, in the time that is all time," I wrote, "is Q'ntana's nightmare ended…now and for all time."

The brilliant light from the story that had permeated the Scriving Rock and shone out from it dissipated and faded. My eyes were wet with tears. I glanced at Da'nay. The fur around his eyes was moist.

"Well done, Ben Ko'lar…Ben Kano'ha. Well done."

Janq'a stared into the blank rock and shook his head. "My master? It can't be. It just can't."

"I hate to agree with Janq'a," Panesh said. "But I must. That cannot be Bo'Rà K'n."

"It can be and will be," Da'nay countered. "Here in Kea Kana, it already is."

"Then we're finished?" My'leen asked. "Our SunQuest is over?"

Da'nay laughed, a hissing, purring sort of chortle. "Not hardly. Ben?"

I wet the quill and touched its tip to the rock. This time, I said nothing. The quill moved my hand for me, so rapidly that my arm and shoulder ached from the exertion. The scene it sketched out for us was horrifying and disheartening.

A village sleeps. The sole light present is that reflected by M'nor off white-washed houses. The late-night scene is peaceful, serene. Unusual for these times, not even nayla disturb the stillness. If the initial dreams of these villagers have drifted down from Na'an's loom, the terrors that await them can only have been cranked by Bo'Rà K'n's manufacture of shadows.

A sound intrudes into the silence: a distant, barely audible rumble. As it nears, the rumble grows louder, more distinct. Horseshoes, pounding into the earth, raising clouds of dust that veil the moon and darken the village. The thunder approaches, the dust thickens. Bloodthirsty whoops and hollers merge with the crash of hooves. Torches illuminate the night, revealing masked men, their blood racing feverishly as they brandish sabers, daggers and whips and urge their pitch-black stallions toward the no-longer-sleeping village.

First one orange light, then a dozen, then a dozen more flicker behind curtained windows, silhouetting a flurry of panicked activity. Then, one by one, the lights extinguish as the villagers huddle in the darkness, awaiting the onslaught. Awaiting the slaughter.

What can these villagers do? No more than other villagers have been able to do. There is never any escape from these nightmare marauders. Every horse and conveyance in the village was confiscated long ago. And there is no out-running the Black Riders, who descend as one onto the main square, torches aloft, their laughter a chilling blend of menace and mockery.

Mothers and fathers do what they can to both comfort and silence their weeping children, praying that this one time, their house will be passed over… that this one time, they will not be noticed and will survive the carnage. They tremble as light flares outside their window…flinch as they hear neighbors howl, friends keen, kinsmen plead for mercy…as the acrid smell of burning wood, burning fabric, burning flesh assaults their nostrils.

Black Riders pass their house once…twice…three times. The villagers hold their breath and pray to be spared…pray that if they must die their children will be spared…pray that if their children must die that it will be quick and painless…pray as they have never prayed before. More Black Riders. More shouts. More prayers.

Then, silence…the absolute stillness that can mean only one of two things: that the danger has passed or that the terror is about to escalate.

A flaming torch bursts through the window. It strikes the father across the head. His hair catches fire. The mother screams. The children scream. Black Riders storm the house, drag the mother out. The house erupts in flame. The village explodes in flame.

The Scriving Rock is a mass of conflagration. When it has burned itself out, there is nothing left, only the sour smell of death.

My'leen sobbed in Panesh's arms. Panesh glared at Janq'a, who shook uncontrollably. I stared up blankly from the now-empty rock. Da'nay stood in front of me, gazing at each of us in turn. Janq'a could not meet his eyes.

"You have seen what is," he said. "That cannot be changed." He padded over to Janq'a. Janq'a cringed. Da'nay licked him, and he started to cry. "You have also seen what the what can become, if you let it."

"How?" Panesh whispered.

"That will take care of itself." Da'nay paused. "If you let it."

"What happens now?" I asked.

"Now it is time for you to return," Da'nay replied. He looked pointedly at Panesh and Janq'a. "All of you. Together."

"How?" Janq'a asked, practical considerations overtaking his distress. "Will we get clothes again? We can't go back like this." He covered his genitals. "People will laugh."

Da'nay ignored Janq'a. He drilled his eyes into mine. "You know what to do," he said.

I did? I stared back, deep into his eyes. Yes, I did.

I dipped Kumba's quill into the well of stories one final time and traced a large circle onto the Scriving Rock, around the area where the stories had played themselves out. From outside the perimeter, I shook out the feather, letting four drops fall inside the circle. As they hit the stone, they expanded, multiplied and spiraled into a brilliantly colored kaleidoscope swirl. I stood back and gestured for Panesh, Janq'a and My'leen to join me. When they did, I took Janq'a's hand and My'leen's. Panesh, though closest to Janq'a, moved away to take My'leen's other hand.

Da'nay circled us, stopping before each of us to lick us from head to toe, front and back. When he had finished, we were each cleaned up, clothed and carrying a shoulder bag stuffed with food and supplies.

"Are you ready?" he asked.

Janq'a, My'leen and Panesh turned to me. I nodded.

Da'nay stepped back. "You know what to do?"

I pulled the others forward and, together, we stepped into the circle. I thought I saw Da'nay's eyes right in front of mine, watching me. Then everything went black.

DREAMS

I awoke on a grassy slope by the embered coals of a dying fire. M'nor had not yet set, and the suns were just pushing up over the horizon. My'leen and Janq'a were already awake. My'leen eyed Janq'a closely as he poked the fire back to life. His eyes were puffy, and he seemed more frightened than I had ever before seen him.

"As soon as Panesh is up," she announced to him in a voice that brooked no argument. Janq'a nodded miserably.

"What happens as soon as Panesh gets up?" I yawned and sat up. My'leen's eyes flared with a fury directed only at Janq'a. Had they already forgotten about our time in Kea Kana? Our time at the Scriving Rock with Da'nay? Or had it been a dream that only I had experienced? It was still so fresh in my mind that it was as though *this* was the dream and Prithi's Garden the only reality. If I had dreamed it, how had we found ourselves here, wherever here was? How did we get these clothes, these supplies?

"What's going on?" I asked again.

"Janq'a will tell you when Panesh is awake," My'leen repeated. "Right, Janq'a?"

His eyes on the ground, he mumbled an incomprehensible reply.

"Kea Kana. Did you…?" I asked.

My'leen nodded. She poked Janq'a.

"Me too," he muttered.

"It wasn't a dream, then." I was relieved. I desperately wanted it to have been real. I desperately wanted to have visited the Scriving Rock, to have penned my story into it.

"If it was a dream," My'leen said, "we all had it. Panesh, too, probably."

"Panesh what?" he grunted, squinting at us through confused, half-awake eyes.

"Da'nay."

He looked around, trying to match what he expected to see with what was in front of him. He rubbed his eyes. "Where is he? Where are we?"

I shrugged. "Wherever Da'nay sent us."

We were all so powerfully hungry that My'leen reluctantly agreed to postpone whatever it was Janq'a was to tell us until after we had eaten. He sat apart throughout the meal, fidgeting nervously, and he kept to himself as we packed up our few things.

"Time to go," I called out. Without Rykka and Ta'ar, it would now be up to us alone to chart our course. We would need to make our way on foot and follow Aygra west. It was the only direction that made sense in a land that continued to make none at all.

Janq'a jumped up, eager to hit the road.

"Janq'a," My'leen snapped.

He dropped to his haunches and etched circles with a stick in the dirt by his feet.

"Janq'a has something to say," she announced to me and Panesh. "Isn't that so?"

"Uh…" He smudged his drawings with his foot.

I gazed up at the suns, already higher in the sky than I would have liked. "We should probably get moving. Can we hear about it while we walk?"

Janq'a leapt to his feet. "Sure," he said. He smiled nervously.

"No," My'leen countered. "It cannot wait. Not another minim." She glared at Janq'a. "Can it?"

"Umm. Uh…" He sat down again, only for an instant. A moment later he was back on his feet, pacing anxiously, refusing to meet anyone's eyes.

"Janq'a…" There was an edge to My'leen's voice I had never heard before.

"I had a dream." He stretched each sound as though every letter was its own word and every word its own story. Then he sped up and spit the rest out in a single breath. "And I talked in my sleep. And My'leen heard me. And it wasn't good." He dropped to his knees and gouged at the dirt with his index finger.

"Was it a dream?" My'leen asked. "Or was it real?"

"I don't know. It's not always easy to tell…l-like with Da'nay." He scrutinized a tiny, green, six-legged fllia that was burrowing into the ground by his finger. Clearly, he wished he could follow it. When the fllia had disappeared, he continued. "Maybe it was a dream. Maybe it was real."

Panesh shot Janq'a an exasperated look. "Will you just tell us what you are talking about? Ben is right. We need to get going. If we are still in Q'ntana, we must not stay in any one place for too long. Black Riders."

"This sounds important," I said. "What is it, Janq'a?"

He said nothing.

"Janq'a?"

He stood up. "Maybe Panesh is right. Maybe it's better if we go now. I can tell you later. It can wait."

"Janq'a!" My'leen pushed him to ground. Hard.

Still, he said nothing.

"Okay," she said. "I will start for him. I woke up when it was still dark out. This one," she pointed at Janq'a, "was tossing and turning, talking in his sleep. He sounded the most upset ever."

"No…I can't…Take me back…Let me come home…Please…I can't. I can't. I can't!"

"When he woke up, I asked him what it had been about, even though, somehow, I already knew."

"You can't what?"

"What?"

"In your sleep. You said you can't. You said you want to go home. Was that a dream? Who were you talking to?"

"Go on, Janq'a," she said.

"Like I said," he said, all his attention focused on the stone he worried at with his hands, "it could have been a dream. It could have been real. You can't always tell with— Whichever it was, it didn't matter. I didn't want to tell her. I didn't want her to know."

"I think you had better tell me, Janq'a."

"I didn't say anything at first. I wanted her to drop it. I hoped she would drop it. Then I realized it was too late. She already knew. I don't know how she knew, or how I knew that she knew. But I was sure she did."

"Why tell you? You know, don't you?"

"I thought you were done with him. That's what you told us. That's what you keep telling us."

"No one is ever done with Bo'Rà K'n."

My'leen turned away from Janq'a, her face twisted in disgust.

"No one? What about people who are tortured and killed by his Black Riders? What about the village we saw in Ben's story. You saw it too. You know it was real. You know those people were really burned alive. You know that woman was raped and murdered."

"They're not his Black Riders."

"They're not, you know." Janq'a looked miserable.

Panesh glared at him with contempt.

"Well, they're not."

"It's not like I had a choice, My'leen. You don't have a choice with Bo'Rà K'n. Not never. Maybe you pretend you do. But you don't. You can't."

"You didn't answer my question. Are you done with him or not?"

"You have to understand." Janq'a focused only on me now, his eyes begging for understanding, for forgiveness. *"I've never known anyone except Bo'Rà K'n. No family. No friends. Nothing. No one. Not until now. Until now, I have only ever seen the world through his eyes. Why wouldn't I believe that he's right and you're wrong? Why wouldn't I?"*

"Is that what you believe?"

"Yes. No. I don't know anymore. It seemed so simple once—"

"Once upon a time?"

*"*I didn't know what to say to that. So I turned away and tried to go back to sleep. My'leen wouldn't let me.*"*

"What about now, Janq'a? What do you believe now?"

"I just want to go home. That's all I want."

"Me too. Only I have no home to go back to. No one to go back to. My father is dead. My sister is gone, maybe dead. My mother too. And my friends. They are all gone. Every one of them. Everything I ever knew is gone. There is nothing left of my life. Nothing at all, thanks to your Bo'Rà K'n."

"He's not my Bo'Rà K'n."

"Are you sure?"

"I—"

"What if you are home, Janq'a? What if this is it? What if there is no going back?"

"He's not my Bo'Rà K'n." Janq'a began to cry.

*"*Tell them, Janq'a,*"* My'leen said, compassion in her voice for the first time since I had woken up. *"*You have to tell them. We can't go on unless you do. You can't go on unless you do.*"*

Janq'a swallowed hard. He turned away and kept his back to us.

"I— I lied," he said in barely a whisper. "He sent me. Bo'Rà K'n sent me. To betray you. I didn't want to come. But-but—"

Panesh leapt up. He growled menacingly. If I had not stopped him, I cannot know what he might have done.

"*Was* your master?" he mimicked. "Not now? No more? Nohow?" He dropped back down, his face red with fury.

"I know, Janq'a," I said to him. "I know Bo'Rà K'n sent you. I know you came here to betray us. I have known it for some time. But My'leen and Panesh don't know your story. Go on. Tell it."

"You knew?" My'leen, Janq'a and Panesh exclaimed in unison.

"Go on," I said, ignoring My'leen and Panesh. "Now is the time for everyone to hear it. All of it."

Janq'a stared blankly into the distance, his voice dull and expressionless. "I'm here with you to make sure that Bo'Rà K'n gets the Ring of Unity. That's all he wants." He looked at me pleadingly. "Couldn't you just give it to him? Is it that important, really?"

This time, I couldn't hold Panesh back. He roared to his feet, towering over Janq'a. "Give it to him? Ben should just give it to him? Why you—" He grabbed Janq'a by the collar and jerked him up over his head. "Let me kill him," he begged. "Slowly."

"Put him down."

"But—"

"Put him down and let him be."

Panesh glowered and started to open his fist to let Janq'a fall to the ground.

"Gently," I said

With mock solicitude, Panesh set Janq'a back on the ground and brushed him off. Janq'a ducked out of reach and backed as far away from him as he could.

"He lied to us," Panesh cried. "He *is* Bo'Rà K'n's spy. He has been telling Bo'Rà K'n everything about us. You have, haven't you?"

"Please. I had to. Don't you understand? I didn't have a choice." He turned to me. "You saw what he's like."

"I see what *you* are like," Panesh retorted.

I gestured for Janq'a to sit next to me. He did, reluctantly. "What are you going to do now?" I asked. "It is time for you to decide."

He studied his feet. "I don't know. Really, I don't. Bo'Rà K'n says you're bad. You aren't. I know that now. But if I don't do what he says..." He hugged himself and again began to cry. "I just want to go home," he wailed. "Then I won't be able to hurt you. Any of you." Sobbing hysterically, he pointed at Panesh. "Even him."

My'leen put her arm around him, trying to console him.

"I know everything," I said. "I have known who you were since before we found you in Yeerg'a's field."

Janq'a stopped crying. He stared at me in horror.

"How? Why—?"

"I didn't know why at first. I only knew that I was not to do anything about you or to say anything about you, as much as Panesh tried to convince me otherwise." I paused, recalling all my dreams and visions. "Then I did know. Panesh knew too, even though he did not want to admit it. Panesh knew because Na'an told him. I knew because I witnessed the dream she sent him about you."

"Na'an? Sent a dream about me? What did she say?"

"That you are as much a part of this SunQuest as any of us. Can you believe that?"

"No. That can't be at all right. How can I be any part of your SunQuest when I'm a traitor and a spy?"

"Believe what you will, Janq'a. It's true. I don't know how or in what way. All I know is that The SunQuest needs you. If The SunQuest needs you, I need you. That means we all need you. Even Panesh."

"Why? How? For what?"

I shook my head. "All I know is that when the time comes, you will do what you must, whether you want to or not…whether I want you to or not. That, too, is part of The SunQuest."

"Oh," he said, in a tiny voice.

"You are still welcome to continue with us, if that is your choice. Only you can choose."

He bobbed his head, not looking at either My'leen or Panesh, and wiped his tears on his sleeve.

I smiled and shook his hand. "Good. Is everyone okay with that?"

My'leen nodded.

"Panesh?"

He grunted.

The others stood to go. "Wait," I said. "I know we have already lost too much time. But I think you need to hear this dream I had early this morning." I turned to Janq'a. "You, especially. It was about Bo'Rà K'n."

He shuddered and stared at his feet again.

Bo'Rà K'n broods in his armchair, the same chair in the same room where I first saw him, where I first also saw Janq'a. The fireplace is cold and smells of stale ash. Every few moments, he stands, walks to the fireplace, then returns uncertainly to his seat.

He is glaring at the food putrefying on the tray at his side when Na'an materializes by the dining table. Even her radiant brightness is dulled in this space. She glances around the chamber with distaste, contemplates pulling over the solitary dining chair so she can sit next to Bo'Rà K'n. When she sees how dusty it is, she wrinkles her nose. She is even reluctant to step onto the carpet, so dirty is it. So she stands in place until Bo'Rà K'n notices her.

"What do you want?" he growls.

"The story moves forward."

Bo'Rà K'n scowls into the fireplace. "Do I not know that?"

"You could prevent much unhappiness, even death, if—"

Bo'Rà K'n leaps from his chair and unfurls his cloak. He glares at his sister then strides across the room to where she stands. "You think you know every-thing. You always have." He leans into her. She neither flinches nor budges. "This time you are wrong, Na'an. You know nothing. This time I will prevail. This time I cannot be stopped. I will not be stopped." He turns his back on her.

"You know that is not true," she says, softly but firmly.

He spins around in a cold fury. "What I know is not your business. It never has been. It never will be. I will fix the truth of that for all time when the moment is ripe. For now, you are not welcome here. Go."

Na'an nods her head, slightly. "As you say, brother. Regardless, the story moves forward. As for its conclusion, it—"

"Leave," he shouts. "Now."

Na'an fades, disappears.

Bo'Rà K'n storms back to his armchair, drops back into it.

"Janq'a," he shouts. "Janq'a!"

No reply.

A brooding frown is just visible through the dusky mist that swirls around his face. He stands and marches to the circle at the center of the carpet. He stares into the spiral. Nothing changes. Then, suddenly, brilliant sunlight spikes through it, into his face. For an instant it clears the mist. He shields his eyes from the brightness, curses and stomps out of the room.

"What does it mean?" My'leen asked.

"That we must be on the right track," I replied. I smiled at Janq'a. "And that Janq'a's place is here, with us."

twenty -six

The next several days were uneventful. We trekked west through loamy meadows, light woodlands and verdant lake country, and at Panesh's insistence we skirted established roads and villages to avoid encountering Black Riders. Not that we saw any…or any evidence of their pillage. The countryside here was peaceful, untouched by any sign of evil. Some mornings we spied distant chimney smoke or if the wind was right, smelled fresh-baked bread. Other days, we passed along the far edge of farm fields, where muscular horses grazed lazily and plump gita'as bleated noisily. We spoke little, either of the trials of the past or the uncertainties of the future. Instead, we bathed in sparkling streams, dove splashingly into gently flowing rivers and raced down grassy hillocks. It could almost be the idyllic land of Karenna Kihanna's reign, those days in lifetimes past when I was Q'ntana's first Elderbard.

If our days were pleasantly uneventful, the nights were not. At least mine were not. Most nights I would be barely asleep before I started thrashing restlessly, clutched by nightmare visions I could not shake loose. Multiple times a night, those first nights, I forced myself awake, my breath ragged and my body soaked, to evade scenes I refused to see, experiences I refused to relive — all from my previous Ben-lifetime in Q'ntana.

I assumed it was Bo'Rà K'n who sent me the nightmare. Where else could they have come from? Just because he could not harm me during daylight hours didn't mean he lacked the power to torment me during dreamtime. Night after night I called out to Na'an to override painful remembrances that grew more distorted and exaggerated the longer I resisted them. Either Na'an was not listening or she lacked the power to intervene, for nothing changed.

After four consecutive nights of this, my eyes red and my head throbbing with anxiety, Na'an came to me. M'nor had set and the suns had yet to shoot rays of dawn into the sky. Stars winked in their usual constellations, but that familiarity brought me no comfort.

"Just like your grandfather," Na'an pronounced sharply, even before she had fully glittered into view. The others still slept.

"Na'an," I breathed. "Thank you. Thank you for coming." I sat up, more grateful for her presence than I could express.

"I have come to you every night these past four nights, Ben. Every night." With a handkerchief retrieved from her cloak, she whisked invisible dirt from a nearby rock and lowered herself onto a corner of its dawn-chilled surface. "Just like your grandfather," she repeated.

"Every night? I have had nothing but nightmares, Na'an. Grim, horrible nightmares."

She folded the handkerchief into neat squares and rested it on her knee. "And?"

"Bo'Rà K'n had to have sent them. Must still be sending them. Isn't there anything you can do?"

"My brother has sent nothing." She pulled back her hood and her silver hair tumbled free, glittering in the starlight. "He has no power over your dreamtime, though I am certain he would wish otherwise."

"But—"

"Even had he that power, there is little he will do now to impede your progress." She flicked a piece of lint from her dress. It fluttered away on the breeze. "It is no longer in his best interests."

"I don't understand." I reached for my water skin and gulped half of it down. My nights of nightmare-avoidance had also kept me insatiably thirsty.

"That much is all too clear."

"If it is not Bo'Rà K'n, then—" I stared at her in shock.

She nodded.

"Why?"

"My brother's nightmares serve but a single purpose: to control the dreamer. There is only one way to guarantee absolute control: to instill absolute terror."

"That's just what those dreams were doing. They were terrifying me."

"How do you know?"

"What do you mean, how do I know? I was so frightened that I forced myself awake before they could play out."

Na'an stared at me, waiting for me to grasp what my mind refused to see. She plucked two more pieces of lint from her cloak then drummed her fingers on the rock. When she tired of waiting, she rose, smoothing her dress.

"Truly, Ben, how can you know the value of a dream unless you let it run its course? Are you Tikkan, that you can prejudge the value of what I send you?" She shook her head in wonder. "You were braver than this once…once upon a time. Wiser too. What has become of you?"

I bundled my blanket around me and stood next to her. "You know what has become of me, Na'an."

She scrutinized me then raised an eyebrow.

"I am no longer B'na…or even recently B'na. I am Ben. I am human."

"Precisely." She sat down and gestured for me to join to her on the rock. "Let me speak, as Tikkan, to you as the mortal human you are once again. Let me speak to you as I spoke to your grandfather, to Toshar."

She pulled a mug of steaming tea from inside her cloak and offered it to me. I shook my head. She pressed it into my hand and extracted another, for herself. After a few sips, she continued. "You must trust, first, that these dreams come from me, that I have woven them most specifically for you. These are not Bo'Rà K'n's, could not be Bo'Rà K'n's. Even if my brother possessed the power to torment you at night, his manufactures lack the necessary subtlety."

"You call what you have sent me *subtle*?" I shot back. It was insolent, but I could not help myself.

Na'an hesitated, trying to determine the most appropriate tone for her reply. In the end, she ignored my outburst and continued without rebuke. "You must not run from the dreams I send you, Ben. Whatever you think of them, whatever you think of me, you must trust in their value as you trust in the value of your stories. You must allow them to unfold freely, as you allow your stories that same autonomy…as you allow your SunQuest that same autonomy."

She finished her tea and returned her mug to the dark recesses of her cloak. She peered into my mug. I had hardly touched the brew. She tapped a long fingernail on the side of the mug. "It will help," she said, "with everything."

I sighed, drank down the tea and returned the mug.

"Do you presume to know what lies ahead on your SunQuest?" she asked, her tone a touch less stern.

I shook my head.

"Then how can you know what purpose these dreams serve? How can you know for which purpose they prepare you?"

"They're just so...so..." I felt tears welling up in my eyes. "All you send is visions of past horrors...of my mother...of what happened to my mother...of S'kryssna S'kyaga and her torture chambers...and her snakes." I shuddered. "Of all the emptiness of those missing years...of Y'glana and—" I choked. I couldn't continue.

"I know," she said, and took my hand with a gentleness I had never known her to display. "She died in childbirth."

"I was there, right there. I watched her suffer. I watched her die." My body quaked as I sobbed. "I watched our daughter nearly die with her." I pulled my hand free and jumped to my feet, eyes blazing. "It was unbearable the first time. Excruciating. I never got over it. Never. I died never having gotten over it. Why must I revisit it now?"

Na'an rose slowly. She pressed her right hand into my shoulder. My tears and anger dissolved, but not the pain. Why not the pain? "Do you remember what I said to you when Panesh first brought you to me?"

I nodded. "My humanness. You said it would prove to be my greatest strength. I didn't understand then and I don't understand now. It does not make any sense."

"It does not have to. Sense is not its purpose. Nonetheless, you must trust it." She stared thoughtfully into the distance. Bands of dawn were pushing up through the velvet blackness. "Listen to me, Ben. Little time remains. Your companions will wake presently, and this dream is for you alone. Only for you." For the first time in a long time, nayla howled in the far distance. She pressed a finger to her lips. They stopped. "Yes, you felt those sorrows in your previous lifetime so many lifetimes ago. But you have lived in the sky as B'na since that time, as a glorious ball of light that illuminates all yet needs not feel anything. That is not a criticism. A sun's purpose is not an emotional one. Man's purpose is. Woman's too, of course." She studied me before continuing. "Now you are once again in a human body." She touched my arm. "And you are on a human journey where your humanness is key to the success of your SunQuest. You must learn how to feel again. Fully, deeply and, yes, painfully."

"Why only the pain? Why not the joy? Being human is as much about the joy as it is about the pain."

"Yes, it is. But it is through the pain that you will gain your strength most quickly, the strength you will need to face my brother and do what you are destined to do, what only *you* can do. What only Ben Ko'leya can do. The SunQuest is not a journey for B'na the sun. B'na has his own journeys." She pointed to the western horizon, where B'na peeked tentatively into the sky. "It is a journey for Ben, for the man who is Ben."

I followed her gaze and for the first time since my return to Q'ntana felt homesick for the simpler journeys that had been mine as B'na.

"You ask why I do not send you dreams of the joys of your past?"

I nodded.

"It is true that man grows from his joys as well as from his sorrows, that joy is at least as important to the human tapestry as sorrow. Yet sorrow offers an acceleration that joy cannot in these times match. Perhaps one day it will be otherwise…" She paused in thought. "That is Prithi's domain, not mine. On *your* journey, Ben, on your SunQuest, there is no time for the leisurely learning of a lifetime. That would be an impossible luxury when you are on the odyssey of the ages, when you are readying yourself to come face-to-face with Bo'Rà K'n, when you are preparing to be the agent of his ultimate healing, which must also be yours, which, if your SunQuest achieves Crowning, will also be Q'ntana's."

Panesh stirred. Often the first up, his eyes would soon open to the day. My'leen would follow quickly after. Janq'a would sleep until someone shook him awake.

"Do you understand now?" Na'an asked.

I did. I was not happy with my understanding, but I understood.

"I will not send you any more dreams of Y'glana's death. You have felt what you needed to feel, here with me. As such, there is no longer any need. However, there will be other dreams, and the sooner you surrender to them and free them to run their course, the sooner they will be done…and the sooner you will be free. Is that understood?"

"Yes, Na'an."

She nodded and began to dissolve into the light of dawn.

"Na'an?"

"Yes, Ko'lar Kano'ha?"

"Thank you."

twenty-seven

I said little the next day, for I knew that night would bring with it harrowing trials. I knew, too, that I would have to surrender to whatever Na'an sent, however much I longed to avoid it. If any of the others noticed my discomfort, nothing was said. Fortunately, it was another easy day's walking with no intrusions or interruptions. For the first time in our time together, Panesh, Janq'a and My'leen all acted at ease with one another. Panesh even joked playfully with Janq'a, who took no offense and bantered back lightheartedly. For her part, My'leen hummed and sang her way through the day, a faraway smile playing on her lips.

That night, I waited until the others had fallen asleep before leaving my place at the fire. I knew what was ahead: a journey back to the time of Q'nta's StarQuest, to my worst times of that time. Knowing that, I wanted to muster all the strength and courage I could before traveling into the Dream Realms. I gazed into the sky and asked the stars for their help, reminding them that I had once played a role, albeit a minor one, in their world. Then I stretched out on my back and made a similar request to M'nor, now rising in the north. Within a few breaths of closing my eyes, I was asleep, yet fully aware of all I was seeing and feeling.

I stand atop Ko'Ba Rock, high above the frothing wrath of the Ma. I hear nothing but the crash of waves pounding relentlessly against stone. It grows louder…nearer…louder…nearer…

Then, I hear a thunderous boom as a single breaker thrusts itself over the edge of the cliff. As it recedes, a solitary sun dances off the water droplets suspended in midair. The droplets come together to form a woman.

"Ben!" she cries as she sees me. A sob later, she crumples to the ground in a faint.

Two thoughts collide in my head. "I have a name!" and "Who is this woman that she knows me?"

Time passes. The woman — I now know her name to be Q'nta — sits across from me in the shadow of Ko'Ba Rock. It is the night of a different day, although so much has just taken place that it could easily be a different lifetime. That is because in this moment, I know Q'nta to be my mother. I do not know how I know this, but know it I do. The fact that she does not herself know this infuriates me as much as if she had known it and had kept it hidden. My rage is a cold one, icier than anything I have experienced in the brief period of my life that is available to my memory.

When rage ebbs and love at last takes its place, I know myself to be at home — in the eyes of the mother I have not seen since infancy. I know myself to be at home, even as I continue to wander through an unknown time and place, stripped of my past. Sadly, this new home is short-lived. The StarQuest wrenches it from me when it demands that mother and son separate — Q'nta on her journey and I—

I woke up drenched in sweat. I had not forced my eyes open as I had the other nights, yet something within me must have been reluctant to face the next ordeal because M'nor had halfway crossed the sky before I was able to sleep again and continue into the worst of the nightmare.

Snakes. Writhing…hissing…red tongues spitting poison at me. Snakes… thicker than my arm…longer than I am tall…snakes all around me…a circle of snakes pressing in on me. Tighter. Tighter. Tighter.

Tighter.

Behind them, on the terrace of a craggy, sinister castle and dressed in a black, hooded, fur-trimmed robe decorated with dulled-gray runic markings, stands a woman whose countenance I can barely make out. What I do see is startlingly beautiful: a straight nose, rosebud lips and high cheekbones on a face whose creamy, unblemished complexion shines in the drizzle I have barely noticed through my panic. Then I notice her eyes. There is nothing beautiful about her eyes. Dull blue, glass-like and soulless, they drill into me with an undiluted hatred that might terrify me if I were not already paralyzed by the snakes.

The serpentine circle draws tighter…tighter…tighter. S'kryssna S'kyaga disappears behind it as the twisting wall of terror closes in on me.

My hands. They are pressed to my forehead. Why are they pressed to my forehead? Then I remember: Astel Elohia. Was it only moments ago that I held the Ring of Unity against my forehead and it absorbed into me? Was it only moments ago that I stood with Q'nta and Eulisha and Toshar? Was it only moments ago?

"Hoss eeyah ka-am seeya na sempah." The hissing chant comes from beyond the snakes...from S'kryssna S'kyaga. She repeats it, more softly. "Hoss eeyah ka-am seeya na sempah." A third time, barely a whisper: "Hoss eeyah ka-am seeya na sempah."

The snakes squeeze closer. All I see are darting tongues and cruel snake eyes indistinguishable from S'kryssna Skyaga's.

"Ka-hass," she shrieks...and everything goes black...

I am curled up on a damp, filthy bedroll in the corner of a dark, dank cell, my eyes fixed on the only source of light, a rusty-barred skylight open not only to the sky but to all the elements. The sky is now, rarely, cloudless and blue. Earlier, a thunderstorm flooded the cell and drenched me. The rain's only benefit was to cleanse some of the putridness from both me and this space, which has been my home for longer than I can recollect.

At the beginning of my time here, whenever that is, I mark the days with a stone, scraping a vertical line through the dried blood that cakes these walls. After a while, I often forget the ritual. A while after that, it becomes just as effective to note time's passage by the way my ragged clothes hang more and more loosely on my increasingly skeletal frame as by any other measure.

At the beginning, too, I am left alone. A guardsman carries in one meal at midday, either a clear, watery broth or a thin watery gruel. Each day's guardsman is different...yet each day's guardsman is identical to every other day's. Head shaved, he wears washed-out gray chain mail emblazoned with a coiled black snake, with the same mark tattooed on his wrist. A second tattoo, a crossed club and dagger, brands his left cheek immediately below the eye socket. His eyes, twins to S'kryssna S'kyaga's and those of her snakes, are the same shade of empty. Silent as the dead, he refuses to utter a single sound, not even a grunt.

One day my cell clangs open and S'kryssna S'kyaga strides in, accompanied by two guardsmen who jerk me to my feet. She says nothing to me that first day. She just glares at me and pulls back the sleeve of her cloak to reveal the black-snake tattoo on her right wrist. She strokes the tattoo, hissing a few tender lines of sibilance. The snake wriggles to life at her touch. It uncoils from her arm and snaps at me. I try to back away, but the guardsmen hold me in place. I don't know why I should be so terror-struck by S'kryssna S'kyaga's snakes. Nothing else has ever sparked such a primal fear within me. Even watching her kep'chas destroy Co'anra and Co'anri's house — and Co'anra and Co'anri with it — was not as frightening, even as I wondered whether it was me and Q'nta that they had really been after.

S'kryssna S'kyaga shakes the snake off her arm and watches impassively as it puffs up in size, slithers toward me. It coils first around one leg then around both, then around my torso, squeezing me until I can barely breathe, all the while flicking its venomous tongue at me. When S'kryssna S'kyaga grows bored, she extends her arm. The snake disentangles from me and returns to its mistress, shrinking and coiling back into its tattoo. The guardsmen heave me back onto my bedroll and my tormentors leave, as wordlessly as they came in.

This continues daily, though not always in silence. Some days S'kryssna S'kyaga taunts me. She tells me that my mother is in a nearby cell being tortured. Or she threatens to fill my cell with snakes and leave them to have their way with me. Or she moves other prisoner and their torturers into adjoining cells so that I must listen to whips cracking and bones snapping, so that I must listen to unending screaming, crying and pleading, so that I cannot avoid the smell of blood, vomit, urine and feces.

"I am Ben Ko'leya, son of Q'nta Ko'lar Fayr'Owyn, grandson of Toshar Ko'lar, great-grandson of Eulisha Ko'lar." My days are now filled with this chant. I pace my tiny cell repeating it again and again, all day long, and all night long when sounds, smells or fears prevent me from sleeping.

"I am Ben Ko'leya, son of Q'nta Ko'lar Fayr'Owyn, grandson of Toshar Ko'lar, great-grandson of Eulisha Ko'lar." It is the one thing that keeps me sane, although I wonder most days whether madness might not be preferable.

On this day, S'kryssna S'kyaga and her guardsmen march in, interrupting my chant. This is the first time she has heard it.

"I am Ben Ko'leya, son of Q'nta Ko'lar Fayr'Owyn, grandson of Toshar Ko'lar, great-grandson of Eulisha Ko'lar. I am Ben Ko'leya, son of Q'nta Ko'lar—"

"Is that lineage supposed to impress me?" Contempt drips from her voice.

I ignore her. "— Fayr'Owyn, grandson of Toshar—" One of the guardsmen jerks my arm behind my back, holds me still, forces me to look at her. "— Ko'lar, great-grandson of Eulisha Ko'lar." I complete my round.

"It should," I reply when I am done.

S'kryssna S'kyaga laughs. It is a dainty, delicate laugh that is even more chilling issuing from someone like her in a setting such as this. "It will take more than a doomed line of bards to impress me," she says.

"I still have nothing to say to you. Why are you here?"

"To remind myself why I despise you and your mother. I will get my hands on her too. Don't you doubt it. When I do, the Heart of the Star will be mine. This land too. All of it. Forever. Then, I will find a more permanent way to deal with you. For right now, I have a friend who so wants to keep you company."

Once again, she pulls her sleeve back to reveal her snake tattoo on her right wrist. She strokes it, brings it too life. I back away.

"The Ring of Unity," S'kryssna S'kyaga snarls suddenly. "What is it? What does it do?"

"I told you. I don't know."

She shakes the snake from her wrist and watches it tangle around me, her mouth arranging itself into the hint of a smirk. This time, the guardsmen release me when I try to wriggle free. My back is to the wall. Sweat pours down my face.

"Give it to me. I want it. I will have it."

"I don't know how."

The snake's tale coils around my leg. I cannot to shake it off.

"I-I am Ben Ko'leya, son of Q'nta Ko'lar—"

The snake's tongue scrapes my cheek.

"— Fayr'Owyn, grandson of— I don't know how!"

"No," she says with icy calm, "Perhaps you do not." She lets the snake torment me for a few eternity-filled moments longer, then extends her arm. "Not that you would help me if you could. Would you, bard?" The snake coils onto her wrist and shrinks back into the tattoo. "I shall return. Count on it." She spins around and leaves, followed by her guardsmen. The cell door clangs shut behind them.

"…Toshar Ko'lar," I whisper, "great-grandson of Eulisha Ko'lar…" I fall back onto my bedroll. "I am Ben—" I burst into tears and hiccup the rest of the chant through my sobs. Then I curl into as tight a ball as a I can, as daylight dissolves into night and night fades back into day.

*   *   *

Night was fading into day when, curled into that same fetal ball, I woke up, my face drenched with tears. Even during my centuries as B'na, that endless-seeming time in the Castle Do'am dungeon had never disappeared from my memory. Nor had I forgotten the snakes and the terror they had ignited in me. As B'na and before the nightmare as Ben, I had remembered them as events not as feelings. I had remembered them almost as though they had been part of someone else's life. Now I remembered them as having happened to me. More than that, it felt was as though I had not only revisited experiences from another lifetime in my dreams but that I had lived them in this lifetime, for the first time this past night. My hands trembled, my heart raced and I shivered, chilled. I was human…and I was scared.

twenty-eight

Somehow, I managed to fall back asleep. Mercifully, Na'an spared me any further dreams or visitations.

When I awoke a short while later, I felt surprisingly rested…and ravenous. It was Janq'a's turn to prepare the morning meal, something we all generally dreaded. Bo'Rà K'n was lucky that Tikkan eat by choice not out of need and that they cannot die, because had he been mortal and reliant on Janq'a's culinary skills, he would have been dead long before. On this morning, I did not care. I wolfed down seconds and thirds of his questionable, gray-green concoction, even as My'leen and Panesh played halfheartedly with the heaping serving Janq'a had ladled into their bowls.

I slept dreamlessly the next night and was grateful for the gift. The following night, Na'an returned.

"You have done well, Ko'lar Kano'ha, so well that I need send you no more sorrowful dreams," she said as I was drifting off to sleep.

Even half-awake, I was grateful. "Thank you, Na'an."

"There is nothing to thank me for. It is you who have done the work. It is you have relived the pain and thus strengthened yourself against more. It is you…all you." Her face slowly dissolved from my awareness then with jarring suddenness returned.

"Ben Ko'leya."

My eyes shot open. Na'an sat next to me on a wooden stool drinking a sweet, scented tea. She did not offer me a cup.

"Na'an?" I sat up.

"As a rule," she said, "I do not do this." She held the mug up to her face. The rising steam distorted her features. She pondered me silently through the aromatic mist. I waited. Impatient though I was to know what she was talking about, it was never wise to hurry a Tikkan dreamwalker.

After a lengthy interlude, she set the mug on her knee and stared off into the night. The steam lingered around her face, then dissipated. Once it had, she continued. "These are extraordinary times, and you are not an ordinary dreamer." She hesitated. "Yes," she said at last. "Yes." The mug disappeared from her hand and she looked down at me.

"Joy may not be as potent an accelerant as sorrow, but it is an accelerant nonetheless. I can offer you a dream of pleasures past this night…a dream of your own choosing."

These truly must be extraordinary times, I thought. Na'an had never been known to give her dreamers any sort of choice.

"Astel Elohia is about many things," she went on to explain. "Perhaps most, it is about balance and the unity that derives from that balance. Thus, as the bearer of the Ring of Unity, you must always strive for balance. Joyful dreams from the same past as your distressing dreams will help you achieve and maintain that balance." She paused. "Have you chosen?"

I had and was ready to share my choice when she held her hand up. "There is nothing you need tell me. My loom will do all that needs doing. You will do the rest."

With that, she vanished as swiftly as she had reappeared.

I didn't fall back asleep right away. Instead, I lay with my eyes open to the stars that winked down at me from the moonless sky. I had known these constellations intimately once upon a time. They had been new to both me and the sky when I became Q'ntana's first Elderbard all those uncountable seasons ago. As such, it had fallen to me to name them, not by making up random names but by using the Elderbard's gift of Naming, of knowing and speaking the truth name of all living things, including the constellations. During my time as Elderbard, I had passed those names on to the people of Q'ntana, as well as to my daughter, Mîr'gn'ma, who would ultimately succeed me under the Law of Balance established under my tenure.

From father to daughter, mother to son,
The mantle passes, the Balance is done.

Balance. How perfect that balance should once again be critical to a lifetime of mine in Q'ntana.

I traced the celestial patterns with my finger, silently mouthing each name: Ky'nar, the constellation of the ancient bard…Thyra the Eagle, with Aris serving as its single "sun-eye"…The Traveler…

The Harpist...The Dreamer...The Wise Woman, a diadem of stars crowning her head...

I was remembering and relearning the constellations this night after having passed so many generations as B'na, a star so bright that no others were visible while I and my father, Aygra, journeyed across the sky. The twinkling stars felt like old friends, gathered to welcome me back after a lengthy time in other realms. They were old friends, and I felt their support as my eyelids, heavy with fatigue, dropped shut and, finally, I slept.

The moment is bittersweet. Q'nta, her StarQuest complete, has returned to her own time, leaving me motherless once again. Yet there is no time now to dwell on a past that, in the twisted ways of time, is also the future. The sun is nearly overhead, the sun I will one day know to have been the father I never met. Soon it will beam down onto the center of the dais that rises up from the courtyard of the new Castle Rose in a joyous ceremony that will be repeated countless times in the centuries to come: the Naming of an Elderbard.

For now, the joy-filled people of this newly renamed land of Q'ntana sing and dance around the dais, watched over by the trumpet-bearing heralds stationed in the courtyard's archways. Outside the castle, on the smooth, sloping Great Lawn that has magically replaced Castle Do'am's craggy setting, long trestle tables spill over with food and wine for the celebration that will span this day and two more. For not only is Q'ntana gaining its first Elderbard, it is also set to crown its first monarch.

On the dais, O'ric stands motionless by a small cloth-covered table that holds only The Nayr. Karenna Kihanna, all traces of the S'kryssna S'kyaga she was washed from her countenance, stands across the table. Although her beauty is still striking, it is now tempered by a compassionate humility that I know will serve Q'ntana well in the seasons ahead. O'ric tips his head so slightly that no one but I and Karenna Kihanna notice. She spots me at the fringes of the crowd and smiles with such genuine heartedness that I immediately forget who she was and focus only on who she has become. As I make my way through the throng, well-wishers stop me to shake my hand and embrace me, tears of gratitude streaming down their faces. They are grateful not for what I have done, but for who I am and for the promise I bring to this renewed land.

When I reach the dais, the heralds blast their trumpets in a fanfare that carries strains of Reesa Kam'ana's Star Chant. The sun is nearly directly overhead. O'ric raises his clawed hand. The crowd falls silent. Everyone edges as near to the dais as possible.

How do I feel? A strange blend of conflicting emotions: humbled by the honor about to be bestowed on me and by the challenge and opportunity it represents...and overwhelmed and hesitant for all the same reasons. There is no time to feel much of anything as O'ric lifts The Nayr over his head with both hands in the moment that Aygra hovers above it. A ray of sunlight shines into the chalice, filling it with radiance. O'ric lowers The Nayr to chest level and calls out to the crowd.

"Let the people name their queen!"

There is an instant of silence as her soon-to-be-subjects evaluate this woman who, so recently as Sk'ryssna S'kyaga and Bo'Rà K'n's handmaiden, had terrorized and tyrannized them. No one now gazing into her face could deny the transformation that has occurred.

"Karenna Kihanna!" they call out in one voice.

She bows her head modestly and the crowd erupts in cheers. She smiles warmly and steps back, bareheaded. She has the crown that Reesa Kam'ana and the stars granted her, but she has requested that it not be part of this ceremony. Throughout her reign, she will wear it only rarely, reserving it for the most important of state occasions.

O'ric silences the crowd again. "Let the people name their Elderbard."

"Ben Ko'leya! Ben Ko'leya!"

"Karenna Kihanna, mother to the line of kings and queens who will rule Q'ntana in times both prosperous and painful, and Ben Ko'leya, father to the line of Elderbards who will keep story alive for all Q'ntanans in times both prosperous and painful: Do you swear allegiance to this land, to Aygra that lights her by day, to M'nor that lights her by night, to the stars that have brought you both to this place at this time, and to Prithi who lights her always?"

"I do," we reply in unison.

"Then take The Nayr, each of you. Take it and drink from its light that you too may radiate wisdom, mercy and compassion, and that you may pass those same qualities forward to those who succeed you."

O'ric passes The Nayr first to Karenna Kihanna then to me. We each drink the sunlight that fills it. I cannot know what Karenna Kihanna feels. For me, it is a homecoming, a reunion with a past I never knew and with the destiny that is my future, even as I cannot yet know the joys, pains and perils that await me. The light pours down my throat and I am humbled, even as, for the first time, I know I am ready.

"Yes." I heard Na'an's voice drifting in over the edges of my dream. "You are ready."

When I woke, the cheers from that long-ago day still echoed in my head, along with O'ric's closing invocation:

"In Prithi's name, I therefore name you Ko'lar Ben Ko'leya, Elderbard over all Q'ntana. Long may your stories, visions and dreams awaken and inspire your people. Long may you serve this land in peace."

ARRUKKA

twenty-nine

Whatever it was that Na'an declared me ready for did not show up that morning or the next, or the one after that. We continued our westward trek through the empty, rolling Plains of Aq'anor, seeing no one but each other and speaking little. We knew that we moved toward something. We could not guess what it was, even as we could feel its oncoming menace and peril. As for my nights, Na'an was true to her word. No further nightmare visions disturbed my sleep, and whatever dreams she sent were forgotten by daybreak.

By the end of the seventh day, the landscape began to shift. Gentle slopes sharpened into more angularity, and jagged rocks now poked out from grasses that were brown and brittle instead of velvety green. Soon, the grasses disappeared altogether and we found ourselves on a craggy, upward-sloping mesa bisected by a clear serpentine stream. Mature pika'a trees cast a lush canopy over the stream, creating a suns-dappled home for the silver kromii-fish that darted wrigglingly through its crystal waters. We camped by the stream that night, and when we fell asleep to its soothing burblings, our bellies were stuffed with the kromii that Janq'a, with surprising dexterity, had caught and that Panesh had cooked up with herbs he had found growing wild along the water's edge.

Next morning we chose to follow the stream, which meandered in a westerly sort of way. The other option would have been a more direct route along the open mesa. There, though, the suns beat cruelly down on increasingly cracked, barren earth. Although it was cooler under the pika'as, Panesh worried that we might have to pass through villages that way. Any settlements in this part of the country would surely be in gentler riverbank territory. He was right, though it turned out not to matter. Black Riders had preceded us, with sickening thoroughness. Of the five villages we passed, in not one did a single building still stand. Most were burnt-out husks, eerily devoid of life. A few were nothing but timber and ash. Any horses and cattle that might once have been corralled here had been brutally slaughtered, their remains left to the vulture ants, black, eight-legged insects as big as a child's hand and noisily efficient. Of people, there remained not a single sign. Either they had burned with their homes or had been carried off by the horsemen...or Bo'Rà K'n had taken them. At the fifth village, the timbers were still warm and a few embers glowed.

That night was our last by the stream. It veered sharply north just beyond our campsite, and our direction needed to remain westerly. I was reluctant to build a fire, despite the cold. Black Riders could still be close by. But after surveying the area with Janq'a perched on his shoulder, Panesh declared it to be safe. It was odd to see those two getting along after so much bickering and bitterness. Since Janq'a's confession, they had been easier with each other, at least some of the time.

Our plan for the next morning was to continue toward the edge of the mesa, which rose sharply into the sky in the middle distance. Somehow, there would be a way down. For now, we huddled by the warmth of a welcome fire and slept.

*   *   *

Something woke me in the middle of the night. When I opened my eyes, I saw My'leen staring into flames that she had prodded back into life.

"Something wrong?" I asked. It was rare for My'leen not to sleep undisturbed through the night. She was the most solid sleeper of the four of us, rarely budging from the moment she closed her eyes to the moment, the next morning, when she reopened them.

My'leen shook her head, without shifting her eyes from the fire.

"Are you sure?"

"Go back to sleep, Ben. I'm fine. Really."

I wrapped myself in my blanket and moved closer to the fire. "Is that why you're wide awake in the middle of the night?"

She glanced at me wordlessly, then stared back into the flames. "I'm scared," she confessed.

"Of what?"

"It's silly."

"It can't be any sillier than my fears."

"It's silly because I don't know what I'm afraid of. Something woke me up. I don't know what it was. It wasn't a nightmare or anything like that. I hardly ever have bad dreams. In that first moment, with my eyes still shut, I felt fine. I opened them just to make sure everyone was okay then closed them again, ready to go back to sleep. I couldn't."

I waited.

"I don't know what happened or what changed. Something did. I was terrified...of nothing in particular. Of everything. I pulled the blanket over my head, thinking that might help. The dark only made it worse. So I got up and got the fire going."

"Does it help?"

"What?"

"The fire."

She shrugged. "Starting it up gave me something to do. Watching the flames helps. It also gives me something to do."

I hugged my blanket more tightly around me and leaned into the fire. The heat felt good. "Is it all right if I sit here with you for a while and watch too?"

She shrugged again. We sat quietly as sparks crackled into the sky.

"How do you do it?" she asked after a long silence.

"How do I do what?"

"How do you keep going, day after day? How are you not scared from the past...or terrified by the future? Every day for the past days, we have seen what Black Riders can do, will do. I grew up seeing it, hating it, being frightened of it. I lost my parents because of it. Now, I have seen even more of it, and I've also seen what Bo'Rà K'n can do. I didn't think I could be more afraid than I was after...after my parents died. But I am. I'm more scared than ever of the Black Riders. I'm scared even more, every day, by Bo'Rà K'n." She shuddered. "Yet, that appears to be where we're going, to find Bo'Rà K'n, naively ready to walk right into whatever he is about...wherever that is. Why? It doesn't make any sense."

"No," I said, "it doesn't." I tossed a few twigs onto the fire. They sputtered uncertainly then burst into flame. "But it's not naive, My'leen. Whatever else it is, it's not naive."

My'leen shook her head, unconvinced.

"You're right to be afraid," I said. "You would not be human if you weren't. None of us knows what awaits us or what Bo'Rà K'n might be capable of." I paused, gathering my thoughts. "Somehow, we are the ultimate threat to whatever it is he seeks. We are also the only key to it."

My'leen pondered that. "He cannot succeed without us, and we cannot succeed without him."

"Something like that."

"Doesn't that scare you?"

It did. As B'na, I had been fearless. As the Ben I had been when I first returned to Q'ntana, I had also been largely fearless, because I was still more B'na than Ben. Now, after all this journeying, I was more Ben than B'na. Yes, I could feel fear. Na'an's dreams had proven it, and S'kryssna S'kyaga's snakes had reawakened it. But Na'an had also reminded me of something else.

"Our greatest gift and strength," I said, quoting Na'an, "is something that Bo'Rà K'n will view as our greatest weakness."

"Our fear?"

"Not fear by itself. Fear by itself is what Bo'Rà K'n counts on, what he feeds on. Our greatest strength is our humanness, which, for better or worse, includes our fear. Janq'a and Panesh are not fully human. You and I are. If what Na'an says is true, only by embracing that humanness — all of it — can we succeed."

"That doesn't make any sense either." Her lips trembled.

"That doesn't make it any less true. Whatever you are afraid of, you have to let it in. You have to let yourself see it. You have to let yourself feel it." I thought back, not happily, to S'kryssna S'kyaga and her snakes. "If you do that, Bo'Rà K'n cannot hurt you. Oh, he will try. He will try very hard...as hard as he knows how. But feeling your fear carries you to the other side of it and starves Bo'Rà K'n of the only fuel that feeds him."

"What are you scared of, Ben?"

"Lots of things. Like you, it seems, more every day. That we won't succeed...that by coming back I will have made things in Q'ntana worse not better." There was more. "That we will succeed. That what everyone says is true, that I will be king...that in becoming king I will fail as badly as my mother did as queen...and then we won't have succeeded at all." I threw a rock into the fire, then another and another, to break the tension and shatter my own anxiety. Then I added, grinning, "I'm also afraid that Panesh and Janq'a will kill each other before we get wherever we're going and you and I will have to finish up Bo'Rà K'n by ourselves."

My'leen giggled. "Thank you for that, Ben. For all of it." A moment later, she was serious again. "I think I know what I'm afraid of, apart from the obvious."

"The obvious?"

"Bo'Rà K'n and the Black Riders."

"And the not-so obvious?"

"I'm also afraid that we'll fail, but…but that isn't really it either." She spoke slowly now, weighing each word. "I knew what my life was before Yzythq'a sent me off with you. It was not a good life. But it was a life. Oh, I loved the children I taught, even though I hated having to teach them lies. And I loved B'tha…love B'tha. In that life, I knew what to expect, which was nothing. I knew who I could trust, which was no one. I knew when change would come, which was never. No, it was not a good life. It was a terrible life, an unbearable life. But whatever that life was, I knew it." The tears she had held back flowed freely now. "It's gone now. All of it. This, this…whatever it is, will be gone soon too. Then what? What will become of me?"

What would become of any of us? I knew my destiny, but that did not stop me from wondering the same thing. I didn't speak that. Instead, I pulled My'leen next to me and held her head on my shoulder while she wept.

"Only good things," I murmured, with no idea what I meant or whether it was even true. "Only good things."

*　　*　　*

In the morning, we devoured one final kromii breakfast, refilled our water skins and set off. When we reached the top of the mesa we were both grateful and dispirited. Grateful, because as sheer and steep as was the escarpment, a narrow switchback jackknifed down through the talus. Dispirited, because the base of the path opened out to a vast wasteland that stretched forever, disappearing into the swirling dirt of a distant dust storm. We spotted not a single oasis, only twisted, half-dead co'aqas, their black-mottled gray-green skin spiked with poisonous thorns, and an occasional cluster of dun-colored boulders that might serve for shade from the relentless heat that rose visibly from the desert floor. A lonely road punched west through this yellow-skied wilderness, frequently disappearing under sand drifts and towering dunes.

"There is no other way," I said, even as I wondered silently how

189

we would make it across. Then, as if to offer us a hint of hope, a flash storm struck the desert below. When it cleared, dirt and dust had been washed from the sky, revealing a thin blue line of sea at the edge of a distant horizon. Beyond it, so barely visible that it might have been a mirage, a pyramid-shape mountain rose from the water, its summit obscured by a lenticular cloud.

"Does touch the point where earth meets sky..." I murmured.

"What?" Janq'a asked.

"Can you see it?" I pointed to the island.

He squinted, shook his head.

My'leen leaned forward, balancing precariously over the lip of the cliff. "I do," she said softly. She hummed Yzythq'a's song. "Beyond the west," she whispered when she was done.

"Yes," I said. "Beyond the west."

thirty

As harsh as the desert had seemed from the top of the mesa, it was appreciably worse when we stepped off the escarpment path. Fortunately, Da'nay had outfitted us with light boots, because the sand was so hot to the touch that our previously sandaled feet would never have made it beyond a few steps. The wind gusted sand and grit into our eyes, mouths and hair, up our noses, under our fingernails and through our clothing. The boulders too, when we reached them, were searing enough to roast meat on. Not that any of us could stomach the thought of hot food…or any food. All we craved was water — severely rationed, given that there was no telling how long we would be forced to trudge through the extreme heat and brutal gales of this place.

If the days were blistering, the nights were their radical opposite. We huddled together in a giant ball, praying that our thin blankets and the heat from our blended bodies would ward off the bitter chill and keep us alive until morning. Even following Aygra's path west proved difficult. The road grew increasingly patchy the farther we traveled. And the pall of ocher dust that nearly always hung from the sky masked all but a tiny of dot of struggling light. That was Aygra. B'na remained hidden altogether.

By our third day, all we could do was stumble from one rocky outcropping to the next. The shade wasn't cool, or even comfortable, but nor was it as scorching as the unprotected sand. Panesh suffered the most. His size and Angarusha constitution demanded constant hydration. Yet we lacked even enough water for normal human needs. At some point on that third day, Panesh drained his last water skin. He chose not to tell us, and by suns-merge on the fourth day, he was so weak he could barely limp. Too tall for any of us to support him, not that he would have permitted it even were it possible, he collapsed in a tiny slice of shade, next to a sickly knot of co'aqas.

"You have to…go on…without me," he croaked. He fell into a fit of dry, hacking coughs. "You have to." His lips were cracked and bleeding, and despite the ravages of desert sun and wind, his skin was so pale that it was nearly translucent.

"What do we do?" My'leen cried.

While she rummaged in her pack for a water skin, I forced mine to Panesh's mouth. Had he been stronger, he would have pushed it away. He didn't have to. Janq'a wrenched it from my hands before a single drop could touch Panesh's lips. I was stunned. I had believed the two to have resolved their differences. Yet here was Janq'a, ready to let Panesh die of thirst. Had they been playacting? All the suppressed rage from our journeying — not only toward Janq'a but toward Na'an and Bo'Rà K'n and all the way back to O'ric, Toshar, Eulisha and Q'nta — roiled inside me. My face must have revealed my fury because My'leen looked at me and blanched. Before I had a chance to explode, Janq'a had corked my water skin and uncorked his own, thrusting its spout into Panesh's mouth. With uncharacteristic tenderness, he carefully poured the remaining contents down the giant's throat.

"He needs you more than he needs me," Janq'a said gently to Panesh.

Panesh stared at the little man with amazement. We all did. Janq'a daubed Panesh's mouth with his sleeve then turned to me. "You have to make it through, Ben, even if I don't…even if no one of us does. *You* have to make it through. You have to."

Panesh cleared his throat. Tears filled his eyes. I had never seen him cry, never knew that Angarusha could cry. "You are a fool," he said warmly to Janq'a. "And you are wrong. You are important. More important on this SunQuest than I am." He wiped his eyes with the back of his hairy hand. "Thank you."

We plodded on. Panesh managed better than he had done earlier, but he remained frail. Janq'a, though, soon began to weaken. He adamantly refused water from either me or My'leen and only let Panesh carry him because he had grown too feeble to resist. By suns-set we were drenched in sweat and caked with dirt from a sandstorm that had erupted out of nowhere. And we were out of water.

*   *   *

In the way of this desert, the temperature plummeted almost instantly from blazing to wintry, and our teeth clacked loudly with the cold. We had no blankets. We had abandoned them, along with all packs but My'leen's, on the second day. Carrying them in the heat consumed too much energy, made us need too much of our rapidly depleting water. Previous nights, we had managed with shared body heat alone. That would not work this night. We were soaked with sweat. Without a miracle, we would die, and this night would be The SunQuest's last.

My'leen collapsed by the nearest boulder, curled into a fetal ball and lay on the cooling sand, shivering uncontrollably. Gently, Panesh laid Janq'a, barely conscious, next to her. He lowered himself to the ground, his back against the rock.

I tugged first on My'leen's arm then on Panesh's. "Get up. If we stop now it's all over. You'll die. We'll all die. We have to keep moving. Somehow, we have to keep moving. If we don't, we will freeze to death, right here in this spot."

"We're going to f-freeze to death either way," My'leen stammered through chattering teeth. "Let's just get it over with." She shut her eyes. "I'm so tired."

"My'leen is right," Panesh rasped. "We cannot keep going like this."

I was astounded. I had never known Panesh to give up, on anything.

"Look," I said, pointing to the sky. "The moon is out. We can see the moon." Every other night the sky had been so cloudy or dirty, or both, that M'nor had been as invisible to us as she had been to all of Q'ntana in Toshar's time.

"What of it?" Panesh asked.

"We can finally see where west is. If we rest till morning and the winds start up again, we will be traveling blind. Again. If that happens, we will never get out of here."

"We'll never get out of here anyhow," My'leen moaned.

Janq'a opened one eye. He stared up at the moon, then back down at me. "A story."

"What?" we all responded together.

"A story," he repeated.

"A story? No. This can't be the time. We have to keep moving."

Janq'a forced himself up to a sitting position. "Look at us. None of us has got the strength to take another step. You know that. Even you couldn't make it very far."

He was right, but...

"What can a story do?"

Panesh eyed Janq'a with surprised admiration. He turned to me. "A bard — an Elderbard — asks that question?"

"Remember what you did at the Scriving Rock?" Janq'a asked. "Maybe you can write something that gets us out of here…or at least conjures us up some dry clothes and a fire."

Maybe I could at that. It was worth a try. A story had gotten us through the Xa'qìa Mountains. Could a story save us again? It might work. It would have to work.

"Where would I write it?"

"Over there." Janq'a pointed to a nearby dune, smoothed by the day's winds. "Write it in that."

Panesh stumblingly carried first My'leen then Janq'a to the slope of sand. I pulled the quill from my waistband and started to scratch a story into the dirt.

"Once upon a time," I began, "in a cold, ill-tempered desert, four weary travelers rested next to a giant sand dune under the gaze of a watchful, compassionate moon…"

The story was dull, designed with a single purpose: to ensure that we survived the night and gained the strength to keep going when daylight returned. By the time I scraped the final words into the dust — "And they were warm, dry and safe…at last" — only M'nor had progressed on her journey. For us, nothing had changed. We were still cold, wet and, if possible, even more miserable than when I had begun.

"The end," I added, hoping these two words might prove as magical as "once upon a time" had…once upon a time.

"The end," I repeated, louder. Nothing.

"The end. The end. The end!" I shouted it over and over — at the desert, at Prithi, at Bo'Rà K'n, at Na'an, at O'ric, even at Pryma. Then I stabbed the quill into the dune and burst into tears.

thirty-one

After emotional goodnights — none of us expected to wake to another morning — the others slept, Janq'a and My'leen curled up in Panesh's giant arms. I couldn't. I had failed my friends. I had failed my ancestors. I had failed Q'ntana. There would be no Crowning for The SunQuest and, certainly, none for me. Whatever my reluctant destiny was to have been, it would end this night, here in this unforgiving wasteland. Human that I now was, I would die with my friends. I slipped from the bundle of bodies and paced around our encampment, hoping that the movement would still my shivering.

"You either trust or you do not." The voice came from both within me and the sky, all at the same time. It was a woman's voice. "You either trust or you do not," she repeated.

"M'nor?"

"You either trust or you do not. There is no halfway in between. Do you not know that by now, Ben Ko'leya?"

"What do you mean?"

"Where is your quill?"

I walked back to the dune, pulled it from the sand and held it up to the moonlight.

"When you trust the quill to tell you *its* story," she said, "you will find what it is that you seek. Until then..." M'nor passed behind a large cloud, her light growing diffuse.

Its story. Isn't that what I just wrote?

No. If I am truly honest, I have to admit that I wrote what I wanted to write because I was trying to achieve a particular result. I did not write the quill's story at all.

I stared at the quill in the now-dimmer moonlight. It glimmered faintly. "What is your story?" I asked it. Without waiting for an answer, I knelt down, wiped the dune clean of my previous attempt and started again.

"Once upon a time," I wrote...and waited. M'nor reemerged from her cloud and cast a moonbeam onto the dune. The letters I had scratched into the sand lit up and flickered. As I continued, that same light illuminated all my words.

"Once upon a time," I began again, speaking as I wrote, "in the desert kingdom of Ardyyn, there lived a prince by the name of Bonda'ar...a wise prince too old to still be a prince. Old, because his father the king and mother the queen still lived and ruled, though their years numbered in the many score. The prince loved his parents and wished them no ill. But he wished, too, that what he saw as his life and destiny would finally begin to unfold. Because it did not or would not, and because he had little else to do, he spent most of his days wandering through the Ardyyn deserts. Wandering and wondering.

"One day, on his aimless meanderings, he came upon an ancient tartaruca, Arrukka by name. Tartarucas do not, as a rule, live in the desert. As a rule, tartarucas live exclusively in the sea. Bonda'ar knew this and was astounded to see the dust-covered creature sunning himself atop a dune, his face tilted up to B'na. He was even more astonished that this tartaruca had two eyes, for everyone knows that tartarucas have but a single eye that sits at the center of their forehead.

"'What are *you* doing here?' the prince asked. It was an impertinent question impertinently asked. Tartarucas are as ancient as the sea itself and expect concomitant respect.

"The tartaruca ignored Bonda'ar at first then slowly dropped his head, opened his eyes and gazed down at the prince, his left eye hooded with boredom, his right eye wide and bright with interest.

"'What are *you* doing here?' Arrukka asked in return.

"'Not much of anything, alas,' Bonda'ar replied sadly.

"'Ah,' the tartaruca said, and tilted his face once more up to the sun.

"'You did not answer my question,' Bonda'ar pressed, with yet more impertinence.

"'Indeed,' Arrukka said, without moving his head.

"'Shouldn't you be in the water?'

"'Do you see any water here?' Arrukka asked, his voice tinged with annoyance.

"'No.'

"'Well, then.'

"Feeling snubbed, Bonda'ar started to walk away. After a few paces, though, he stopped and turned back.

"'Is it true, sir, that tartarucas are the wisest creatures of the sea?'

"'So it is said. Two-eyed tartarucas are said to be even wiser still.'

"'Would you also be the wisest creature of the desert?'

"Arrukka said nothing.

"'Sir?'

"Arrukka angled his head ever so slightly in Bonda'ar's direction.

"'I ask because if you are, I would truly appreciate your counsel.'

"Tartarucas are wise. They are also easily flattered. You might take from that that they are not as wise as they seem. You would be wrong. So certain are they of their wisdom and grace, that they are wise enough to recognize the wisdom in those others who recognize it as well.

"Arrukka turned his ancient, wrinkled head back toward the prince. Again, one eye was hooded; the other, wide and bright. He nodded slowly.

"'Go on,' he said.

"Bonda'ar strode back to the dune, stood as close to the tartaruca as he dared and recounted his story. He spoke lovingly of his parents and of his home. Others, he said, disparaged, the stark, colorless, dusty-aired Ardyyn lands. For his part, he could not imagine any other home.

"'But I am weary with boredom. And I am lonely'

"'That,' the tartaruca pronounced, 'is your problem.'

"'That I am bored or that I am lonely?'

"Arrukka issued a honking laugh. 'Neither, young prince. That you cannot imagine. If you imagined, you would never be bored. Or lonely.'

"'Young?' the prince retorted incredulously. 'Look at me.' He touched the furrows etched into his face and the brow from which thick black curls had long ago fled.

"The tartaruca honked again. 'Look at you? Look at me!'

"'I take your point. But human princes do not live as long as tartarucas.'

"'Bollocks. That none has yet proves naught. They do if they choose to. It is all about choice. All of it. Everything.'

"'But that means—' Bonda'ar began, more astonished than he had ever been in all his years.

"'Indeed,' Arrukka interjected. He opened both his eyes so wide that his gold-flecked, sea-green eyeballs bulged from his head. 'What, then, do you imagine, young Bonda'ar? What do you imagine, and what do you choose?'

"Prince Bonda'ar shut his eyes and thought and thought. And thought some more. When he at last reopened them, they were wet with tears. 'I don't know,' he replied sadly.

"'Wrong answer,' Arrukka countered. 'Of course, you know.'

"'I do?'

"'As sure as I am the wisest tartaruca in the desert.' Arrukka erupted with a blasting, blare of a laugh then, just as suddenly, turned serious. 'Try again.'

"Bonda'ar squeezed his eyes shut, gritted his teeth and screwed his face up into a maze of knotty lines.

"'Not so hard,' the tartaruca counseled. 'There is no call to hurt yourself. Hurting yourself is not at all necessary. You might also want to breathe. Breathing is absolutely necessary.'

"The prince relaxed. He inhaled slowly and exhaled more slowly still. As he did, his shoulders dropped, the lines around his eyes softened and the slightest hint of a grin tickled at his lips.

"'Oh,' he whispered, letting his eyes open — first a slit, then wide in wonderment.

"'Indeed,' said the tartaruca. He raised himself up on claw-tipped leathery legs and stretched, his mouth distending into a gaping yawn. Then with a giant push, he slid down the dune in a cloud of sandy dust.

"'Have you imagined?' he asked.

"Bonda'ar nodded.

"'Have you chosen?'

"'I have.'

"'And?'

"'I have imagined the home you have come to carry me to. I have imagined, too, the true love who waits for me there. And I have chosen to journey there with you.'

"Arrukka nodded, satisfied. 'Then climb aboard, young prince. It is time to say goodbye to all that you have known in order that you may travel to all that you are growing to. It is time to step into the destiny you never dared imagine. It is time to become.'

"With quiet confidence, Prince Bonda'ar climbed onto the

tartaruca's back. Before he could settle comfortably, the tartaruca leapt forward with a speed unknown to any tartarucas the prince had ever heard of.

"'Goodbye…and thank you,' Bonda'ar murmured as his desert home melted into a blur.

"After what might have been seasons but felt like the breath between breaths, Arrukka stopped, so abruptly that Bonda'ar toppled from his back.

"For an instant, the prince feared that they had traveled nowhere at all, for he landed, face-first, in a soft cushion of familiar-seeming sand. But when he turned his head, he saw that this was the sand of beach not desert. Seashore stretched in a vast expanse to his left and right. Behind him, a tree-fringed dirt path cut through a flower-studded meadow to a massive stone circle. Above meadow and stone circle unfurled a thick forest of gurja trees that obscured all views beyond it. Ahead of him and just out of reach, the ocean exhaled its surf in a gentle ebb and flow of froth-tipped waves. As he gazed out toward the foggy horizon, an island peeked through swirls of mist, a cloud-topped pyramid-shape mountain at its center.

"'Hana Mar Ò Q'inaya,' he whispered. 'The Land of Dreams.'

"'Your new home,' Arrukka replied. 'Is it as you imagined it?'

"'It is just as I imagined it.'

"'Good.' The tartaruca nodded and padded toward the sea.

"'Wait,' Prince Bonda'ar cried. 'Will you not take me there?'

"'This is as far as the story will allow me to carry you,' Arrukka replied, already in the water and swimming away. 'You will find your way, King Bonda'ar, in your own way, which will be the perfect way, and in your own time, which will be the perfect time.'

"'*King* Bonda'ar?' he shouted back in amazement.

"'Indeed,' the tartaruca replied before dropping into the ocean and out of sight.

"You might wonder what became of Bonda'ar, whether he ever made it across the Hana Mar Ò Q'inaya Channel to the Land of Dreams, whether he assumed his kingship and lived happily ever after with his true love. The answer, of course, is yes. As to the how… that, my friends, is a story for another day."

*　*　*

The dune glowed with the letters of my story, of the quill's story, its

199

light shining into the tearstained faces of Janq'a and My'leen…into mine, too, no doubt. That same light generated sufficient heat to dry our clothes and keep us warm. Suddenly, somehow, we were also no longer thirsty.

Panesh, Janq'a and My'leen had awoken at some point during my telling. As each of them later recounted it, they woke from a dream about a prince and a tartaruca, only to hear my voice continuing the same story that had begun for each them in the identical dream. Now it was just past dawn. Both Aygra and B'na hung low in the clear, dust-free sky.

"That island that Bonda'ar sees," Janq'a said excitedly, "Hana—Hana Mar—"

"Hana Mar Ò Q'inaya," Panesh said. "The Land of Dreams."

"Is that the island we saw from the mesa?" My'leen asked.

Was it? Could it be?

"Indeed." The voice came from atop a second dune, behind us. The voice was Arrukka's.

thirty-two

The tartaruca sunned himself on top of the dune, his face angled toward B'na. As in the story, his left eye was hooded with boredom, while his right bulged opened, its gold flecks glinting in the sun. Janq'a jumped up and down, pointing at Arrukka.

"How— You— Here? How? How? It was just a story!"

Arrukka yawned, licked his lips and dipped his head lazily toward us. "Tell him, Ko'leya," he said to me. "Tell him what, truly, he should, by rights, already know by now."

I laughed. "Nothing is 'just' a story, Janq'a. Even I had to be reminded of that at the Scriving Rock, and I was an Elderbard once upon a time."

"But— Does that mean— It can't mean— Does it?"

"Indeed," Arrukka replied. He yawned again, noisily this time, opening his mouth so wide and keeping it open so long that we could count all his teeth — twenty-seven on the top, twenty-two on the bottom — and see deep into the back of his throat. Then he stretched each of his legs in turn and raised himself up on the tips of his three-clawed toes, arching his back as much as a hard-shelled tartaruca can. Finally, with a powerful shove from his back legs, he slid down the dune in a cloud of dust.

Tartarucas are giant creatures. Pryma, for example, who had scooped me up out of the ocean at the start of this SunQuest, had easily carried Toshar, Yhoshi, Fynda and Garan on an earlier journey, on The MoonQuest. Arrukka was no smaller than his one-eyed cousin. But as diminutive as Janq'a was, his lack of size could not compensate for Panesh's heft. There could be no room for all four of us on the tartaruca's back. We tried, but Panesh was too hulking and ungainly to fit.

"Well?" Arrukka demanded, tapping his right front foot

impatiently. "Are you coming or are you not? I have a schedule to keep."

My'leen, Janq'a and I dismounted and glanced anxiously from one to the other. Panesh stepped away.

"What about Panesh?" I asked the tartaruca.

"Panesh is not my concern," he replied. "My concern extends only to transporting those of you who climb aboard. Nothing more, nothing less. Did I mention that I have a schedule to keep?"

"You must go without me," Panesh said. He lifted each of us in turn onto Arrukka's back. "See? There is no room for me. Period. No argument."

"No," Janq'a wailed. He jumped back down, wrapped his arms around Panesh's leg and refused to let go. "I won't go without Panesh. I won't. I won't. I won't."

"If that is your choice," Arrukka said, "that is fine with me." He extended his legs to their full height.

"It is not fine with me," Panesh growled.

Arrukka dismissed Panesh with a disdainful shake of the head. "Whatever it is you think you are going to do, get on with it. I have a schedule to keep. Did I mention that?"

"You did," Panesh replied, "and I, for one, will not prevent you from keeping it." He pried Janq'a's arms free, gathered him up and, though Janq'a wriggled fiercely, dropped him next to me.

"You can go, Janq'a. You must," Panesh insisted. "You have a role to play in what is to happen next. I cannot know exactly what it is, and I do not much like what I do know of it. But I know it to be true. Ben needs you. The SunQuest needs you. You must go. Now."

"But you'll die here! I don't want you to die," Janq'a whimpered.

"I would rather not die here, if it can be helped. If it cannot, I will die knowing that I have done what needed doing and that I served my king in doing it." He bowed his head to me. "Kano'ha."

My'leen burst into tears. "Oh, Panesh!" She pulled Janq'a to her in a smothering hug.

My eyes were wet too, as were Panesh's. For only the second time on our journey, he wept.

"One more moment, Arrukka," I said. "Please."

The tartaruca grunted.

I climbed down and embraced Panesh. "I will miss you, my friend. But I will see you again. I know I will."

Panesh returned me to the tartaruca's back.

"If I am needed," he said, "Na'an will find a way to send for me. If not…" He shrugged.

"It is time," Arrukka said.

"But—" Janq'a cried.

We were off.

"Panesh…" Janq'a moaned. But Panesh was gone.

thirty-three

We traveled as Bonda'ar had, with such speed that everything around us was a blur. At first the color of the blur matched the grayish-brown of the desert. After a while that faded into a neutral, cloudy off-white. Now and again, a shock of red, orange or blue would stab through the smudge, but only for an instant. Then it would dissolve back into colorlessness. Nor was there any indication of the passage of time. When we were tired, we slept. When we were hungry or thirsty, whatever we needed appeared in front of us. At the beginning, we passed the time by sharing stories about Panesh. When the stories made us too sad, we continued on without conversation.

Arrukka, for his part, was the opposite of Pryma, though the effect was the same. It had been impossible to ask Pryma anything because he talked so much. Arrukka spoke not at all, ignoring all questions posed to him. Throughout the entire journey, however long it lasted, he said only one word.

We had lapsed into silence after our Panesh stories were done when Arrukka bobbed his head once and barked, "Sing."

Although startled, we obeyed. My'leen led us in one melody after another, each opening differently than the last. Oddly, all songs always returned to the one I had first heard her sing at Castle Rose, the same melody that Yzythq'a had used for his song. When we weren't sleeping, we sang. When we weren't eating, we sang. We sang until Arrukka stopped, as abruptly as he had for Bonda'ar in the story I had scrawled into the desert dune. We tumbled off his back and onto the same sandy beach to which he had delivered the prince. To my amazement, it was the same sandy beach where I had first met Panesh.

Like that first beach and Bonda'ar's, ours extended infinitely north and south. To the east, behind us, a tree-fringed path wound up to a broad, raised meadow studded with brilliantly colored wildflowers. In its center stood a vast stone circle formed by an upside-down-V pattern of white rocks topped by slabs of dark gray stone. Crystalline specks embedded in the rocks glittered in the light from Aygra and B'na, which were nearly at suns-merge. Were I to pass beyond the stone circle and into the forest dense with majestic gurja trees, would I once again find my way to the Maya Ko?

To the west across the still-as-glass channel, a thick, swirling fog veiled the sky…but only until Aygra and B'na joined overhead in suns-merge. Then the fog vanished as though it had never been, revealing Bonda'ar's pyramid-shape island, so far distant that it might have been sketched onto the horizon. A broad lenticular cloud hovered just above the summit.

"Hana Mar— Hana Mar Ò—" Janq'a squinted at the island.

"Hana Mar Ò Q'inaya," I said.

"Yeah. Is that it?"

"About time it showed itself," Arrukka muttered. He padded toward the water.

"Wait," Janq'a called. "What about us?"

"I have a schedule to keep," he replied. "Remember?" The tartaruca allowed the next wave to carry him out to sea. "You already know the answers to your questions," he called back. "You will find your way. Indeed, you will." A moment later he was gone.

"Now, what do we do?" Janq'a asked.

"I don't know," I replied. "Wait, I suppose." Hana Mar Ò Q'inaya was too far to swim to. There was nothing else for us to do but wait.

"For what?"

"For an answer to your question, Janq'a. For some sort of direction about what is to happen next."

When neither answer nor direction made itself known, we stripped off our clothes and dove into the ocean. After our time in the desert, we were filthy, with sand caked to nearly every piece of skin. Our clothes were worse. Stiffened from the combination of heat, dirt and sweat, they scraped at the sand that already scraped at our skin. If I could have, I would have burned every piece. Although we had left our clothes behind once before, it had not been by choice, and it did not seem practical here. Instead, we washed them as clean as salt water would allow, laid them on flat rocks to dry and returned to the water. After a time, we returned to shore, got dressed in clothes that were now salt-stiffened instead of sand-stiffened, and strolled up and down the beach. Whenever I gazed west across the water, Hana Mar Ò Q'inaya beckoned. I was certain that it was our destination but still knew of no way to get there. My'leen suggested I tell another story, but it did not feel right. Either it wasn't the way or it was not yet time.

After a while, we climbed partway up the path up from the beach and napped among the grasses, grateful not to have to sleep on sand.

"Janq'a!" Bo'Rà K'n's voice, that unmistakably inhuman rasping growl, always so chilling.

I try to open my eyes but cannot. I try to sit up but cannot. Am I still sleeping? Is this a dream?

I open my mouth to whisper My'leen's name. No sound emerges. Only breath. I try again. Still nothing.

I hear it again. "Janq'a. Answer me!"

"Janq'a," I whisper, or think I do. Again, no sound.

After several more attempts to pry open my eyes, to move or to speak, I give up. Instead, I lie still and listen.

"Janq'a!" Now Bo'Rà K'n shouts. "You will obey me."

No response. Then a vague, shooshing sort of sound. Janq'a. He whispers. I strain to hear.

"There is nothing to tell," he says.

"The Ring. What about the Ring?"

"You keep talking about a ring. I haven't seen any ring. Don't you think I would have told you if I had? What kind of ring is it? Are you even sure there is such a thing down here? Even if it's around, why would they tell me? They know I'm your spy. They think I'm a traitor."

"You are lying. Be careful, Janq'a. Be careful what you say. Be careful what you choose not to say."

"No, master! On my mother's grave. I have seen no ring. There is no ring."

"You never knew your mother. If you had, you would dance on her grave if it would somehow profit you."

"I— No— Yes, master."

"Decide now who you are going to betray, Janq'a. If you betray me, I promise you will wish that you were dead."

"Yes, master. I mean no, master."

"Where are you?"

"By Hana Mar— Hana Mar—"

"Hana Mar Ò Q'inaya."

"That's it."

"Then it will soon be over."

Something shifts. Although I see nothing, Janq'a has left this dream or vision, or whatever it is. Now, Na'an and Bo'Rà K'n speak.

"It will soon be over, brother. For all time. One way or another."

Bo'Rà K'n roars with anger. "I will find a way to kill you, Na'an. I swear I will. The power will soon be mine. When it is, you will wish you had not chosen to defy me."

Bo'Rà K'n's voice fades.

All I hear now is Na'an. "One way or another…for all time," she repeats. Then she too is gone.

"You were talking in your sleep again." My'leen's voice startled me. She was whispering to Janq'a. "Or were you sleeping at all?"

Janq'a said nothing. He lay on the ground, his back to one of the trees that lined the path. My'leen crouched next to him, her face close to his.

"Who were you talking to? I know you were talking to someone. Was it Bo'Rà K'n? Are you still spying on us for him?" She was angry.

Janq'a shook his head.

"I thought you were on our side now," she said.

"I—" He turned away.

I sat up, grateful that my body now agreed to function normally. "There are no sides in this, My'leen," I said. "There is only one side, whatever happens, however The SunQuest ends."

"That doesn't make any sense. What if Bo'Rà K'n wins? Because of him?" she kicked Janq'a lightly. He grunted and tried to melt into the tree trunk.

"He will," I replied. "Because of him."

"No!" My'leen and Janq'a shouted in unison. They stared first at each other then at me in astonished horror.

I joined them by the tree. "We will win too." They looked at me in confusion. "And no one will."

"What do you mean? I don't understand."

I gazed through the trees out to Hana Mar Ò Q'inaya. It was bathed in golden light from Aygra, which was sinking into the ocean on this side of the island, not behind it.

In fearless journey beyond the west…

"I'm not sure I do either. All I know is that it's true."

* * *

"Bo'Rà K'n is really going to get the Ring of Unity?" My'leen asked.

I shrugged. "Apparently."

We sat around a campfire on the beach, munching fruit from the forest, the only food we had been able to find. Our water came from a tiny rill that we had discovered on our explorations. It originated in the gurja forest, flowed through the stone circle, then wound down through the woodland trees before slicing through the sand and into the sea farther down the beach.

"None of this makes any sense. Can't you just give it to him?" Janq'a said.

"No, he can't," My'leen replied. She turned to me. "You can't, can you? Even if you wanted to?"

"What do you mean? Where is this ring? What is it?"

I touched the top of my head. "It's really a crown, not a ring. Remember the light on my forehead, back at the Xa'qìa cliffs?"

Janq'a nodded.

"That was it. It's inside me. I have been carrying it here for a long time. A very long time." I repeated for him The StarQuest story I had shared earlier with My'leen and Panesh.

"The sun?" Janq'a asked. He pinched my arm to convince himself that I was real. "How? You can't be. It isn't possible. How can it be possible?" He stared up to the eastern sky, but B'na had long ago set. "Can it?"

"It must be. I'm here, aren't I?"

"Yes, but…" He scratched his head. "How can you be up there and down here at the same time?"

"I don't know. It does seem odd, doesn't it? Maybe as B'na I know the answer to that riddle. Not as Ben. Definitely not as Ben."

"Can't you get it out?" he asked.

"Get what out?"

"The Ring. The crown. Whatever it is. Can't you just get it out? Then you could give it to Bo'Rà K'n. Then you would be done with all this. Then he wouldn't be mad at me anymore."

I laughed. "It's not as simple as that, Janq'a. It never is. Besides, I have no idea how to get the Ring out. I'm guessing it will come out when it's ready. In its time, not ours. That's why Bo'Rà K'n needs you here."

He eyed me quizzically.

"He needs you to tell him when it appears," I said. "He has no other way of knowing."

"Will bad things happen if he gets it?"

"He would not view them as bad."

"That's not good," Janq'a said.

"Maybe. Maybe not. I wonder if we would view them as bad." I shook my head. "I don't know, Janq'a. If what will happen really is bad, I have to wonder what the point has been of this SunQuest. It's still all a mystery to me. I only know what is. I don't know why it is."

Janq'a pondered on that as he munched on some more fruit. "What if I don't say anything? What if I don't tell him about the Ring when it shows up? Wouldn't that make it so the bad things never happen?"

Poor Janq'a. He was trying so hard to figure out a way for The SunQuest to play out in a way he could understand, in a way that worked for him. I didn't blame him. If there was some way I could have controlled the process and outcome, I would have. That was another choice that had not been given to me.

"You must tell him," I said.

"What if you don't let it out?"

"When the time comes," I said, "over there—" I pointed to the island "—I will have no choice." I paused. "Neither will you."

HANA MAR Ò Q'INAYA

We set up camp that night by the bottom of the path, with a clear view to the water. I wanted Hana Mar Ò Q'inaya to be the last thing I saw before falling asleep. Then, perhaps, Na'an would send me a dream with clear instructions on how we were to get there.

She did not. Not that night, nor the next. Nor the one after that.

Each morning, I prayed that the new day would bring a sign. Nothing showed itself. Now, Janq'a added his urgings to My'leen's for a story. Both hoped I could recreate the magic that had saved us in the desert. I did, as well, and although I frequently pulled out my quill, I never felt inspired to use it. The time was still not right.

When Janq'a was not begging for stories, he was asking whether I knew what had happened to Panesh. I wished I had an answer, for my peace of mind as well as for his. I did not: Na'an ignored that request of mine too. As for Astel Elohia, Janq'a was convinced that if he stared at the top of my head often enough, long enough and fixedly enough, he could will the Ring to appear. Of course, it never did.

By suns-merge on the fourth day, we were so bored by the beach, by our diet and from doing nothing that we even discussed what it would take to build a raft to get across the channel…or to swim it. We weren't serious. We had no tools, and the distance was not only too great, it was not fixed. One morning we would wake to find Hana Mar Ò Q'inaya frustratingly close, only to watch it drift off into the distance as the day progressed. The next morning, it might not be visible at all, reappearing at dusk as if by magic. Yet these options, unrealistic though they were, offered new possibilities for us to consider at a time when all others had long since been exhausted.

We had just about talked this one out that afternoon when a savage gust blew a violent squall in from the sea. In an instant, a clear suns-lit sky turned pitch. Angry blasts of icy wind stripped trees of their leaves and convulsed their naked limbs. The ocean frothed and foamed, and stinging saltwater sprays joined the brutal lashings of rain and hail. For all our boredom, we had still largely avoided the stone circle. I had never felt comfortable around it. Now, we raced up the teeming cascade of muck that had once been the sandy path to take shelter under the stone circle's rock-slab overhangs. From there, shivering with cold, we watched as wildflowers, too delicate for the storm's vicious pounding, were trampled into the mud.

On the next cyclone-like burst, a giant crow charged out of the roiling clouds, cawing so loudly that it overpowered the thunder's echoing boom. The bird swooped toward us, its steely wings slicing through the trees that climbed up from the beach. When all had been reduced to clean-edged stumps, it soared into the air, cut a swath through the gurja forest and then took aim for the stone circle…and us.

"Bo'Rà K'n," I whispered.

Janq'a ducked behind me. "It's just a temper tantrum," he said, his teeth chattering as much from fear as from cold. "It will pass." He poked me. "Do you think it will pass?"

The crow, its massive wings outspread and barely moving, plunged toward us. It was not going to stop.

"I'm not waiting to find out," I replied.

Maybe Bo'Rà K'n couldn't kill us. That didn't mean he couldn't seriously harm us. I dragged My'leen and Janq'a into the center of the circle and fell to the ground, just as the crow shattered the plinth that, seconds earlier, had been sheltering us. In an explosive crash, the entire circle collapsed into rubble. The crow flew low over the debris, pulverizing any stray chunks into dust. When it had completed its circuit, it flapped its wings in front of us, transforming into Bo'Rà K'n as it landed.

I stood, My'leen by my side. Janq'a, again, ducked behind me.

"The fearsome Bo'Rà K'n," I said.

"The foolish bard," he replied. He unfurled his cloak. Rain and hail ceased, but water still coursed down my face from my sopping hair. The sky was as grimly gray as ever, as was Bo'Rà K'n's gaze. "At last I stand before the legendary Ko'leya." He bowed mockingly. "You do not look particularly sunny today, son of Aygra."

I glanced up at the sky. Two faint dots of light poked through the low, dark clouds. "The sun always prevails in a contest between sun and storm, Bo'Rà K'n. It will be no different here, in the end."

"The end will be more different than you know, bard. Once I possess the Ring of Unity—"

"I look forward to that moment, Rev'Àn."

"Prithi save me," Janq'a whispered from behind me. He pressed so close to my legs that I could feel him trembling.

Bo'Rà K'n roared, louder than the thunder, louder than his cawing. A giant tidal wave surged up in mid-ocean. It heaved explosively toward shore, then flung itself up the beach and toward us.

"You dare use that name?" Bo'Rà K'n boomed.

"I do more than dare," I replied evenly, not at all sure where my fearless certainty was coming from. "I have no choice but to speak your truth name. It is my duty." I stared directly into eyes that burned at me through the swirling mist that still largely veiled his features. "I know my duty, Rev'Àn, as I know you to know yours."

The tidal wave crashed up toward the rubble of the stone circle, hung motionless for an instant, then, just as noisily, hurtled back into the sea.

"Once I wear the Ring as crown," Bo'Rà K'n stated with cool confidence, "no sun, or son of sun, will ever again have the temerity to speak to me so arrogantly nor possess the power to withstand the eternal storm I will unleash. With Astel Elohia I will gain absolute dominion over Q'ntana. Absolute power and absolute control. It will, at last, give me the power to kill. I will enjoy that power. You will be the first to die, bard. After him." He pointed a finger at Janq'a, who peered shakily out from behind me.

"Master?" he whimpered. "I— I didn't… I couldn't…" Bo'Rà K'n ignored him.

"Do your worst," I challenged.

"Count on it," Bo'Rà K'n spat. He spread his cloak. It reshaped itself into giant, outstretched black wings. His body transformed immediately afterward. The crow issued a bloodcurdling shriek and took off out to sea, pulling the storm clouds with it.

A moment later the suns reemerged and we trudged uneasily back to the beach.

thirty - five

While Janq'a and My'leen warmed themselves by the smoky bonfire we had built on the beach from the damp woodland debris, I paced by the water, letting the cool ocean wash over my feet and watching M'nor's silvery luminescence undulate in the waves. We had been in this place for four days, and we still had no way to get to Hana Mar Ò Q'inaya, which felt increasingly remote and inaccessible. The only thing of consequence that had shown up for us in that time was Bo'Rà K'n. Maybe My'leen had been right. Maybe it was time for a story.

"A story brought us here, Ben." I had not heard My'leen join me.

Janq'a huddled by the fire, still shivering — not from the cold and wet of the storm, but from our encounter with his master.

"I knew he could be mean," he had said tremblingly afterward. "He's been mean to me. Real mean. Not like that, though. If I had ever seen him like that, I would never, ever, ever have dared to talk back to him. And I did. A lot. Like I told you, he is all that I ever knew. I don't know how I ended up with him. I know nothing about my parents… if I even had any. When I asked about my past, he would never say. I don't know why he put up with me for as long as he did. When I think of what he has done…what he might have done to me…" He shuddered and edged closer to the nascent flames. "What is going to happen to me? I can't go back now…even if he would have me, which he wouldn't. Not anymore. Not that I could be with him again. Not knowing what I know."

He turned to My'leen, his eyes sad and pleading. "I didn't know what he was really like, how bad he really was. I didn't. You have to believe me. Do you?"

She opened her arms to him. He snuggled in. "Yes," she said. "Of course, I do."

Although temporarily comforted, Janq'a remained fearful about the future. I was certain that My'leen did as well, even though she had never mentioned it after our earlier conversation. Sitting around doing nothing for days on end didn't help. Nor did Bo'Rà K'n's threats.

Yes, a story had brought us here. I had not been in charge of that story any more than I could be in charge of a new one. "I can't just make up a story because I want it to do something for us," I said. "You saw what happened last time I tried that."

My'leen and I walked side-by-side in silence, the only sound the soft lap of the waves and the distant crackle of the fire.

"Are you sorry you came back, Ben? Wouldn't it have been simpler, easier, for you if you had stayed up there." She nodded up at the sky.

I skipped a rock into the sea. I didn't mean for it to land in M'nor's reflection, but it did, shattering the moon into an abstraction of ripples. I reflected back on Toshar, on his journey to rekindle M'nor's light and on Q'nta's to restore the stars to their night patterns. Why was I here in Q'ntana? Why had I returned, and in human form? Why had I agreed with O'ric that it was the right thing to do? Unlike the moon in The MoonQuest and the stars in The StarQuest, the suns needed no help from me. They continued to rise and set freely, as they always had, without restriction. Would they continue to do so if Bo'Rà K'n's reign of tyranny were allowed to remain in place? Would the suns be threatened next? I did not know, could not know.

As B'na I had observed Q'ntana's affairs with an impartial detachment that had never required any action. I saw everything, yet lacked any power to intervene, a power I had never desired and so had never missed. My time as B'na had also been devoid of pain, hunger and fear…of all human sensation and emotion. I had experienced no courage, no loss, no love. Now that I had experienced both ways of being, the human and the celestial, which was better? *Was* one better?

I skipped a second rock into the water, then a third, taking care to aim them away from M'nor's reflection. My'leen watched me silently from a few paces back. I stared out to sea, out to where Hana Mar Ò Q'inaya hid in the night, and asked myself the question My'leen had asked me: Would it have been simpler to have stayed where I was, as I was?

Perhaps. But like my mother and grandfather before me — and like the Ben I had been once before — I doubted that I had any meaningful choice in the matter. Eulisha spoke of choice as though it were an exercise of free will. I no longer viewed it that way. How could it be when, in the end, there seemed always but a single choice: whether or not to be true to oneself and one's vision. Once Toshar had made that choice, his MoonQuest was inevitable. The same had been true for Q'nta and her StarQuest…and her death. The same had been true for me — as B'na and as Ben. Would it have been easier to have remained celestially aloof? Undoubtedly. Could I have ignored the imperative that called me back here? Not unless I had also been prepared to ignore the essence of who and what I was. No. I was here because being here was the only choice I could have made.

"Ben. Ben?" My'leen nudged me. "Do you hear it?" She pointed out to sea. "You must hear it." She began to sing softly. "Something is coming toward us. Something out there is singing."

Something was out there. More than a single "something." A chorus of high-pitched, whistle-like tones drifted to us from the dark ocean. They were voice-like, though not voices. Haunting, though definitely not human. Another sound too. The sound of something skimming on the water. A boat? If it was, there was also more than one.

"Janq'a," I called up to the fire. "Come down. Hurry." I could now just make out four incandescent sea creatures, sailing toward us in diamond formation. "I think maybe our ride is here."

They were o'tria, sleek, lustrous water beings that swam upright on their tail fins. Their side fins flapped like wings, making them always appear as though they were about to launch into flight, although as creatures of sea not sky, they never did. On only rare occasions would they travel or sing alone. For the most part, they sang only together, in a spellbinding blend of unusual harmonies that pulsed tinglingly throughout my body. Curiously, My'leen understood the meaning of their sounds.

"It's not words so much as feelings," she explained hesitatingly, challenged to express in words what she knew in her heart to be true. "I can't tell you exactly what they are saying. What I can do, I think, is give you a sense of it. I might even be able to get them to understand me. I just have to have an idea of what I want to say and then not try to say it."

"I don't get it," Janq'a said. He had joined us and watched, mesmerized as we were, as the o'tria approached.

"Me neither." My'leen smiled. She touched her heart. "If I sing from here without trying to communicate what I am trying to communicate—" She giggled. "I'm not making any sense, am I?"

"Some things don't," I said. "Ever."

"I'm sure learning that," Janq'a said.

"All I have to do," My'leen tried again, "is take what I hope to communicate out of my mind and sing it from my heart. At least that's what I think I understand from them."

The o'tria were just offshore now, skimming the water, flapping their fins and singing. Dancing too, in a sense, for their bodies twisted sinuously in time to the music.

"What are they saying?" I asked.

My'leen inserted her voice into the chorus of song as naturally as if she were an o'tria herself. Her body began to undulate. Her eyes closed. She continued, trancelike.

"My'leen?"

"Oh. Sorry! It's just so—" She shrugged. "No words." She sang a few more sounds at the o'tria, pointing to Janq'a then to me.

They replied and danced closer to shore.

"You were right, Ben," she said. "This is our ride. They have come to take us to Hana Mar Ò Q'inaya. They say that we will have to wade out to them. The only land they can be on is the land of Hana Mar Ò Q'inaya. They are also asking that we sing with them as they carry us." She paused to listen. "They say our singing will give them the energy they need to bear our weight."

With the water too deep for Janq'a, I knelt down so he could climb onto my back and I waded toward the nearest o'tria.

"No!" My'leen pushed in front of me to stop me from setting Janq'a down on the lead creature. He and I tumbled into the water. "I'm sorry," she said, helping us up. "But no one sits on the o'tria prima. Ever."

Apparently, the o'tria had already predetermined which of them would carry which of us. My'leen directed me to place Janq'a on the left o'tria, and I was to sit on the creature in the rear. My'leen climbed onto the one next to Janq'a's. Once we had settled comfortably, the o'tria moved off in an elaborate pattern, weaving in and out of each other as they glided through the water.

"The pattern is part of the song," My'leen explained.

The next time she passed near me and Janq'a, she chided us. "You aren't singing. You must. You promised. They need our help."

"Right," I said. I shut my eyes, doing my best to melt into the rhythm and sound of the o'tria, to the rhythm and sound of the sea. Although I don't think that I fell asleep, I lost all awareness of everything but the music and the motion. Only when I sensed a change in the creature's cadence did I open my eyes again. The o'tria had ceased their dance. Instead, they bobbed in place as they sang.

Behind us, B'na was rising out of the ocean. Farther behind, on the distant eastern horizon, Aygra also rose. Ahead of us, Hana Mar Ò Q'inaya, bathed in the pinkish glow of dawn, soared up from the water, its cone-shape volcano disappearing into clouds still thick at its summit. A thin ribbon of sand and pastel-hued rocky beach, barely visible through the thin layer of mist that wafted over it, was all that separated mountain from sea.

"What's happening?" I asked My'leen.

She shrugged and continued singing.

Janq'a had fallen asleep. His arms were still wrapped around his o'tria's neck and he snored softly. I grinned. Maybe that was his song. My eyelids drooped shut and I thought I might also fall asleep to the cradled rocking and lullaby-like song. But just as I was drifting into oblivion, the o'tria thrust their necks forward and trumpeted a complex, blaring fanfare. My eyes jerked open to a large o'tria, double the size of the one I rode, pushing silently toward us out of the mist. Astride it was Bonda'ar.

thirty-six

"Yo!" Bonda'ar shouted. "Yo! I'm coming. I'm coming." He pulled off his crown and waved it at us.

Our o'tria dipped their heads as Bonda'ar approached. When he reached us, he plopped the crown back onto his head. It sat at an awkward angle, ready to slide off at any moment.

"Your Highness," I said, bowing my head. My'leen bowed hers too, at the same time kicking Janq'a, who had, improbably, slept through the fanfare.

"Uh? What?" He looked around, confused, then, without knowing what was going on, aped our actions.

"*Your* Highness," Bonda'ar replied. "Kano'ha."

I smiled. "Not yet, sir."

He grinned back, a boyish smile of limitless enthusiasm. "Soon! Very soon. Until that day, my kingdom is your kingdom. My home is your home. My story is your story." He acknowledged Janq'a and My'leen, especially My'leen. "You too. Welcome, my friends!"

I introduced them and My'leen smiled back shyly. Janq'a couldn't respond. His mouth gaped open as, incredulous, he stabbed his finger at the island. Hana Mar Ò Q'inaya whizzed toward us with determined speed.

Now that it was nearer, however curiously that was occurring, more of the volcanic island was visible. The mist had mostly burned away and the beach, as meager as it had first appeared, consisted almost entirely of rock slabs arranged in a pale mosaic of pinks, yellows and greens. The only sand was right at the water's edge. It sparkled the same blue-green as the water that lapped gently up against it. Beyond the beach, dense trees and scrub scaled the mountain, interrupted only by the gravel path that spiraled increasingly steeply around and up it, passing multiple times behind a teeming waterfall that tumbled down in a cloud of mist from some hidden place near the still-shrouded summit.

"Had I known you were already here and waiting," Bonda'ar continued, paying no heed either to Janq'a or the approaching island, "I would have come for you earlier. I am so terribly sorry, Your Highness. You too, My'leen. And…and…Jinqy."

"Janq'a," Janq'a muttered.

"Yes. Janq'a. Of course. How inhospitable you all must think me."

"I am certain the timing was perfect," I said.

"Yes, yes. Now, it is. Now, it is."

"You must stop calling me 'Your Highness,' Your Highness."

Bonda'ar laughed so hard that his crown slipped off his head and onto the o'tria's, which made him laugh all the louder. "If you call me Bonda'ar," he managed to spurt out between guffaws, "I will call you…I will call you…whatever you wish me to call you."

"Ben will do fine," I said.

"My'leen, please."

"Janq'a. That's *Janq'a*. Have you got that?"

"A little respect, Janq'a," I snapped.

"No, no," Bonda'ar replied, still laughing. "He is right, absolutely right." He addressed Janq'a directly. "You are correct, sir. I am terrible with names. Just terrible. Next time I get yours wrong, you have my royal permission to get mine wrong too. Or to forget it altogether. How is that?"

Janq'a grinned, mollified. "It's a deal your Bonda'ar-ness."

Bonda'ar peered up at B'na, crossed his eyes as he did some sort of mental calculation, straightened them again as he glanced back at Hana Mar Ò Q'inaya, which had halted about a quarter of a league away, then gazed far across the sky at Aygra. After that, he studied each of us in turn, counted off twelve on his fingers, looked up again at the suns, measured the size of the cloud at the summit with his thumb and index finger and shook his head.

"Hmm," he said. He shook his head again.

"What is it?" I asked. "Is something wrong?"

"Wrong? Oh, no. Nothing is wrong. Nothing is ever wrong on Hana Mar Ò Q'inaya. I would not permit it to be wrong. A privilege of kingship." He grinned. "Still, we had best be going ashore if the timing is to be right."

"The timing? For what?" My'leen asked.

Bonda'ar smiled at her, ignoring her question. "I understand you sing like an o'tria, My'leen. Just like an o'tria. Is that true?"

My'leen blushed, stammered and, in the end, said nothing.

"That is what Anariy'a tells me." He stroked the side of his o'tria's head. It leaned into his hand. "Anariy'a is never wrong." He paused, tilting his head in thought. "Except...? No, that's right. Never." He nodded his head resolutely. "Well?" he asked My'leen.

"Sir?"

"No, no, no, no, no! No highness, no sir. Bonda'ar. Or I will have to call you Princess My'leen."

My'leen blushed again.

"Just Bonda'ar. Only Bonda'ar. Ask Ji— Janq'a."

Janq'a giggled.

"Well?"

My'leen looked perplexed. "I'm sorry. I don't know what you are asking me."

"Will you sing us to shore? Someone must do it." Bonda'ar patted his o'tria. "Anariy'a insists that yours is the finest voice in the kingdom."

"I don't know. I wouldn't know what to sing."

Bonda'ar winked at her. "I cannot believe that for a minim. No, not even for a minim. Anariy'a knows that you know. Don't you, Anariy'a?"

The o'tria trilled.

My'leen looked at me helplessly, if flattered.

"You will know what to sing when you open your mouth and let the song happen," I said. "Like a story. Right?"

"I guess so."

If Bonda'ar had been smitten with her before, My'leen voice completed the job. Without understanding what she was singing, I knew she sang The SunQuest. She sang it in a wordless melody that encompassed everything we had experienced since leaving the spectral remains of Castle Rose. There was joy in her song, as well as fear, courage, sorrow, love, uncertainty and hope. Panesh, too, was part of the song. Even the o'tria were moved, remaining uncharacteristically silent for much of her performance. In the rare moments they joined in, it was in soft whispers that heightened the emotional impact of her performance. Bonda'ar's eyes were moist with tears as he let Anariy'a guide us toward the island and its beach. Mine were too. Janq'a wept openly. It was as though we needed to relive our experience together before we could set foot on Hana Mar Ò Q'inaya, before we could continue our journey, before we could carry our SunQuest to Crowning.

The song ended just as the o'tria skimmed onto the island. Anariy'a glistened, glittered and dissolved, leaving Bonda'ar standing on the beach. Our arrival was not nearly as smooth or elegant. When our o'tria vanished without warning from underneath us, we tumbled onto the rocks. Fortunately, the rocks only looked like rocks. In fact, they were made of a spongy substance that easily cushioned the fall. A flustered Bonda'ar rushed to My'leen's assistance.

"I am so sorry, my dear. I should have cautioned you." It took a few moments before he noticed that we had fallen too. Embarrassed, he hurried first to assist me, then Janq'a.

"I should have cautioned all of you." He brushed me and Janq'a off, then he reached out to do the same for My'leen but pulled back the instant his hand made contact. His face reddened. My'leen's did, as well. I covered my mouth to stifle a laugh.

"I did that my first time too," Bonda'ar explained once he had regained his composure. "I fell, just like you did. Not at all kingly. How was I to know that o'tria did that? Arrukka could have told me. But that tartaruca said not a word on our journey together. Not a word." He brushed his hand against My'leen's back and gently guided her up the beach. Janq'a and I followed behind. "O'tria take practice, they do," he explained to her. "I am certain that you will get the hang of it in no time, if…if…if you need to, that is."

Janq'a and I giggled, not only at Bonda'ar, but at My'leen, who was as flustered around the king as he clearly was around her.

When we reached the bottom of the gravel path, Bonda'ar stopped.

"Here, I must leave you, I am both sad and sorry to say," he said, directing this last phrase mostly at My'leen.

"You won't be coming with us, Bonda'ar?" I asked. I was surprised and disappointed. As this was his kingdom, I had expected him to guide us to the summit.

"This is your SunQuest not mine, Ben Ko'leya. I have other journeys to make before we meet again. But meet again we shall." He took My'leen's hand, then dropped it, his face pink with embarrassment. "If that is your wish."

My'leen smiled shyly.

Bonda'ar grinned like a schoolboy, then coughed and grew serious.

He removed the ring from his left index finger and handed it to me. The band was braided gold and silver, etched with tiny runic markings and set with a mirror-polished, milky blue stone. Within the stone sat a second, equally glassy, fiery orange, in the shape of a sunburst.

"Put it on, Ben Ko'leya, Ko'lar Kano'ha." He closed my fist over it. "Do not worry," he said, when I started to argue. "If the ring has a need to, it will know how to find its way back to me, in the right time. For now, it must travel with you. With it, you will be able to open the final p'rtulle of your SunQuest, the Maya Elohia, the doorway of unity."

I slipped it on my right index finger. It fit perfectly. "Is it…?" I raised my eyes toward the summit.

"Yes," Bonda'ar replied. "That is where the Maya Elohia will find you." He followed my gaze. "Your destiny will find you there too." After a solemn pause, he grasped both my hands in his. "Journey well. When next I see you, we shall both be kings. For now, though…" He whistled and Anariy'a materialized beneath him. "For now, we must part." He leaned down and heartily shook Janq'a's hand.

"Janq'a." He winked. He then reached for My'leen's, this time holding it tightly. "When I see you again," he said quietly, "I pray that you shall consent to be my queen."

Only when Bonda'ar and Anariy'a had vanished into the ocean haze did we realize that the island was once again on the move. It continued west, with increasing speed, toward two clouds that hung high in the distant sky: one, snowy white; the other, dark as coal.

thirty-seven

The path up the mountain began easily, a gentle grade that was wide enough for us to walk side-by-side-by side. My'leen sang dreamily, and Janq'a and I walked along in companionable silence, this, after his first attempt to tease My'leen about Bonda'ar ended with a kick from her and a glare from me. If others lived on the island, they kept to themselves, for we saw no one. Even the animals that peeked out at us from behind the trees and shrubs did so warily. We rarely caught sight of more than a furry head or a pair of blinking eyes and then only for an instant.

After a while we discovered where the waterfall we had seen from the beach ended: it cascaded with sweet, unwaterfall-like music into a large irregular-shaped pool lined with clear, crystalline rocks, its water so limpid that we could clearly see its far-distant, equally crystalline bottom. Milk-white do'ra birds, their silky wings flapping in an almost invisible blur, swooped playfully through the surging water, chirping a song that complemented the cataract's unusual melody. Occasionally, the flock would dive as one, deep into the lake. They would emerge long breaths later completely dry, orange-and-gray bratta fish wriggling in their long blue beaks.

We did not expect to emerge dry as the do'ras, but we did need a bath. After our swim we feasted on exotic-looking fruits, nuts and vegetables that grew wild in a nearby grove. The fruits were sweet, soft and squishy, all in different colors, with sticky crimson juices that guaranteed the need for a wash-up before we could continue our climb. The vegetables, crunchy, green and spiral-shaped, abounded on runners that twisted and trailed along the ground. We tripped over them frequently. The nuts were the strangest of all. Their pocked orange shells were rind-like: pliable, porous and too bitter to eat. Although tough to break through, the effort was worth the trouble. Inside, the pearl-colored nugget was an addictive blend of sweet and sour that melted on the tongue. We collected as many as our pockets would hold for the next leg of our journey.

"Panesh would have loved this place," Janq'a sighed, taking in the idyllic setting one last time before we resumed our climb.

"I hope we will see him again. Do you think we will?" My'leen asked me.

"We'd better," Janq'a growled. "If anything happens to him because of Bo'Rà K'n, I'll…I'll…" He shook his head impotently then cried softly. "I don't know what I'll do."

The path soon steepened and narrowed, forcing us to walk single-file and, increasingly often, scramble over rock-fall rubble with a nervous eye to the precipitous drop should we slip. The trees, majestic and full near the mountain's base, were now scrubby and prickly, their gnarled, exposed roots clinging fiercely to the rocky talus. The ascent was hardest on Janq'a, whose stubby legs were challenged to keep pace with me and My'leen. When I offered to carry him, he adamantly refused, insisting that I not waste my strength on him.

"You will need it," he predicted ominously, "for what's up there." He pointed up to the cloud that still veiled the summit.

I didn't want to think about it. Instead, I marveled at Aygra and B'na, both journeying through the sky to the east of us — a strange sight to see. We were beyond the west. Equally bizarre was the waterfall, which we passed behind whenever we spiraled back to the east side of the mountain. From the beach and the crystal pool, it had shown itself to be an ordinary, if magnificent, cascade: a blend of clear water and froth, throwing off clouds of sparkling mist. Its music, when it tumbled into the pool, was peculiar enough. Even more peculiar was that from the back, it was not at all wet. It wasn't even water. It was a cascade of multicolored light, a prismatic flow that awed us each of the half-dozen times we encountered it.

* * *

"Are you going to marry that Bonda'ar fellow?" Janq'a asked. We had stopped to rest just below the cloud. Its misty tendrils wafted down toward us as we sat, backs to the mountain wall, munching on the last of the nuts. Janq'a still huffed and wheezed from the climb.

"Janq'a…" I threw him a warning glare.

"No, it's all right," My'leen said. "After all we've been through together, we are family now, and it's a fair question for my brothers to ask." She smiled at us, but the smile was strained. "I have been wondering the same thing most of the way up here. I know we keep saying that nothing on this SunQuest makes any sense. This *really* doesn't make any sense."

"Why not?" I asked.

Janq'a nodded enthusiastically.

"Lots of reasons. *Lots.*"

"Like…" Janq'a prompted her.

"Like, is he even real? After all, he first showed up in a story."

"Do you remember King Kyri?" I asked.

"Of course. How could I forget the only happy times I have ever known in Q'ntana, when he was king."

"The *only* happy times?" Janq'a asked.

My'leen giggled.

"What about all this?" I added with a teasing grin, stretching my arms out to take in all of Hana Mar Ò Q'inaya and beyond.

"Oh," she replied, grinning back, "*nothing* compares to trekking up mountains, nearly dying in deserts, fighting off Black Riders and being terrorized by vicious crows. That's why I saw no point in mentioning it."

We laughed long and hard. We needed it, to erase the tensions of the past and to ease our anxiety over what lay ahead.

"Do you know Kyri's story?" I asked. "Do you know the story of The MoonQuest?"

"Some of it."

"Do you, Janq'a?"

He shook his head.

"While Toshar, Fynda, Yhoshi and Garan were traveling on their MoonQuest, Toshar told them the story of a grizzled old man who had lived, barely surviving, in a desert oasis for so long that he had forgotten who he was or where he came from. One day, a sandstorm threw itself at his oasis so viciously that he had no choice but to throw himself into the storm and leave, despite his immense fear. When the sand cleared, he found himself, to his astonishment, standing next to the Castle Rose moat. Even more surprising, the face staring back up at him from the water was his, a much younger version of him. He was Prince Kyri, and he had returned to his home, to Castle Rose.

"As Toshar tells it in The MoonQuest, he and his companions fell asleep soon after the story was done, on the slabs of river rock where they had been camping. Can you guess where they woke the next morning?"

Janq'a and My'leen stared back at me blankly.

"On the ferry dock on the far side of the River Alanda from Castle Rose." I turned to Janq'a. "You couldn't know the place I'm talking about. My'leen does. Don't you, My'leen."

"Of course. It has been a long time since there was a ferry there, but I have swum across to that dock many, many times. It's the only part of the river near the castle that is still clean."

"Can you guess what day that was, the morning they found themselves on that ferry dock, without knowing how they got there?"

My'leen shook her head.

"It was the morning of Kyri's coronation. Fortas, his father, had abdicated when Kyri returned. Kyri was to be crowned king that very suns-merge. As he was. His sister, Dafna, by the way, was my grandmother."

"Interesting story," Janq'a said. "What does it have to do with My'leen and Bonda'ar?"

I turned to My'leen. "Do you know?"

She looked back at me, mystified. "No. I—"

"Wait," Janq'a jumped up. "I know, I know. Can I tell?"

My'leen and I laughed. "Go ahead," I said.

"Kyri was in a story, but he was also real. You even knew him, for real. That's how really real he was. Right?"

I nodded.

"So Bonda'ar must be real too," My'leen said slowly.

"Yes! Yes! And you're the true love of his story." Janq'a pirouetted around us. I pulled him back to the ground. There was little dancing space on this path. Any slip could be deadly.

"I have two other reasons to be unsure," My'leen said.

"Name 'em," Janq'a shouted. "I'll knock 'em down too. I swear I will."

My'leen laughed again, in spite of her unease. "How do I know I love him? How can I love him? We've only just met. We've barely spoken."

"And the other reason?" I asked.

"Is there something wrong with that one?"

"Yes. To quote Arrukka, it's bollocks."

"That isn't fair."

"Do you know when it was that Toshar fell in love with Dafna and she with him?"

My'leen shook her head.

"At Kyri's coronation, when he was seated next to her at the ceremony. That was the first they had ever set eyes on each other."

My'leen gazed into the waterfall that tumbled next to where we sat. Its multicolored light danced on her face.

"Yes, you have only just met," I continued. "But what I saw in your face when you were with him was no schoolgirl crush. That was your heart glowing in your face. Anyone can see the same in his face whenever his eyes light on you. I don't know why you should love each other or why it should happen so quickly, without warning. I do know not to question it."

I had experienced love like that too, once upon a time.

"The first time I saw Y'glana…"

I do not know why I have come here, to this bonfire. This is a night of music and dancing, part of the twelvemonth festivities marking the return of the Heart of the Star to Reesa Kam'ana. It also celebrates the end of Castle Do'am and the transformation of S'kryssna S'kyaga into Karenna Kihanna. It is bound to be loud and raucous. I hate loud and raucous. I would rather stay in my study and write under M'nor's silver light. But Karenna Kihanna has insisted. She would never order me to go, of course, though she could. She is queen, after all. All she will offer, with a pixie-twinkle in her eye, is her guarantee that I will not regret attending, despite my misgivings.

When I arrive, a huge cheer erupts. I am Elderbard, after all, and I am loved. I find the nearest approximation to a quiet corner and watch the tops of the flames lick at the sky. The tips are all I can see over the silhouetted bodies that frolic joyfully around it. As I sip from my tankard, a woman's voice asks if she can join me. I do not recognize the voice, nor can I initially see her face, shaded as it is by the firelight behind her.

"I am Y'glana," she says, "Marutha's daughter." Once she realizes who I am, she is embarrassed.

"Oh, Ko'lar." She jumps up. "I did not know it was you. Forgive me for intruding."

I know Marutha's daughter or, rather, I have seen her often. I have watched her from my castle window while she is down in the courtyard helping her father on market days. Her mother is dead, killed during S'kryssna S'kyaga's reign of terror. She has no brothers or sisters, only her father. You can tell, even from a distance, how much she adores him. From that same distance, you cannot help but notice that Y'glana is lovely, with long chestnut hair that falls in waves down her back. She moves with elegant grace and smiles with heart-stopping radiance.

Now I am the one who is embarrassed. I stammer an invitation for her to remain. At first we are awkward together. Neither of us knows what to say, how to act. Those discomfiting moments must pass quickly, because my next awareness is of Aygra's earliest light illuminating her face. It is even more comely than I recall from market days. Without either of us knowing how it could have happened, we have talked nonstop through the night.

"We were married on the next full moon," I continued, "and there was not a day we were together that I failed to look at her the same way that Bonda'ar looks at you, the same way you look at Bonda'ar. When she died—" I swallowed hard. "When she died, I didn't think I could go on living…didn't want to go on living. But there was Mìr'gn'ma to watch over. And there were stories to tell…happy ones too, again…after a time." I wiped my eyes. "If love has found you, My'leen, however it has found you, don't ever turn your back on it."

My'leen squeezed my hand then looked away.

"There is one more thing, isn't there," I said.

"You and Y'glana," she asked. "Only a few seasons separated you?"

I nodded.

"Bonda'ar…well, he is nearly old enough to be my father. Isn't he?"

"Do you love him?"

My'leen paused. Her eyes softened dreamily. She nodded.

"Then be his queen. When all this is over, be his queen. He could be old enough to be your grandfather, or you could be old enough to be his grandmother. It does not matter. It cannot matter. Years don't matter. Love matters. Only love."

My'leen wept. Janq'a too. Then I burst into tears as well. Y'glana…the love…the loss…the joy…the pain…the ecstasy…the sorrow… All the first Ben's memories flooded back into my heart as though, once again, it was this lifetime I was remembering, not another. If this is what it felt to be fully human, I wasn't sure I liked it. Yet, strangely, I welcomed it.

If I was destined to be fully human, this was the perfect opportunity to step into that role. Moments later, we passed through the cloud and stepped up onto the summit of Hana Mar Ò Q'inaya. Here, somewhere soon, the human Ben would face the dreamwalker Bo'Rà K'n. Here, one way or another, The SunQuest would come to an end.

THE CROWNING

<h1 style="text-align:center">thirty-eight</h1>

I'm not certain what we expected. It was not this. The broad, empty, rock-slab plateau that floated just above the cloud was larger than the island itself, stretching endlessly in all directions. Only a single boulder in the distance, coal-black, jagged and sloping at a sharp angle, broke the unrelenting gray flatness of the place. Above, the azure sky was clear and unblemished, with no trace of either Aygra or B'na.

"Sing, My'leen," I said. "Sing us to the p'rtulle as you sang us to the island."

This time she did not argue. She nodded slightly, opened her mouth and let a song emerge that was so hauntingly resonant, so powerfully stirring that I couldn't move. I didn't need to. She was singing the p'rtulle to us. Seduced by her voice, the boulder slid slowly in our direction. It stopped a few paces away, as broad as two houses and three times as tall, just as My'leen finished. The moment it did, two clouds materialized in the far distance: one white and puffy, the other, dark, angry and brooding. Within the space of a breath, both had sped toward us and were hovering overhead, one on either side of us, with only a narrow slice of blue separating them.

My right hand tingled. It was Bonda'ar's ring. Its stones buzzed, vibrated and glowed, most vividly in the center point of the fiery sunburst. I touched stone to rock at the level of my forehead. The ring sparked and an opening melted into the boulder, wide enough for the three of us and a few hairs taller than me. We stepped through together. The doorway sealed behind us. As it did, the ring vanished from my finger.

"Now," I said. "Now, it is time for a story."

*　*　*

We stood in an enormous circular chamber lit by the luminescent gold and silver chips that flecked its smooth, semigloss, black-stone walls. Its floor was a sheet of smoked, mirrored glass, unbroken but for the black-marble top surface of Kol Kolai, the Table of Prophecy, which was set into the center, its red veins pulsing lightly. High above, braids of gold and silver rope ringed the domed ceiling: a single pane also smoked and mirrored that, with the looking-glass floor, projected infinite and infinitely dizzying reflections.

Slowly, the tabletop began to revolve and rise, unsupported, to its full height. I knew that I had to go to it. Somehow, despite the nausea-making vertigo of the chamber's all-mirrored surfaces, I managed to shuffle over to it without tripping over my reflection. Somehow, Janq'a and My'leen managed to follow.

I pulled Kumba's quill from my waistband and touched it to the table's surface. "Now," I repeated. "Now, it is time for a story." The red veins throbbed insistently then faded.

"I have waited a long time to know this story." Toshar's face formed in the smooth blackness of the tabletop. "Lifetimes," he said.

Eulisha's face joined Toshar's. "Now is the time," she said, "for all time."

The quill in my hand hovered uncertainly over the table, much as Toshar's had over the parchment laid on this same table, when Na'an had insisted that he set his MoonQuest in ink. "Where do I begin?" I asked, as my grandfather had, but with none of his fear and uncertainty.

Toshar and Eulisha's faces dissolved back into the table. It remained dark for an instant. Then a tiny pinprick of light illuminated its center. Within the space of my next breath, the light ballooned and brightened until it formed a sun — Aygra, whose flaming radiance pulsed as strongly as had the table's veins. Within Aygra's fiery center, a man's face took shape: blond, wavy hair framing a smiling, strikingly handsome face.

"Father?" I whispered, startled.

He nodded. His smile broadened. "Begin with the beginning you know, my son. The ending will take care of itself. It always does, when you let it."

"Once upon a time?"

"Once upon a time. Always, once upon a time."

Aygra slowly dimmed to black, taking Akila's face with it. The chamber's walls dimmed too. I touched quill to table, penned "once upon a time" and waited for a story to unfold, waited for the truth of The SunQuest to at last reveal itself to me.

"Once upon a time," I wrote as I spoke, "in the time of Kumba, the great dragon, it was said that Aygra, sole sun in the sky, would bear a son of a human woman."

Within the table, the sun formed again, a radiant orb of light that shone down on the Q'ntana of King Kyri and Toshar Ko'lar. From that light, a single ray so bright it would have blinded anyone looking directly into it beamed down to a deserted spot near Castle Rose. Where the sunbeam dusted the earth, Akila emerged from it. He touched his arms, chest and face to make certain he was solid and real. Then he glanced around to ensure that no one had noticed his arrival, straightened his clothes and casually ambled up the Great Lawn toward the castle gate.

"I knew everyone in the area, inside the castle and out, so it was not difficult to notice Akila, a stranger…an extraordinarily luminous and handsome stranger." Q'nta's voice spoke from the table, and a younger Q'nta could seen be seen on the castle's Great Lawn.

"Mother?"

"It was dawn," she continued, perhaps unaware of my presence. "I saw him climbing the hill from the ferry dock as I returned from an early morning stroll into the village. There was something about him… I know now what it was. But then… But then he was the most striking man I had ever seen, and not just because of his bright, suns-bleached hair, unusual in Q'ntana. His smile, too, was extraordinary: beamingly wide and totally unguarded. He laughed easily, and heartily. He never took anything too seriously, yet he was not at all flippant. But I skip ahead. My knowingness of those qualities was not to come until later.

"I must have fallen in love with him the instant I set eyes on him that morning, even from a distance. Now, in this moment out of time, I know that we were destined to be together and that nothing I did or neglected to do would likely have changed that. That morning, though, all I knew was that I was drawn to strike up a conversation with this stranger.

"Oddly, though not in retrospect, I learned little of who he was that day…or any other. All he would say was that he had traveled to Castle Rose from a far-distant land because of the legends sung about its greatness, because he had heard about The MoonQuest and was inspired to meet its architect.

"Mother and Father took to him right away. Father probably sensed more about this amiable young man than Akila's attractive aspect could divulge. Father certainly sensed more than his own unconscious awareness was prepared to reveal. Even Garan, so jealous of anyone's special attention to me, quickly warmed to him. Two moons later, we were wed."

Q'nta paused. The scene in the table, which had closely followed her story, paused too. "Alas," she proceeded with a sigh, "my joy dissipated rapidly. Death followed death as, in rapid succession, Mother, Garan, Father and Kyri died. By the time my son was born, you, Ben…" For the first time, she looked out from the table directly at me. "By then, Akila had also vanished from my life."

The table now revealed Q'nta nursing her newborn son, as the story continued, now in an otherworldly voice that I had never before heard, the voice of Kol Kolai, the voice of the prophecy itself.

"Born near the end times, this child would die in the beginning times, straddling all time as B'na, second sun in the heavens and filial sun to Aygra.

"B'na, this second sun, was integral to that prophecy, in that time of Kumba. B'na's return to earth as Ben to restore Elohia to the land was also integral to the prophecy. For the prophecy, it was said, could only be fulfilled by a human. Only a human could carry within him the capacity to feel all that would power both the prophecy's fulfillment, known as the Crowning, and the prophecy's aftermath."

Thunder exploded noisily from somewhere beyond the chamber, rattling the mirrored dome.

"Speak, Ben Ko'leya," the table urged. "Speak of the prophecy that is now yours to speak…that is now yours alone to fulfill."

More thunderclaps, immediately outside. The chamber quaked. I barely noticed.

"This is the time of balance," I said, not knowing where the words came from or what their consequences might be. The thunder exploded again, more viciously still. "This is the time of Elohia. This is the time of unity. This is the time when dark and light come together as one, when dream and nightmare join in wholeness. This is the time when vision and power unite. This is the time of the human and celestial in a single body, of the union of king and elderbard…of Ko'lar and Kano'ha."

I released Kumba's quill. It fluttered onto the Table of Prophecy and dissolved into it. Before I could grasp the import of all that I had seen and said, My'leen placed my right hand on the table, palm down. Janq'a did the same with my left. The table glowed, brighter and brighter as the thunder outside grew fiercer and more violent. I inhaled deeply. Again. I ignored the noise, focusing all my senses on my hands. As I did, more and more light focused under my palms, until my hands glowed brilliantly and my bones were disconcertingly visible through my skin. Although what I saw suggested a searing heat, all I felt was a slight buzzing warmth. My breathing deepened even more, slowed even more. Deepened…slowed…deepened… slowed. It was as though I breathed in the essence of this Table of Prophecy, as though I breathed in the prophecy itself. Perhaps I did, for the light that had gathered under my palms now traveled tinglingly up through my arms and into my shoulders. The two strands joined in my neck, where they twined then spun around my head, creating a braided circlet of light that must have been similar to the one My'leen had seen early on in our journey. Not only could I feel the circlet, at once natural and unnerving, I could see it as well, reflected in a tabletop that was now as smoothly mirrored as were the chamber's floor and ceiling.

I touched my right index finger to my forehead. The Ring of Unity was not solid. Not yet. But it pulsed with a light throb that I could only feel when my finger was in contact with it. I knelt next to Janq'a.

"It is time," I said to him. "Do you know what you must do?"

"I can't. Don't ask me to. Please don't ask me to."

"You must, my friend. You are the only one who can. That is why you are here. That is why you journeyed with us to this place. That is why Bo'Rà K'n sent you. That is why Rev'Àn sent you."

Janq'a stepped behind me and touched the crown of light with his right index finger. It solidified into the same simple coronet of braided white and yellow gold that I had first seen with Q'nta beneath Ko'Ba Rock. I had never worn it before and, to my surprise, it sat lightly on my head.

"Call him, Janq'a."

"But—"

"He is waiting."

"But if I do…"

"This is part of The SunQuest, part of the prophecy, part of the story. In this story we must all play our role. This is yours, possibly the most important role of all."

Sobbing, Janq'a lifted the crown from my head. With his touch, it lost its luster and glow. "Master," he whispered through his tears. "It is time."

thirty-nine

Thunder crashed just outside the chamber. It rumbled into laughter; cruel, menacing laughter so piercing, harsh and dissonant that the ceiling imploded, raining shards of mirrored glass down toward us. The glass never made it to the ground. Halfway down, it flew together into a new shape, that of Bo'Rà K'n, taller and more malevolently imposing than ever.

In that same instant, a blurred whoosh of silver wings swept swiftly across the sky, now visible through the chamber's open roof. *Kumba?* It couldn't be. The thought passed from my mind a moment later when O'ric entered. He passed through the chamber's solid stone wall as though it were air.

"You cannot stop me now, old man," Bo'Rà K'n growled at O'ric, reaching greedily for the crown in Janq'a's hands.

O'ric moved toward us purposefully but without haste. "It has never been my role to stop you."

Bo'Rà K'n turned to me. "You will not stop me either, bard. You were foolish to take on this SunQuest, foolish to come to this place, foolish to give up Astel Elohia to this fool, Janq'a. Without the Ring of Unity, you will be powerless. Soon you will be dead. Your friends too. Foolish friends who invest their faith in one foolish enough to willingly abdicate the source of his power."

Growing paler with every breath, My'leen backed away.

For the first time since I had fully embodied my humanness, Bo'Rà K'n ignited not the slightest spark of fear in me. "Foolish dreamwalker," I said, "who believes that a thing can be the source of anyone's power."

"Ha! We shall see who is right, presently. I know where I would stake my wager."

"I know where you would too," I countered. "That does not make it a winning one."

My'leen swallowed hard, stepped forward and looked directly at Bo'Rà K'n. "I am not frightened of you," she said, her voice trembling.

"No?" He unfurled his cloak, revealing thousands of monochromatic specters — men, women and children of all ages, all blank-eyed and hollow-faced, many with their mouths distended into a perpetual scream. One young woman stepped out in front of the rest. She was thin, almost skeletal, and stooped, her scalp a patchwork of scaly baldness and clumps of long, stringy hair. My'leen gasped.

"B'tha!"

My'leen's sister reached toward her, her arm extending beyond Bo'Rà K'n's cloak, as though trying to pull her in or have My'leen pull her out. My'leen covered her face and screamed. When she stopped, still trembling and her voice rasping from the strain, she opened her eyes. B'tha and the others were gone.

"You will join them soon enough, foolish friend of a foolish bard. You will join them in an eternal nightmare that will make all terrors you have ever experienced seem like playtime. First, however, this place must be destroyed, and all pretense of a mythical Elohia with it."

Bo'Rà K'n pulled his gaze from Janq'a, who still clutched the crown in shaking hands, and strode around the chamber's perimeter, barking a deep, throaty laugh. The walls collapsed noisily into dust as he passed. Outside, only a single, small, distant coin of blue sky could now be seen among the black roiling turbulence that had gathered overhead. Scores of spectral bodies floated down from the storm cloud and into his cloak. He completed his circuit at Janq'a.

"Place Astel Elohia on the table," I said to Janq'a. Janq'a did, relieved to be rid of it. The crown immediately regained its luster.

"Do you think a table can stop me?" Bo'Rà K'n sneered. "Your SunQuest was doomed from the outset. Now it is over. No table will stop me. Nor will you."

"It has never been my role to stop you."

Bo'Rà K'n regarded me incredulously then burst into gales of hideous laughter. "Whose role would it be?"

"Yours," I said.

He laughed again, stopping abruptly. "You have lost more than your power and your crown, bard. You have lost your senses." He stared covetously at the Ring of Unity. "I have waited through all time for this," he continued. "No king or sorceress will ever disappoint me again. No bard or Elderbard will ever thwart me again. Not ever."

"You speak the truth, Rev'Àn."

Bo'Rà K'n spun around angrily. "I have warned you once before, bard." He glowered at me, then his rage dissolved back into laughter. "Try as you may, you will neither distract nor delay me. The future is come. My destiny is realized. With this." His finger touched the crown. Its glow leached into his hand. He yowled and leapt back, clutching his still-flickering finger. "No," he whispered. "No, it cannot be. It was not meant to be thus. Not after all this time. Not after all I have—"

He gazed at the crown, longing to touch it again but not daring. "It is the table," he pronounced at last. "I will see it turned to dust before this day is done." He prodded Janq'a. "Pick it up, Janq'a. Pick up the crown and hand it to me."

A blast of warm wind gusted toward us from beyond the rubbled walls. It eddied and swirled sparklingly, taking shape as Na'an when it reached Bo'Rà K'n.

"Allow me, brother," she said. "Please." When she picked up the crown, it glowed even more brightly in her hands.

"What chicanery is this?" Bo'Rà K'n roared. "What are you doing here? How dare you?"

"This is no chicanery, brother. You know I cannot lie, any more than you can. Dreamwalkers speak only the truth of the human heart. The dark words you speak through your nightmares are no less true for their darkness. That is the way of the world in these times."

She polished the crown on her sleeve and handed it to him. He reached for it, then pulled his hand back.

"This is a trick. You have enchanted it in some way. You will die for this, Na'an. I swear it."

"You know better than I that I carry not a smidge of trickery in me. You are no different than I am…in that respect, at least. If I possessed the power to enchant Astel Elohia, which I do not, any more than you do, you would know, as a brother must know the heart of his sister. No, I am here to offer you this Ring of Unity, not because that is my wish but because that is how the story must play out. That is also the way of the world in these times."

Bo'Rà K'n considered Na'an's words. "Let the story play out, then," he said. "Crown me, sister. Make me eternally powerful, eternally supreme. Give me dominion over all of Q'ntana. Give me the power to see you dead. Do you dare?"

Na'an stepped toward him, holding the crown out in front of her. "Do you, brother?"

"I dare that and more. Much more." He knelt before her. She raised the crown over his head, then lowered it slowly. O'ric watched disinterestedly. My'leen and Janq'a held their breath. I suspected what was going to happen next. But I couldn't be certain.

Na'an released the crown just above the top of her brother's head. It hovered there without moving.

"*On* my head, sister" he snarled.

"You must do the rest," Na'an said. She stepped away.

"Very well." He reached for the crown. "You will pay, sister. Dearly. I promise you that."

"As you say."

He grasped the crown with both hands and pulled it down. When it touched his head, a brilliant flash of lightning shot through him, jolting him to his feet. He clenched his fists until they were white. He writhed in pain but could not budge from where he stood. His mouth yawned open. No sound emerged.

His mouth clamped shut and his eyes bulged, but not from pain. The pain had lasted the briefest of instants, barely a breath. His new expression was one of astonishment, and it was visible to all, for most of the black mist that had swirled around his face, largely masking his features, had cleared. Also gone was the hard, contemptuous sneer I had last seen when Rev'Àn had turned his back on the Tikkan to become Bo'Rà K'n. Now, his face was softer, his hair was lighter and he had regained some of Rev'Àn's strong but boyishly gentle countenance. Most of the cruel arrogance had vanished too. That was not the source of his astonishment, for he was not yet aware of it. His disbelief came from watching much of his clothing brighten from black to gold. Only when that transformation had neared its conclusion did he glance into the mirrored surface of the Table of Prophecy and see his face. He touched it, not quite convinced by what his eyes were showing him.

"I thought…" he began. His voice petered out.

"You think altogether too much, brother," Na'an said, smiling. Her voice carried a deep-hearted tenderness I had never before heard from her. She stepped toward him, her arms outstretched. Alarmed, Bo'Rà K'n recoiled.

"The crown," she said softly. "It is not yours to keep. You do know that, do you not?"

He studied himself again in the mirrored table. The metamorphosis was nearly complete. His cloak was still black, strands of black still streaked his blond hair, and a few hard lines still etched his brow and scarred his mouth. Despite that, he looked striking, and the crown suited him. It glowed and glinted under the dark, overcast sky that still brooded overhead. He reached longingly for the crown, yet was reluctant to touch it. He turned to Na'an, his eyes moist. "If I remove it, what will happen? Will I go back...?"

O'ric, who had watched impassively from the background, moved forward to join us. "Not if your heart is pure."

Bo'Rà K'n leaned into the table's mirrored surface. He traced the remaining lines on his face, which deepened with worry. Then he tried to remove his cloak, but the clasp had fused shut. "It isn't," he said sadly. "Is it?"

"It is best not to know too much too soon," O'ric replied. "The story must continue for you to find out. The story must always continue."

Bo'Rà K'n sighed. He took one final look at himself wearing the crown then lifted it from his head and tried to give it to O'ric.

O'ric shook his head. "Kumba passed this on long, long ago. Now it is for you to do likewise. If your heart is pure, you will know what to do."

Bo'Rà K'n scrutinized each of us in turn, beginning with me. He then turned to My'leen, who met his stare unblinkingly, to Janq'a, who wilted fearfully under his gaze, and to Na'an, who smiled and shook her head.

"I don't know. I don't know who it belongs to. I don't know what to do."

Then he did. He returned the crown to the table and, one last time, unfurled his cloak. The clasp released freely and, this time the cloak pulled no one in. Instead, all the spectral people within it — thousands upon thousands of them — swarmed out, regaining their color, substance, wholeness and humanity as they did. The last to exit was B'tha. She stepped free, unhunched her shoulders and shook out her legs. When she stood straight, her hair and figure restored to their fullness, she scrutinized the crowd, spotted My'leen and ran to her in tears. The sisters fell into each other's arms, sobbing.

With the last of Bo'Rà K'n's captives freed, the last of the black leached from his now-silver cloak and bleached from his golden hair, and the remaining lines smoothed from his face. He was no longer Bo'Rà K'n. He was Rev'Àn.

Rev'Àn smiled, and his smile was so bright and genuine that it dispersed the dark clouds that still loomed over us. The sky turned as blue and unblemished as we had seen it what seemed lifetimes ago, when we had first climbed onto the summit of Hana Mar Ò Q'inaya. Still smiling, Rev'Àn at last picked up the crown from the table. The table dropped back into the mirrored floor and regained its normal countenance. Its red veins, pulsing so subtly in the black marble as to be almost unnoticeable, slowly reshaped themselves into an image of Castle Rose, a Castle Rose revitalized to its storied greatness and splendor.

Together, Rev'Àn and I stepped onto the tabletop, which spiraled out and expanded, spreading under the feet of all present: Janq'a and My'leen, Na'an and O'ric, and the thousands upon thousands of men, women and children, once Bo'Rà K'n's victims, who had been freed from his cloak. It continued to broaden infinitely in all directions as Rev'Àn smiled and raised Astel Elohia over my head.

forty

"Let the people name their Elderbard," Rev'Àn shouted.

"Ben Ko'leya," the crowd shouted back and, suddenly, we no longer stood in the remains of the Chamber of Elohia atop Hana Mar Ò Q'inaya. We stood on a raised dais in the center of the Castle Rose courtyard, moments before suns-merge.

Rev'Àn still held the crown over my head. I was dressed in white pants and tunic threaded with silver and gold. O'ric hung behind me to one side, his clawed hands clasped in front of him. Na'an stood next to her brother. Above us, filling the courtyard's many flag-festooned arches, heralds stood erect, gold-and-silver trumpets pressed to their lips. Before us, it seemed as though all of Q'ntana, dressed in holiday finest, filled the benches that crammed the courtyard. The seats I was most aware of were in the front row, where Janq'a sat next to Panesh and My'leen was flanked by B'tha on one side and King Bonda'ar on the other.

"Ben Ko'leya," the crowd cried out again, even louder, yet without anywhere near the force and passion displayed by my old friends.

Rev'Àn waited until the courtyard had stilled. "Let the people name their king," he said, this time in a whisper so soft that it was hard to believe anyone could hear him. Everyone did.

The crowd erupted. "Ben Ko'leya. Ben Ko'lar. Ben Kano'ha!"

Again, Rev'Àn waited for silence. "The people have spoken," he said, "and the people's will be done. Ben Ko'leya, heir to Eulisha, Toshar and Q'nta, rightful heir to Kyri, I name you, Ko'lar and Kano'ha, King and Elderbard." As Aygra and B'na joined together in the sky, Rev'Àn gently lowered the Ring of Unity onto my head. "Long may you serve Q'ntana in unity and wisdom, guided by story, vision and love." He paused, smiled humbly at me and raised his voice to the crowd.

"Long live Ben Ko'leya, Ko'lar and Kano'ha! Long live Ben Ko'leya, King and Elderbard of Q'ntana."

An explosion of cheers overpowered the heralds' fanfare as I turned to face the crowd, my people.

"You will teach me what it means to be king," I said when the cheering had subsided, "and, together, we will usher in the greatest era in Q'ntana's history." Tears streamed down my face as I let The SunQuest replay not only in my mind, but in my heart. Against all reason, I had achieved in human form what my sun-self could never have accomplished: unity, balance and a Crowning that would guarantee peace and prosperity to the land I had once cherished and had again come to hold dear. I tore my gaze from the crowd to smile down at the center of the front row, at Janq'a, My'leen and Panesh, who grinned up at me through their uncontrolled weeping. "Thank you," I mouthed, touching my hand to my heart.

Then in a voice stronger and more sure than it had ever been, either as this Ben or the other, I shouted, "Long live Q'ntana! Long live Q'ntana! Long live Q'ntana!"

"Long live Q'ntana!" the crowd echoed back, leaping up from their seats.

Behind me, Na'an and Rev'Àn, embraced. As they held each other in renewed love and respect, they dissolved into gold and silver sparkles that gamboled out into the crowd and were gone. O'ric, for his part, nodded at me, the traces of a rare smile once more playing on his lips. In the next instant, he was no longer O'ric but a giant, green-scaled creature with silver-feathered wings. It spread those wings, plucked a feather from one with its teeth and dropped it in front of me. As I picked it up, the dragon leapt into the sky, growing larger and larger until, as Kumba, he disappeared into the still-separating suns.

EPILOGUE

I never saw O'ric again, for he never again took human form. But his quill — Kumba's quill — served me well throughout my long reign, reminding me of the stories I knew but had forgotten, reminding me of The SunQuest that had brought me back to life, reminding me of all I had been and all I was becoming.

My companions had their own happy endings. My'leen and Bonda'ar were married the next day, by me, in the Castle Rose courtyard and lived long, passion-filled lives as king and queen of Hana Mar Ò Q'inaya. Panesh chose to remain with me in Castle Rose, becoming my Chamberlain, most trusted advisor and closest friend. Janq'a stayed too, though not for long. When Rev'Àn sent for him a few moons later, he did not hesitate to return to his true home, despite a tearful leave-taking from Panesh. As for Rev'Àn, from the instant he and Na'an embraced, they worked their looms together, weaving rich dream tapestries for all, including for me through this second life as Ko'lar and Kano'ha, king and Elderbard.

It was a good life. A rich life. A life overflowing with the unity, wisdom, vision and love that Rev'Àn had anticipated for me in my coronation. And alive with story. Always alive with story. And although love was never absent from my life, I never married. Prithi deemed it best not to send me another Y'glana, and I was content with that. Nor did I leave any heirs. That too was Prithi's wise design.

I will die tonight, as I recorded at the start of this story. I will die moments from now, when, with Kumba's quill, I scratch my final word onto this parchment. B'na calls me home, and I welcome the journey.

But what of the Law of Balance, you ask. What will become of Elderbards, of Castle Rose, of Q'ntana?

I puzzled over that too for many years. Now, finally, in reliving my story and setting it down in ink and parchment, as much for me as for you, I see the answer and I see Prithi's wisdom in it. Q'ntana needs neither Elderbards nor rulers, for the Law of Balance resides fully within it now: in the earth of its land and in the hearts of its people.

Knowing that, I write these final words and take these final breaths in the joy and certainty that the people of Q'ntana are now sovereign and empowered, and that the stories, visions and dreams that live in us all will flow through them forever.

It has been a long journey — for Toshar and Q'nta, for Q'ntana, Bo'Rà K'n and me. But it is over now, done for all time. And I am at peace.

THE WORLDS OF THE SUNQUEST

Akila (ah-*KEE*-lah) — Ben's father

Alanda (a-*LAWN*-dah) — Q'ntana's ancient capital

Anariy'a (ahna-*REE*-yah) — Bonda'ar's o'tria

Angarusha (un-gah-*REW*-shah) — Race of beings that walks between the worlds. See also "Panesh"

Aq'anor (*AHK*-ah-nor) — A region of Q'ntana

Ardyyn (ar-*DINN*) — A desert kingdom in one of Ben's stories

Aris (*AA*-riss) — The north star and eye of the Thyra constellation

Arms of K'varr (kih-*VAR*) — Legendary weapons forged by Prithi

Arrukka (ah-*REW*-kah) — An ancient tartaruca

Astel Elohia (*AA*-stel ell-oh-*HEE*-yah) — The Ring of Unity

Astel Lev (*AA*-stel lev) — The Heart of the Star

Aygra (*AY*-grah) — The larger of Q'ntana's two suns

Ben (*BEN*) — Protagonist of *The SunQuest*

B'na (bih-*NAH*) — The smaller of Q'ntana's two suns

Bonda'ar (*BAWN*-dar) — A character in one of Ben's stories…and more

Bo'Rà K'n (bo-*RAH*-kin) — The dark force at work in Q'ntana

Bratta (*BRAT*-ah) — A type of fish indigenous to Hana Mar Ò Q'inaya

B'tha (bih-*THAW*) — My'leen's younger sister

Castle Do'am (*DOH*-um) — S'kryssna S'kyaga's home

Co'anra (co-*AWN*-rah) — A Co'an and twin brother to Co'anri

Co'anri (co-*AWN*-ree) — A Co'an and twin sister to Co'anra

Co'aqa (coh-*AH*-kah) — A cactus-like desert plant

Dafna (*DAF*-na) — Ben's grandmother

Da'nay (dah-*NAY*) — A giant catlike creature that resides in Kea Kana

Do'ra (*DOH*-rah) — A type of bird that lives on Hana Mar Ò Q'inaya

Elohia (ell-oh-*HEE*-yah) — The unity of all things

Eulisha (you-*LEE*-sha) — Elderbard, Q'nta's great-grandmother and Ben's great-great-grandmother

Fayr'Owyn (fair-*OH*-winn) — M'ranna's storied savior

Fllia (*FLEE*-yah) — A green, six-legged bug

Fortas (*FOUR*-tuhss) — Kyri's father

Fvorag (*FOR*-ag) — A king of Q'ntana

Garan (*GA*-ren) — One of the journeyers on The MoonQuest

Ghorak (*GOH*-rak) — A large, worm-like creature

Gita'a (jee-*TAH*) — A three-legged, single-horned mammal

Grassi (*GRASS*-ee) —Resident of Xa'qìa village; Marq'O's wife

Gravel (gruh-*VELL*) — Fvorag's grandson and a king of Q'ntana

Grizz'm (*GRIZZ*-em) — Gravel's first minister

Gurja (*GOOR*-jah) — A type of tree indigenous to Q'ntana

Hana Mar Ò Q'inaya (*HAH*-na mar oh-kee-*NYE*-ah) — "The Land of Dreams" aka the land "beyond the west"

Horusha (ho-*ROO*-shah) — Mountain range and maze of tunnels in Q'ntana

Hoss eeyah ka-am seeya na sempah (*HOHSS EE*-yah kah-*AHM SEE*-yah *NAH* sem-*PAH*) — Invocation S'kryssna S'kyaga uses to summon her snakes. See also "ka-hass"

Janq'a (*JANK*-ah) — Bo'Rà K'n's manservant

Ka-hass (kah-*HAHSS*) — The word S'kryssna S'kyaga uses to invoke her magic.

Kano'ha (kah-*NO*-hah) — Ancient word for "king"

Karenna Kihanna (ka-*REN*-nah kee-*HAW*-nah) — Q'ntana's first queen

Kea Kana (*KAY*-ah *KAH*-nah) — The otherwordly destination for the souls of the newly dead, aka "Prithi's Garden"

Kep'cha (*KEP*-chah) — Birdlike creature controlled by S'kryssna S'kyaga

King's Men — Gravel's brutal army

Ko'Ba (*KOH*-bah) — Towering rock formation in M'ranna, overlooking the Ma

K'nrah (kin-*RAH*) — Small animal indigenous to Q'ntana

Kol Kolai (kohl koh-*LYE*) — The legendary Table of Prophecy

Ko'lar (*KOH*-lar) — Ancient word for Elderbard

Ko'leya (koh-*LAY*-ah) — Ancient word meaning "son of the sun"

Korb'at (*KOR*-bit) — One of the King's Men

Kromii (*KROH*-mee) — A type of fish

Kumba (*KOOM*-bah) — The Great Dragon of Creation

Ky'nar (kee-*NAR*) — Constellation of the ancient bard

Kyri (*KEE*-ree) — A king of Q'ntana

Lythe (rhymes with "writhe") — Stringed musical instrument

Ma (*MAW*) — Ocean-like body of water in M'ranna

Margolin (mar-*GOH*-lin) — Fvorag's son

Marq'O (*MAR*-ko) — Resident of Xa'qìa village; Grassi's husband

Marutha (mah-*REW*-tah) — Y'glana Tori'à's father

Maya Elohia (maya ell-oh- *HEE*-yah) — A p'rtulle on The SunQuest

Maya Ko (maya *KOH*) — A p'rtulle on The StarQuest and SunQuest

Maysha (*MAY*-sha) — Resident of Xa'qìa village; Rolo'En's wife

Miggy — See "Mig'lanta"

Mig'lanta (mih-*GLAWN*-tah) — Yeerga'a and Ra'ina's granddaughter

Mîr'gn'ma (*MEER*-ghin-mah) — Ben and Y'glana Tori'à's daughter

Mirika'a (mee-ree-*KAH*) — A type of blue-breasted bird

M'nor (mih-*NOR*) — The moon

Moku (*MOH*-koo) — An iridescent-scaled fish that swims in the River Alanda

Mo'Rée (moh-*RAY*) — Resident of the Xa'qìa village

Mokìa (moh-*KEE*-yah) — A fruit-bearing tree; berries from the tree

M'ranna (mih-*RAH*-nah) — The land where The StarQuest takes place

My'leen (my-*LEEN*) — One of the journeyers on The SunQuest

Na'an (rhymes with fawn) — A Tikkan dreamwalker

Nayla (*NAY*-lah) — Vicious animal indigenous to Q'ntana

Nayr (*NAIR*) — Ancient, legendary chalice

Nya (*NYE*-ah) — A k'nrah

O'ric (*OH*-rick) — Timeless oracle who first appears in *The MoonQuest*

O'tria (oh-*TREE*-yah) — Sea creature indigenous to Hana Mar Ò Q'inaya

Panesh (pah-*NESH*) — An Angarusha and one of the journeyers on The SunQuest

Parika (pa-*REE*-kah) — A bird whose call is "pa-REE-ka caaa-ooo-eee"

Pika'a (pee-*KAH*-ah) — A type of tree indigenous to Q'ntana

Pergosà (pear-go-*SAH*) — Eden-like paradise

Prithi (*PRIH*-thee) — Q'ntana's deity

Prak'kà (prah-*KAH*) — A captain in Gravel's King's Men; a descendant of Prak, one of the King's Men in *The MoonQuest*

P'rtulle (purr-*TULL*-ah) — A portal

Pryma (*PREE*-mah) — A tartaruca and messenger to M'nor

Q'nta (kin-*TAH*) — Ben's mother; protagonist of *The StarQuest*
Q'ntana (kin-*TAH*-nah) — The land where The MoonQuest takes place
Q'oroq'i (koe-roh-*KEE*) — A village in Q'ntana

Ra'ina (rah-*EE*-nah) — Yeerg'a's wife, friend of Panesh
Reesa Kam'ana (*REE*-sah ka-*MAW*-nah) — The Star Chantress
Rev'Àn (rih-*VAWN*) — Bo'Rà K'n's truth name
Ro'gàn (roh-*GAWN*) — My'leen's cousin
Rolo'En (*RAWL*-oh-en) — Resident of Xa'qìa village; Maysha's husband
Rykka (*REE*-kah) — With Ta'ar, one of O'ric's magical horses; Toshar's horse on The MoonQuest
Ryolan Ò Garan (*RYE*-o-lun oh *GAR*-en) — See "Garan"

Samson (*SAM*-sun) — Elderly servant in the royal court of Q'ntana
Simeon (*SIMMY*-yun) — Page in the royal court of Q'ntana
S'kala (sih-*KA*-la) — A fire-breathing,f two-headed flying serpent
S'kryssna S'kyaga (*SKRISS*-nah skee-*YAW*-gah) — An evil sorceress

Ta'ar (*TAR*) — With Rykka, one of O'ric's magical horses; Yhoshi's horse on The MoonQuest
Tartaruca (tar-*TAR*-u-kah) — Large, tortoise-like sea creature
Tashek (*TAH*-shek) — Shapeshifter that appears as various creatures
The Nayr — See "Nayr"
Thyra (*THYE*-rah) — Constellation of the eagle; see also "Aris"
Tikkan (tee-*KAWN*) — Ancient race of "dream-weavers"
Toshar (*TOH*-shar) — Q'nta's father and Ben's grandfather; Eulisha's grandson; protagonist of *The MoonQuest*

Vaareq (*FAH*-reck) — Mig'lanta's husband

Xa'qìa (zah-*KEE*-yah) — Mountain range; village in its foothills

Yeerg'a (*YEER*-gah) — A farmer; Ra'ina's husband, friend of Panesh
Y'glana Tori'à (ee-*GLAWN*-ah tor-*YEE*-yah) — Ben's wife
Yhoshi (*YOH*-shee) — One of the four journeyers on The MoonQuest
Yzythq'a (ih-*ZITH*-kah) — A sage and sorcerer

Appreciation

Once upon a time, when the first words of a story I knew nothing about spilled themselves onto my blank page, all I could do was allow them to carry me where they would. I knew nothing then of a *MoonQuest*, let alone a *StarQuest* or a *SunQuest*. All I knew that March evening in 1994 was what an odd-looking man riding an odd-looking coach pulled by two oddly colored horses chose to reveal to me.

From that day until this one, the stories that would ultimately evolve into *The Legend of Q'ntana* never released their gentle but firm grip on me, nor did the Muse who whispered them most insistently into my heart and mind. So my initial thanks must go to the story itself, which chose me to birth it into the world, and to my Muse, who tricked me into becoming a writer and then, with fierce but subtle determination, made certain I was up for the creative journey of a lifetime.

Together, Story and Muse placed many people in my path over the years to ensure both my willingness and readiness to pen these *Q'ntana* books. Among the most significant were my mother, who passed on to me her passion for reading, and Carole H. Leckner, who helped me ignite a now-unquenchable passion for writing. Without them, there might never have been a *Legend of Q'ntana* series.

Unlike *The MoonQuest* and *The StarQuest*, which took more than a decade apiece to travel from conception to publication, the initial release of *The SunQuest* exploded from me to you in less than two years. That I was able to write, revise and complete it with such speed is due in no small measure to Kathleen Messmer, who opened her home to me with unquestioning generosity and who showered me with unfailing enthusiasm for my stories and an unflagging belief in my gifts. Special thanks to Kathleen, as well, for her evocative cover image for this book.

Shoutouts, too, to Denéa West, whose support helped make this new edition possible, and to Sander Freedman, Joan Cerio and Adam Bereki, who, geographically distant though they may be, never hesitated to remind me of the power of my words and the value of my journey in those moments on this *Q'ntana* journey when I questioned both.

Finally, to you my readers: Thank you for all you have shared with me of your experiences with *The MoonQuest* and *The StarQuest*. It remains gratifying to know how deeply my words have touched you. I hope *The SunQuest* offers you as meaningful an addition to your *Q'ntana* journey as it has to mine.

About the Author

Mark David Gerson is the bestselling author of more than twenty books. His nonfiction includes popular titles for writers, inspiring personal growth books and compelling memoirs. As a novelist and screenwriter, he is best known for *The Legend of Q'ntana* fantasy series. His other fiction includes the novels of *The Sara Stories*, set largely in Montreal, his hometown. When not writing, Mark David coaches an international roster of writers and non-writers to help them get their stories onto the page and out into the world with ease.

For more about Mark David Gerson,
to sign up for his newsletter and to learn about
upcoming *Q'ntana* books and other releases,
visit www.markdavidgerson.com